D1038706

THE BOY'S KING ARTHUR

THE BOY'S KING ARTHUR

SIDNEY LANIER

ILLUSTRATIONS BY
N. C. WYETH

DOVER PUBLICATIONS, INC.
MINEOLA, NEW YORK

Bibliographical Note

This Dover edition, first published in 2006, is an unabridged republication of the edition published by Charles Scribner's Sons, New York, in 1917. In this volume, the color plates, originally spaced throughout the text, have been combined in a 16-page insert.

Library of Congress Cataloging-in-Publication Data

Malory, Thomas, Sir, 15th cent.
[Morte d'Arthur. Selections]
The boy's King Arthur / Sidney Lanier ; illustrations by N.C. Wyeth.
p. cm.
"Unabridged republication of the edition published by Charles Scribner's Sons, New York, 1917."—Verso t.p.
Summary: Relates the chivalrous and romantic deeds of King Arthur, Launcelot, Gareth, Tristram, Galahad, and other knights of the Round Table.
ISBN 0-486-44800-2 (pbk.)
1. Arthurian romances—Adaptations. [1. Arthur, King—Legends. 2. Folklore—England. 3. Knights and knighthood—Folklore.] I.Lanier, Sidney, 1842–1881. II. Wyeth, N. C. (Newell Convers), 1882–1945, ill. III. Title.

PZ8.1.M297Boy 2006
823'.2—dc22

2005053789

Manufactured in the United States of America
Dover Publications, Inc., 31 East 2nd Street, Mineola, N.Y. 11501

*** In this edition of Mr. Lanier's classic "Boy's King Arthur" omission has been made of some minor passages and introductory matter — all the greater tales, those of Arthur, Launcelot, Tristram, Gareth, Galahad, Percival, and the Holy Grail, being retained.

CONTENTS

BOOK I

OF KING ARTHUR

OF KING ARTHUR

IT befell in the days of the noble Utherpendragon, when he was King of England, [that there was born to him a son who in after time was King Arthur. Howbeit the boy knew not he was the king's son. For when he was but a babe] the king commanded two knights and two ladies to take the child bound in rich cloth of gold, "and deliver him to what poor man you meet at the postern gate of the castle." So the child was delivered unto Merlin, and so he bare it forth unto Sir Ector, and made an holy man to christen him, and named him Arthur; and so Sir Ector's wife nourished him. Then within two years King Uther fell sick of a great malady; [and thereof he died]. Then stood the realm in great [danger] a long while, for every lord made him strong, and many weened [*thought*] to have been king. [And so, by Merlin's counsel, all the lords of England came together in the greatest church of London on Christmas morn before it was day, to see if God would not show by some miracle who should be king.] And when the first mass was done there was seen in the church-yard, against the high altar, a great stone four-square, like to a marble stone, and in the midst thereof was an anvil of steel, a foot of height, and therein stuck a fair sword naked by the point, and letters of gold were written about the sword that said thus: WHO SO PULLETH OUT THIS SWORD OF THIS STONE AND ANVIL, IS RIGHTWISE KING BORN OF ENGLAND.

So when all the masses were done, all the [lords] went for to behold the stone and the sword. And when they saw the scripture, some assayed [*tried*] such as would have been king. But none might stir the sword nor move it.

"He is not yet here," said the archbishop, "that shall achieve the sword, but doubt not God will make him to be known. But this is my counsel," said the archbishop, "that we let purvey [*provide*] ten knights, men of good fame, and they to keep this sword."

And upon New Year's day the barons let make a tournament for to keep the lords together, for the archbishop trusted that God would make him known that should win the sword. So upon New Year's day when the service was done the barons rode to the field.

And so it happened that Sir Ector rode to the jousts, and with him rode Sir Kay, his son, and young Arthur that was his nourished brother. [But Sir] Kay had lost his sword, for he had left it at his father's lodging, and so he prayed young Arthur to ride for his sword. "I will with a good will," said Arthur, and rode fast after the sword; and when he came home, the lady and all were gone out to see the jousting. Then was Arthur wroth, and said to himself, "I will ride to the church-yard and take the sword with me that sticketh in the stone, for my brother Sir Kay shall not be without a sword this day." And so when he came to the church-yard Arthur alighted, and tied his horse to the stile, and so went to the tent, and found no knights there, for they were all at the jousting; and so he handled the sword by the handles, and lightly and fiercely he pulled it out of the stone, and took his horse and rode his way till he came to his brother Sir Kay, and delivered him the sword. And as soon as Sir Kay saw the sword, he wist [*knew*] well that it was the sword of the stone, and so he rode to his father, Sir Ector, and said: "Sir, lo here is the sword of the stone; wherefore I must be king of this land." When Sir Ector beheld the sword, he returned again and came to the church, and there they alighted, all three, and went into the church, and anon he made Sir Kay to swear upon a book how he came to that sword.

"Sir," said Sir Kay, "by my brother Arthur, for he brought it to me."

"How gate [*got*] you this sword?" said Sir Ector to Arthur.

"Sir, I will tell you. When I came home for my brother's sword, I found nobody at home for to deliver me his sword, and so I thought my brother Sir Kay should not be swordless, and so I came thither eagerly and pulled it out of the stone without any pain."

"Found ye any knights about this sword?" said Sir Ector.

"Nay," said Arthur.

"Now," said Sir Ector to Arthur, "I understand that you must be king of this land."

"Wherefore I?" said Arthur.

"Sir," said Ector, "for there should never man have drawn out this sword but he that shall be rightwise king of this land. Now let me see whether ye can put the sword there as it was and pull it out again."

"That is no mastery," said Arthur; and so he put it in the stone. Therewith Sir Ector assayed to pull out the sword, and failed.

"Now assay," said Sir Ector to Sir Kay. And anon he pulled at the sword with all his might but it would not be. "Now shall ye assay," said Sir Ector to Arthur.

"I will well," said Arthur, and pulled it out easily. And therewithal Sir Ector kneeled down to the earth, and Sir Kay.

"Alas," said Arthur, "mine own dear father and brother, why kneel ye to me?"

"Nay, nay, my lord Arthur, it is not so: I was never your father nor of your blood, but I wote [*know*] well ye are of an higher blood than I weened [*thought*] ye were." And then Sir Ector told him all. Then Arthur made great moan when he understood that Sir Ector was not his father.

"Sir," said Ector unto Arthur, "will ye be my good and gracious lord when ye are king?"

"Else were I to blame," said Arthur, "for ye are the man in the world that I am most beholding [*obliged*] to, and my good lady and mother your wife, that as well as her own hath fostered and kept me. And if ever it be God's will that I be king, as ye say, ye shall desire of me what I may do, and I shall not fail you."

"Sir," said Sir Ector, "I will ask no more of you but that you will make my son, your fostered brother Sir Kay seneschal of all your lands."

"That shall be done, sir," said Arthur, "and more by the faith of my body; and never man shall have that office but he while that he and I live."

Therewithal they went unto the archbishop, and told him how the sword was achieved, and by whom. And upon the twelfth day all the barons came thither for to assay to take the sword. But there afore them all, there might none take it out but only Arthur; wherefore there were many great lords wroth, and said, "It was great shame unto them all and the realm to be governed with a boy of no high blood born." And so they fell out at that time, that it was put off till Candlemas, and then all the barons should meet there again. But always the ten knights were ordained for to watch the sword both day and night; and so they set a pavilion over the stone and the sword, and five always watched. And at Candlemas many more great lords came thither for to have won the sword, but none of them might prevail. And right as Arthur did at Christmas he did at Candlemas, and pulled out the sword easily, whereof the barons were sore aggrieved, and put it in delay till the high feast of Easter. And as Arthur sped afore, so did he at Easter; and yet there were some of the great lords had indignation that Arthur should be their king, and put it off in delay till the feast of Pentecost.

And at the feast of Pentecost all manner of men assayed to pull at the sword that would assay, and none might prevail; but Arthur pulled it out afore all the lords and commons that were there, wherefore all the commons cried at once: "We will have Arthur unto our king; we will put him no more in delay; for we all see that it is God's will that he shall be our king, and who that holdeth against it we will slay him." And therewithal they kneeled down all at once, both rich and poor, and cried Arthur mercy, because they had delayed him so long. And Arthur forgave it them, and took the sword between both his hands, and offered it upon the altar where the archbishop was, and so was he made knight of [1] the best man that was there. And so anon was the coronation made, and there was he sworn to the lords and commons for to be a true king, to stand with true justice from thenceforth all the days of this life. Also then he made all lords that held of the crown to come in, and to do service as they ought to do. And many complaints were made unto King Arthur of great wrongs that were done since the death of King Uther, of many lands that were bereaved of lords, knights, ladies and gentlemen. Wherefore King Arthur made the lands to be given again unto them that owned them. When this was done that the king had stablished all the countries about London, then he let make Sir Kay seneschal of England; and Sir Baudwin of Britain was made constable; and Sir Ulfius was made chamberlain; and Sir Brastias was made warden to wait upon the north from Trent forwards, for it was that time for the most part enemy to the king.

Then on a day there came into the court a squire on horseback, leading a knight before him wounded to the

[1] "Of" was often used for the modern *by* in Sir Thomas Malory's time, and is still so used upon occasion. "Made knight of the best man" thus means *made knight by the best man.*

death, and told him there was a knight in the forest that had reared up a pavilion by a well [*spring*] side, "and hath slain my master, a good knight, and his name was Miles; wherefore I beseech you that my master may be buried, and that some good knight may revenge my master's death." Then was in the court great noise of the knight's death, and every man said his advice. Then came Griflet, that was but a squire, and he was but young, of the age of King Arthur, so he besought the king, for all his service that he had done, to give him the order of knighthood.

"Thou art full young and tender of age," said King Arthur, "for to take so high an order upon thee."

"Sir," said Griflet, "I beseech you to make me a knight."

"Sir," said Merlin, "it were pity to leese [*lose*] Griflet, for he will be a passing good man when he cometh to age, abiding with you the term of his life; and if he adventure his body with yonder knight at the fountain, he shall be in great peril if [1] ever he come again, for he is one of the best knights of the world, and the strongest man of arms."

"Well," said King Arthur. So, at the desire of Griflet, the king made him knight.

"Now," said King Arthur to Sir Griflet, "sithen [*since*] that I have made thee knight, thou must grant me a gift."

"What ye will, my lord," said Sir Griflet.

"Thou shalt promise me, by the faith of thy body, that when thou hast jousted with the knight at the fountain, whether it fall [*happen*] that ye be on foot or on horseback,

[1] "If" here means *whether*. "In great peril if ever he come again," *in great danger of never getting back.*

that in the same manner ye shall come again unto me without any question or making any more debate."

"I will promise you," said Griflet, "as ye desire." Then Sir Griflet took his horse in great haste, and dressed his shield, and took a great spear in his hand, and so he rode a great gallop till he came to the fountain, and thereby he saw a rich pavilion, and thereby under a cloth stood a fair horse well saddled and bridled, and on a tree a shield of divers colors, and a great spear. Then Sir Griflet smote upon the shield with the end of his spear, that the shield fell down to the ground.

With that came the knight out of the pavilion, and said, "Fair knight, why smote ye down my shield?"

"For I will joust with you," said Sir Griflet.

"It were better ye did not," said the knight, "for ye are but young and late made knight, and your might is nothing to mine."

"As for that," said Sir Griflet, "I will joust with you."

"That is me loth," said the knight, "but sith [*since*] I must needs, I will dress me thereto; but of whence be ye?" said the knight.

"Sir, I am of King Arthur's court." So they ran together that Sir Griflet's spear all to-shivered [*shivered all to pieces*], and therewithal he smote Sir Griflet through the shield and the left side, and brake the spear, that the truncheon stuck in his body, that horse and knight fell down.

When the knight saw him lie so on the ground he alighted, and was passing heavy, for he wend [*weened*] he had slain him, and then he unlaced his helm and got him wind, and so with the truncheon he set him on his horse, and betook him to God, and said he had a mighty heart, and if he might live he would prove a passing good knight. And so Sir Griflet rode to the court, whereas great moan was made for him. But through good leeches [*surgeons*] he was healed and his life saved.

And King Arthur was passing wroth for the hurt of Sir Griflet. And by and by he commanded a man of his chamber that his best horse and armor "be without the city or [*before*] to-morrow day." Right so in the morning he met with his man and his horse, and so mounted up and dressed his shield, and took his spear, and bade his chamberlain tarry there till he came again. And so King Arthur rode but a soft pace till it was day, and then was he ware of three churls which chased Merlin, and would have slain him. Then King Arthur rode unto them a good pace, and cried to them: "Flee, churls." Then were they afraid when they saw a knight, and fled away. "O Merlin," said King Arthur, "here hadst thou been slain for[1] all thy craft, had I not been."

"Nay," said Merlin, "not so, for I could save myself if I would, and thou art more near thy death than I am, for thou goest towards thy death, and [2] God be not thy friend."

So, as they went thus talking, they came to the fountain, and the rich pavilion by it. Then King Arthur was ware where a knight sat all armed in a chair. "Sir knight," said

[1] "For" here means *in spite of;* as still used, in certain phrases.

[2] "And" means *if,* here. In later times it becomes contracted into "an," when used in this sense.

King Arthur, "for what cause abidest thou here? That there may no knight ride this way but if he do joust with thee?" said the king. "I rede [*advise*] thee leave that custom," said King Arthur.

"This custom," said the knight, "have I used and will use, maugre [*in spite of*] who saith nay; and who is grieved with my custom, let him amend it that will."

"I will amend it," said King Arthur.

"And I shall defend it," said the knight. Anon he took his horse, and dressed his shield, and took a spear, and they met so hard either on other's shield, that they all to-shivered [*shivered all to pieces*] their spears. Therewith King Arthur drew his sword. "Nay, not so," said the knight, "it is fairer that we twain run more together with sharp spears."

"I will well," said King Arthur, "and [*if*] I had any mo [*more*] spears."

"I have spears enough," said the knight. So there came a squire, and brought two good spears, and King Arthur took one and he another. So they spurred their horses, and came together with all their mights, that either brake their spears to their hands. Then Arthur set hand on his sword. "Nay," said the knight, "ye shall do better; ye are a passing good jouster as ever I met withal, and for the love of the high order of knighthood let us joust once again."

"I assent me," said King Arthur. Anon there were brought two great spears, and every knight gat a spear, and therewith they ran together that Arthur's spear all to-shivered. But the other knight hit him so hard in midst of the shield that horse and man fell to the earth, and therewith Arthur was eager, and pulled out his sword, and said, "I will assay thee, Sir knight, on foot, for I have lost the honor on horseback."

"I will be on horseback," said the knight. Then was Arthur wroth, and dressed his shield towards him with his sword drawn. When the knight saw that, he alight, for him thought no worship to have a knight at such avail, he to be on horseback, and he on foot, and so he alight and dressed his shield unto Arthur. And there began a strong battle with many great strokes, and so hewed with their swords that the cantels [*pieces, of armor or of flesh*] flew in the fields, and much blood they bled both, that all the place there as they fought was over-bled with blood, and thus they fought long, and rested them, and then they went to the battle again, and so hurtled together like two rams that either fell to the earth. So at the last they smote together, that both their swords met even together. But the sword of the knight smote King Arthur's sword in two pieces, wherefore he was heavy. Then said the knight unto Arthur, "Thou art in my danger whether me list to save thee or slay thee, and but thou yield thee as overcome and recreant thou shalt die."

"As for death," said King Arthur, "welcome be it when it cometh, but as to yield me to thee as recreant, I had liever die than to be so shamed." And there withal the king leapt unto Pellinore, and took him by the middle, and threw him down, and raced[1] off his helm. When the knight felt that, he was adread, for he was a passing big man of might, and

[1] "Raced" off: *violently tore off.*

anon he brought King Arthur under him, and raced off his helm, and would have smitten off his head.

Therewithal came Merlin, and said: "Knight, hold thy hand, for and [*if*] thou slay that knight, thou puttest this realm in the greatest damage that ever realm was in, for this knight is a man of more worship than thou wottest of."

"Why, who is he?" said the knight.

"It is King Arthur."

Then would he have slain him for dread of his wrath, and heaved up his sword, and therewith Merlin cast an enchantment on the knight, that he fell to the earth in a great sleep. Then Merlin took up King Arthur, and rode forth upon the knight's horse. "Alas," said King Arthur, "what hast thou done, Merlin? hast thou slain this good knight by thy crafts? There lived not so worshipful a knight as he was; I had liever than the stint [*loss*] of my land a year, that he were on [1] live."

"Care ye not," said Merlin, "for he is wholer than ye, for he is but on [2] sleep, and will awake within three hours. I told you," said Merlin, "what a knight he was; here had ye been slain had I not been. Also, there liveth not a better knight than he is, and he shall do you hereafter right good service, and his name is Pellinore, and he shall have two sons, that shall be passing good men."

Right so the king and he departed, and went unto an hermit that was a good man and a great leech. So the hermit searched all his wounds and gave him good salves; and

[1] "On live": old form of *alive*. [2] "On sleep," *asleep:* as just above "on live," *alive.*

the king was there three days, and then were his wounds well amended that he might ride and go. So Merlin and he departed, and as they rode, Arthur said, "I have no sword."

"No force,"[1] said Merlin, "hereby is a sword that shall be yours, and [*if*] I may." So they rode till they came to a lake, which was a fair water and a broad, and in the middest of the lake King Arthur was ware of an arm clothed in white samite, that held a fair sword in the hand. "Lo," said Merlin, "yonder is that sword that I spake of." With that they saw a damsel going upon the lake.

"What damsel is that?" said Arthur.

"That is the Lady of the Lake," said Merlin; "and this damsel will come to you anon, and then speak ye fair to her that she will give you that sword." Anon withal came the damsel unto Arthur and saluted him, and he her again.

"Damsel," said Arthur, "what sword is that, that yonder the arm holdeth above the water? I would it were mine, for I have no sword."

"Sir king," said the damsel, "that sword is mine, and if ye will give me a gift when I ask it you, ye shall have it."

"By my faith," said Arthur, "I will give you what gift ye will ask."

"Well," said the damsel, "go ye into yonder barge and row yourself to the sword, and take it and the scabbard with you, and I will ask my gift when I see my time."

So King Arthur and Merlin alighted and tied their horses to two trees, and so they went into the ship, and when they came to the sword that the hand held, King Arthur took

[1] "No force," *no matter.*

it up by the handles, and took it with him. And the arm and the hand went under the water; and so they came unto the land and rode forth. And then King Arthur saw a rich pavilion: "What signifieth yonder pavilion?"

"It is the knight's pavilion," said Merlin, "that ye fought with last, Sir Pellinore, but he is out, he is not there; he hath ado with a knight of yours, that hight [*was named*] Egglame, and they have fought together, but at the last Egglame fled, and else he had been dead, and he hath chased him to Caerleon, and we shall anon meet with him in the high way."

"It is well said," quoth King Arthur, "now have I a sword, and now will I wage battle with him and be avenged on him."

"Sir, ye shall not do so," said Merlin, "for the knight is weary of fighting and chasing, so that ye shall have no worship to have ado with him; also he will not lightly be matched of one knight living; and therefore my counsel is that ye let him pass, for he shall do you good service in short time, and his sons after his days. Also ye shall see that day in short space, that ye shall be right glad to give him your sister to wife."

"When I see him," said King Arthur, "I will do as ye advise me."

Then King Arthur looked upon the sword and liked it passing well.

"Whether liketh you better," said Merlin, "the sword or the scabbard?"

"Me liketh better the sword," said King Arthur.

"Ye are more unwise," said Merlin, "for the scabbard is worth ten of the sword, for while ye have the scabbard upon you ye shall leese [*lose*] no blood be ye never so sore wounded, therefore keep well the scabbard alway with you."

So they rode on to Caerleon, and by the way they met with Sir Pellinore. But Merlin had done such a craft that Pellinore saw not Arthur, and so he passed by without any words.

"I marvel," said the king, "that the knight would not speak."

"Sir," said Merlin, "he saw you not, for and [*if*] he had seen you he had not lightly departed."

So they came unto Caerleon, whereof the knights were passing glad; and when they heard of his adventures, they marvelled that he would jeopard his person so alone. But all men of worship said it was merry to be under such a chieftain that would put his person in adventure as other poor knights did.

It befell on a time that King Arthur said to Merlin: "My barons will let me have no rest, but needs they will have that I take a wife, and I will none take but by thy counsel and by thine advice."

"It is well done," said Merlin, "that ye take a wife, for a man of your bounty and nobleness should not be without a wife. Now is there any fair lady that ye love better than another?"

"Yea," said King Arthur, "I love Guenever, the king's daughter Leodegrance[1] of the land of Cameliard, which

[1] "The king's daughter Leodegrance," *King Leodegrance's daughter.*

Leodegrance holdeth in his house the Table Round that ye told he had of my father Uther. And this damsel is the most gentlest and fairest lady that I know living, or yet that ever I could find."

And Merlin went forth to King Leodegrance of Cameliard, and told him of the desire of the king, that he would have to his wife Guenever his daughter.

"That is to me," said King Leodegrance, "the best tidings that ever I heard, that so worthy a king of prowess and of nobleness will wed my daughter. And as for my lands I will give him, wished I that it might please him, but he hath lands enough, he needeth none; but I shall send him a gift that shall please him much more, for I shall give him the Table Round, the which Utherpendragon gave me; and when it is full complete, there is an hundred knights and fifty, and as for an hundred good knights I have myself, but I lack fifty, for so many have been slain in my days."

And so King Leodegrance delivered his daughter Guenever unto Merlin, and the Table Round with the hundred knights; and so they rode freshly with great royalty, what by water and what by land, till they came that night unto London.

When King Arthur heard of the coming of Guenever and the hundred knights with the Table Round, he made great joy for their coming, and said openly, "This fair lady is passing welcome to me, for I loved her long, and therefore there is nothing so pleasing to me. And these knights with the Round Table please me more than right great riches."

Then in all haste the king did ordain for the marriage and the coronation in the most honorablest wise that could be devised.

"Now Merlin," said King Arthur, "go thou and espy me in all this land fifty knights which be of most prowess and worship."

Within short time Merlin had found such knights that should fulfil twenty and eight knights, but no more he could find. Then the bishop of Canterbury was fetched, and he blessed the sieges [*seats*] with great royalty and devotion, and there set the eight and twenty knights in their sieges.

And when this was done Merlin said, "Fair sirs, ye must all arise and come to King Arthur for to do him homage; he will have the better will to maintain you."

And so they arose and did their homage. And when they were gone Merlin found in every siege letters of gold that told the knights' names that had sitten therein. But two sieges were void.

"What is the cause," said King Arthur, "that there be two places void in the sieges?"

"Sir," said Merlin, "there shall no man sit in those places but they that shall be of most worship. But in the Siege Perilous there shall no man sit therein but one, and if there be any so hardy to do it he shall be destroyed, and he that shall sit there shall have no fellow."

And therewith Merlin took King Pellinore by the hand, and, in the one hand next the two sieges and the Siege Perilous, he said in open audience, "This is your place, and best ye be worthy to sit therein of any that is here."

BOOK II

OF SIR LAUNCELOT DU LAKE

OF SIR LAUNCELOT DU LAKE

ANON after that the noble and worthy King Arthur was come from Rome into England, all the knights of the Round Table resorted unto the king, and made many jousts and tournaments, and some there were that were good knights, which increased so in arms and worship that they passed all their fellows in prowess and noble deeds, and that was well proved on many, but especially it was proved on Sir Launcelot du Lake. For in all tournaments and jousts and deeds of arms, both for life and death, he passed all knights, and at no time he was never overcome, but it were by treason or enchantment. Wherefore Queen Guenever had him in great favor above all other knights, and certainly he loved the queen again above all other ladies and damsels all the days of his life, and for her he did many great deeds of arms, and saved her from the fire through his noble chivalry. Thus Sir Launcelot rested him a long while with play and game; and then he thought to prove himself in strange adventures. Then he bade his brother Sir Lionel to make him ready, "for we two will seek adventures."

So they mounted upon their horses armed at all points, and rode into a deep forest; and after they came into a great plain, and then the weather was hot about noon, and Sir Launcelot had great list [*desire*] to sleep.

Then Sir Lionel espied a great apple tree that stood by an hedge, and said: "Brother, yonder is a fair shadow, there may we rest us and our horses."

"It is well said, fair brother," said Sir Launcelot; "for of all this seven year I was not so sleepy as I am now."

And so they there alighted and tied their horses under sundry trees, and so Sir Launcelot laid him down under an apple tree, and his helm he laid under his head. And Sir Lionel waked while he slept. So Sir Launcelot was asleep passing fast. And in the mean while there came three knights riding, as fast fleeing as ever they might ride. And there followed them three but one knight. And when Sir Lionel saw him, him thought he saw never so great a knight nor so well faring a man, neither so well apparelled unto all rights. So within a while this strong knight had overtaken one of these knights, and there he smote him to the cold earth that he lay still. And then he rode unto the second knight, and smote him so that man and horse fell down. And then straight to the third knight he rode, and he smote him behind his horse's tail a spear's length. And then he alighted down, and reined his horse on the bridle, and bound all the three knights fast with the reins of their own bridles. When Sir Lionel saw him do thus, he thought to assay him, and made him ready, and stilly and privily he took his horse, and thought not for to awake Sir Launcelot. And when he was mounted upon his horse he overtook this strong knight and bade him turn: and the other smote

Sir Lionel so hard that horse and man he bare to the earth, and so he alighted down and bound him fast, and threw him overthwart his own horse, and so he served them all four, and rode with them away to his own castle. And when he came there, he made unarm them, and beat them with thorns all naked, and after put them in a deep prison where there were many more knights that made great dolor.

When Sir Ector de Maris wist that Sir Launcelot was past out of the court to seek adventures he was wroth with himself, and made him ready to seek Sir Launcelot, and as he had ridden long in a great forest, he met with a man that was like a forester. "Fair fellow," said Sir Ector, "knowest thou in this country any adventures that be here nigh hand?"

"Sir," said the forester, "this country know I well, and hereby within this mile is a strong manor, and well diked, and by that manor, on the left hand, there is a fair ford for horses to drink of, and over that ford there groweth a fair tree, and thereon hangeth many fair shields that wielded sometime good knights: and at the hole of the tree hangeth a basin of copper and laton [*brass*], and strike upon that basin with the butt of thy spear thrice, and soon after thou shalt hear new tidings, and else hast thou the fairest grace that many a year had ever knight that passed through this forest."

"Gramercy" [*thanks*], said Sir Ector, and departed and came to the tree, and saw many fair shields, and among them he saw his brother's shield, Sir Lionel, and many more that he knew that were his fellows of the Round Table, the which grieved his heart, and he promised to revenge his brother. Then anon Sir Ector beat on the basin as he were wood [*crazy*], and then he gave his horse drink at the ford: and there came a knight behind him and bade him come out of the water and make him ready; and Sir Ector anon turned him shortly, and in fewter cast[1] his spear, and smote the other knight a great buffet that his horse turned twice about.

"This was well done," said the strong knight, "and knightly thou hast stricken me:" and therewith he rushed his horse on Sir Ector and caught him under his right arm, and bare him clean out of the saddle, and rode with him away into his own hall, and threw him down in the midst of the floor. The name of this knight was Sir Turquine. Then he said unto Sir Ector, "For thou hast done this day more unto me than any knight did these twelve years, now will I grant thee thy life, so thou wilt be sworn to be my prisoner all thy life-days."

"Nay," said Sir Ector, "that will I never promise thee, but that I will do mine advantage."

"That me repenteth," said Sir Turquine.

And then he made to unarm him, and beat him with thorns all naked, and after put him down in a deep dungeon, where he knew many of his fellows. But when Sir Ector saw Sir Lionel, then made he great sorrow.

"Alas, brother," said Sir Ector, "where is my brother Sir Launcelot?"

"Fair brother, I left him on sleep when that I from him

[1] "In fewter cast his spear," *in rest placed his spear.*

went, under an apple tree, and what is become of him I cannot tell you."

"Alas," said the knights, "but Sir Launcelot help us we may never be delivered, for we know now no knight that is able to match our master Turquine."

Now leave we these knights prisoners, and speak we of Sir Launcelot du Lake that lieth under the apple tree sleeping. Even about the noon there came by him four queens of great estate; and, for the heat of the sun should not annoy them, there rode four knights about them and bare a cloth of green silk on four squares, betwixt them and the sun, and the queens rode on four white mules.

Thus as they rode they heard by them a great horse grimly neigh, and then were they ware of a sleeping knight that lay all armed under an apple tree; anon as these queens looked on his face they knew that it was Sir Launcelot. Then they began for to strive for that knight; every one said she would have him to her love.

"We shall not strive," said Morgan le Fay that was King Arthur's sister; "I shall put an enchantment upon him that he shall not awake in six hours, and then I will lead him away unto my castle, and when he is surely within my hold I shall take the enchantment from him, and then let him choose which of us he will have for his love."

So this enchantment was cast upon Sir Launcelot, and then they laid him upon his shield, and bare him so on horseback betwixt two knights, and brought him unto the castle Chariot, and there they laid him in a chamber cold, and at night they sent unto him a fair damsel with his supper ready dight. By that the enchantment was past, and when she came she saluted him, and asked him what cheer?

"I cannot say, fair damsel," said Sir Launcelot, "for I wot not how I came into this castle but it be by an enchantment."

"Sir," said she, "ye must make good cheer, and if ye be such a knight as is said ye be, I shall tell you more tomorn [*to-morrow*] by prime [*the first hour*] of the day."

"Gramercy, fair damsel," said Sir Launcelot, "of your good will I require you."

And so she departed. And there he lay all that night without comfort of anybody.

And on the morn early came these four queens, passingly well beseen, all they bidding him good morn, and he them again.

"Sir knight," the four queens said, "thou must understand thou art our prisoner, and we here know thee well, that thou art Sir Launcelot du Lake, King Ban's son. And truly we understand your worthiness that thou art the noblest knight living; and therefore thee behoveth now to choose one of us four. I am the Queen Morgan le Fay, Queen of the land of Gore, and here is the Queen of Northgalis, and the Queen of Eastland, and the Queen of the Out Isles; now choose ye one of us which thou wilt have to thy love, for thou mayst not choose or else in this prison to die."

"This is an hard case," said Sir Launcelot, "that either I must die or else choose one of you, yet had I liever to die in this prison with worship, than to have one of you to my love maugre my head. And therefore ye be answered, for I will have none of you, for ye be false enchantresses."

"Well," said the queens, "is this your answer, that you will refuse us?"

"Yea, upon my life," said Sir Launcelot, "refused ye be of me."

So they departed, and left him there alone that made great sorrow.

Right so at noon came the damsel to him, and brought him his dinner, and asked him what cheer.

"Truly, fair damsel," said Sir Launcelot, "in all my life-days never so ill."

"Sir," said she, "that me repenteth; but and ye will be ruled by me, I shall help you out of this distress, and ye shall have no shame nor villany, so that ye hold me a promise."

"Fair damsel, that I will grant you, and sore I am afeared of these queen's witches, for they have destroyed many a good knight."

"Sir," said she, "that is sooth, and for the renown and bounty they hear of you, they would have your love, and, sir, they say that your name is Sir Launcelot du Lake, the flower of all the knights that been living, and they been passing wroth with you that ye have refused them; but, sir, and ye would promise me for to help my father on Tuesday next coming, that hath made a tournament between him and the King of Northgalis; for the Tuesday last past my father lost the field through three knights of King Arthur's court, and if ye will be there upon Tuesday next coming and help my father, to-morrow or [*ere*] prime, by the grace of God, I shall deliver you clean."

"Fair maiden," said Sir Launcelot, "tell me what is your father's name, and then shall I give you an answer."

"Sir knight," said the damsel, "my father is King Bagdemagus, that was foully rebuked at the last tournament."

"I know your father well," said Sir Launcelot, "for a noble king and a good knight, and by the faith of my body, ye shall have my body ready to do your father and you service at that day."

"Sir," said the damsel, "gramercy, and to-morrow await that ye be ready betimes, and I shall deliver you; and take you your armor and your horse, shield, and spear; and hereby within these ten miles is an abbey of white monks, and there I pray you to abide, and thither shall I bring my father unto you."

"All this shall be done," said Sir Launcelot, "as I am a true knight."

And so she departed, and came on the morrow early and found him ready. Then she brought him out of twelve locks, and brought him unto his armor. And when he was all armed and arrayed, she brought him unto his own horse, and lightly he saddled him, and took a great spear in his hand, and so rode forth, and said, "Fair damsel, I shall not fail you, by the grace of God."

And so he rode into a great forest all that day, and in no wise could he find any highway, and so the night fell on him, and then was he ware in a slade [*glade*] of a pavilion of red sendall.[1] "By my faith," said Sir Launcelot, "in that pavilion will I lodge all this night." And so there he alighted down, and tied his horse to the pavilion, and there he unarmed him, and found there a rich bed and laid him therein, and anon he fell on sleep.

So thus within a while the night passed and the day appeared, and then Sir Launcelot armed him and mounted upon his horse, and took his leave, and they showed him the way towards the abbey, and thither they rode within the space of two hours.

As soon as Sir Launcelot came within the abbey yard, King Bagdemagus' daughter heard a great horse go on the pavement. And then she arose and went unto a window, and there she saw that it was Sir Launcelot, and anon she made men hastily to go to him, which took his horse and led him into a stable, and himself was led into a fair chamber, and there he unarmed him, and the lady sent to him a long gown, and anon she came herself. And then she made Sir Launcelot passing good cheer, and she said he was the knight in the world that was most welcome to her. Then she in all the haste sent for her father King Bagdemagus, that was within twelve miles of that abbey, and before even he came with a fair fellowship of knights with him. And when the king was alighted from his horse, he went straight unto Sir Launcelot's chamber, and there found his daughter, and then the king embraced Sir Launcelot in his arms, and either made other good cheer. Anon Sir Launcelot made his

[1] "Sendall," *a kind of silk.*

complaint unto the king how he was betrayed, and how his brother Sir Lionel was departed from him he wist not whither, and how his daughter had delivered him out of prison, "wherefore I shall while I live do her service and all her friends and kindred."

"Then am I sure of your help," said the king, "now on Tuesday next coming?"

"Ye, sir," said Sir Launcelot, "I shall not fail you, for so have I promised unto my lady, your daughter. As I hear say that the tournament shall be within this three mile of this abbey, ye shall send unto me three knights of yours such as ye trust, and look that the three knights have all white shields, and I also, and no painture on the shields, and we four will come out of a little wood in the midst of both parties, and we shall fall in the front of our enemies and grieve them that we may; and thus shall I not be known what knight I am." So they took their rest that night, and this was on the Sunday. And so the king departed, and sent unto Sir Launcelot three knights, with the four white shields.

And on the Tuesday they lodged them in a little leaved wood beside where the tournament should be. And there were scaffolds that lords and ladies might behold, and to give the prize. Then came into the field the King of Northgalis with eightscore helms. And then the three knights of Arthur stood by themselves. Then came into the field King Bagdemagus with fourscore of helms. And then they fewtred [*placed in rest*] their spears, and came together with a great dash, and there were slain of knights, at the first encounter, twelve of King Bagdemagus' party, and six of the King of Northgalis' party, and King Bagdemagus' party was far set aback.

With that came Sir Launcelot du Lake, and he thrust in with his spear in the thickest of the press, and there he smote down with one spear five knights, and of four of them he brake their backs. And in that throng he smote down the King of Northgalis, and brake his thigh in that fall. All this doing of Sir Launcelot saw the three knights of Arthur.

"Yonder is a shrewd guest," said Sir Mador de la Porte, "therefore have here once at him."

So they encountered, and Sir Launcelot bare him down horse and man, so that his shoulder went out of joint.

"Now befalleth it to me to joust," said Mordred, "for Sir Mador hath a sore fall."

Sir Launcelot was ware of him, and gat a great spear in his hand, and met him, and Sir Mordred brake a spear upon him, and Sir Launcelot gave him such a buffet that the bow of his saddle brake, and so he flew over his horse's tail, that his helm went into the earth a foot and more, that nigh his neck was broken, and there he lay long in a swoon. Then came in Sir Gahalatine with a spear, and Launcelot against him, with all their strength that they might drive, that both their spears to-brast [*burst to pieces*] even to their hands, and then they flung out with their swords, and gave many a grim stroke. Then was Sir Launcelot wroth out of measure, and then he smote Sir Gahalatine on the helm, that his nose burst out on blood, and ears and mouth both, and therewith his head hung low. And therewith his horse ran away with him, and he fell down to the earth.

Anon therewithal Sir Launcelot gat a great spear in his hand, and, or [*ere*] ever that great spear brake, he bare down to the earth sixteen knights, some horse and man, and some the man and not the horse, and there was none but that he hit surely. He bare none arms [*no device to be known by*] that day. And then he gat another great spear, and smote down twelve knights, and the most part of them never throve after. And then the knights of the King of Northgalis would joust no more, and there the prize was given unto King Bagdemagus. So either party departed unto his own place, and Sir Launcelot rode forth with King Bagdemagus unto his castle, and there he had passing good cheer both with the king and with his daughter, and they proffered him great gifts. And on the morn he took his leave, and told King Bagdemagus that he would go and seek his brother Sir Lionel, that went from him when that he slept. So he took his horse, and betaught [*commended*] them all to God. And there he said unto the king's daughter, "If ye have need any time of my service, I pray you let me have knowledge, and I shall not fail you, as I am a true knight."

And so Sir Launcelot departed, and by adventure he came into the same forest where he was taken sleeping. And in the midst of an highway he met a damsel riding on a white palfrey, and there either saluted other.

"Fair damsel," said Sir Launcelot, "know ye in this country any adventures?"

"Sir knight," said that damsel, "here are adventures near hand, and [*if*] thou durst prove them."

"Why should I not prove adventures?" said Sir Launcelot; "for that cause came I hither."

"Well," said she, "thou seemest well to be a good knight, and if thou dare meet with a good knight, I shall bring thee where is the best knight and the mightiest that ever thou foundest, so thou wilt tell me what is thy name, and what knight thou art."

"Damsel, as for to tell thee my name, I take no great force: truly, my name is Sir Launcelot du Lake."

"Sir, thou beseemest well, here be adventures by that fall for thee, for hereby dwelleth a knight that will not be overmatched for no man that I know, unless ye overmatch him, and his name is Sir Turquine. And, as I understand, he hath in his prison of Arthur's court good knights three-score and four that he hath won with his own hands. But when ye have done that day's work ye shall promise me as ye are a true knight for to go with me, and to help me and other damsels that are distressed daily with a false knight."

"All your intent, damsel, and desire I will fulfil, so ye will bring me unto this knight."

"Now, fair knight, come on your way."

And so she brought him unto the ford, and unto the tree where hung the basin. So Sir Launcelot let his horse drink, and then he beat on the basin with the butt of his spear so hard with all his might till the bottom fell out, and long he did so, but he saw nothing. Then he rode along the gates of that manor nigh half an hour. And then was he ware of a great knight that drove an horse afore him, and overthwart the horse there lay an armed knight bound. And ever as they came near and near, Sir Launcelot thought he should know him; then Sir Launcelot was ware that it was Sir Gaheris, Gawaine's brother, a knight of the Table Round.

"Now, fair damsel," said Sir Launcelot, "I see yonder cometh a knight fast bound that is a fellow of mine, and brother he is unto Sir Gawaine. And at the first beginning I promise you, by the leave of God, to rescue that knight; and unless his master sit better in the saddle I shall deliver all the prisoners that he hath out of danger, for I am sure that he hath two brethren of mine prisoners with him."

By that time that either had seen other they gripped their spears unto them.

"Now, fair knight," said Sir Launcelot, "put that wounded knight off the horse, and let him rest awhile, and let us two prove our strengths. For as it is informed me, thou doest and hast done great despite and shame unto knights of the Round Table, and therefore now defend thee."

"And [*if*] thou be of the Table Round," said Turquine, "I defy thee and all thy fellowship."

"That is overmuch said," said Sir Launcelot.

And then they put their spears in the rests, and came together with their horses as fast as they might run, and either smote other in the midst of their shields, that both their horses' backs brast under them, and the knights were both astonied, and as soon as they might avoid their horses they took their shields afore them, and drew out their swords, and came together eagerly, and either gave other many strong strokes, for there might neither shields nor harness hold their strokes. And so within a while they had both grimly wounds, and bled passing grievously. Thus they fared two hours or more, trasing and rasing [*feinting and thrusting*] either other where they might hit any bare place. Then at the last they were breathless both, and stood leaning on their swords.

"Now, fellow," said Sir Turquine, "hold thy hand awhile, and tell me what I shall ask thee."

"Say on."

Then Turquine said, "Thou art the biggest man that ever I met withal, and the best breathed, and like one knight that I hate above all other knights; so be it that thou be not he I will lightly accord with thee, and for thy love I will deliver all the prisoners that I have, that is threescore and four, so thou wilt tell me thy name. And thou and I will be fellows together, and never to fail the while that I live."

"It is well said," said Sir Launcelot, "but since it is so that I may have thy friendship, what knight is he that thou so hatest above all other?"

"Truly," said Sir Turquine, "his name is Launcelot du Lake, for he slew my brother Sir Carados at the Dolorous Tower, which was one of the best knights then living, and therefore him I except of all knights, for and [*if*] I may once meet with him, that one of us shall make an end of another, and do that I make a vow. And for Sir Launcelot's sake I have slain an hundred good knights, and as many I have utterly maimed, that never after they might help themselves, and many have died in my prison, and yet I have threescore and four, and all shall be delivered, so that thou wilt tell me thy name, and so it be that thou be not Sir Launcelot."

"Now see I well," said Sir Launcelot, "that such a man I might be I might have peace, and such a man I might be there should be between us two mortal war; and now, sir knight, at thy request, I will that thou wit and know that I am Sir Launcelot du Lake, King Ban's son of Benwick, and knight of the Round Table. And now I defy thee do thy best."

"Ah!" said Sir Turquine, "Launcelot, thou art unto me most welcome, as ever was any knight, for we shall never depart till the one of us be dead."

And then hurtled they together as two wild bulls, rashing and lashing with their shields and swords, that sometime they fell both on their noses. Thus they fought still two hours and more, and never would rest, and Sir Turquine gave Sir Launcelot many wounds that all the ground there as they fought was all besprinkled with blood.

Then at last Sir Turquine waxed very faint, and gave somewhat back, and bare his shield full low for weariness. That soon espied Sir Launcelot, and then leaped upon him fiercely as a lion, and got him by the banner of his helmet, and so he plucked him down on his knees, and anon he rased [*tore off*] his helm, and then he smote his neck asunder.

So on the third day he rode over a long bridge, and there started upon him suddenly a passing foul churl, and he smote his horse on the nose that he turned about, and asked him why he rode over that bridge without his license.

"Why should I not ride this way?" said Sir Launcelot. "I may not ride beside."

"Thou shalt not choose," said the churl, and lashed at him with a great club shod with iron. Then Sir Launcelot drew a sword, and put the stroke aback, and clave his head unto the breast. At the end of the bridge was a fair village, and all the people men and women cried on Sir Launcelot, and said, "A worse deed didst thou never for thyself, for thou hast slain the chief porter of our castle."

Sir Launcelot let them say what they would, and straight he went into the castle; and when he came into the castle he alighted, and tied his horse to a ring on the wall; and there he saw a fair green court, and thither he dressed himself, for there him thought was a fair place to fight in. So he looked about, and saw much people in doors and windows, that said, "Fair knight, thou art unhappy."

Anon withal came there upon him two great giants, well armed all save the heads, with two horrible clubs in their hands. Sir Launcelot put his shield afore him, and put the stroke away of the one giant, and with his sword he clave his head asunder. When his fellow saw that, he ran away as he were wood [*crazy*], for fear of the horrible strokes, and Sir Launcelot after him with all his might, and smote him on the shoulder, and clave him to the middle. Then Sir Launcelot went into the hall, and there came afore him threescore ladies and damsels, and all kneeled unto him, and thanked God and him of their deliverance.

"For, sir," said they, "the most part of us have been here this seven year their prisoners, and we have worked all manner of silk works for our meat, and we are all great gentle-women born, and blessed be the time, knight, that ever thou wert born; for thou hast done the most worship that ever did knight in the world, that will we bear record, and we all pray you to tell us your name, that we may tell our friends who delivered us out of prison."

"Fair damsels," he said, "my name is Sir Launcelot du Lake."

"Ah, sir," said they all, "well mayest thou be he, for else save yourself, as we deemed, there might never knight have the better of these two giants, for many fair knights have assayed it, and here have ended, and many times have we wished after you, and these two giants dread never knight but you."

"Now may ye say," said Sir Launcelot, "unto your friends, how and who hath delivered you, and greet them all from me, and if that I come in any of your marches [*boundaries*] show me such cheer as ye have cause; and what treasure that there is in this castle I give it you for a reward for your grievance: and the lord that is the owner of this castle I would that he received it as is right."

"Fair sir," said they, "the name of this castle is Tinta-gil and a duke owned it some time that had wedded fair Igraine, and after wedded her Utherpendragon."

"Well," said Sir Launcelot, "I understand to whom this castle belongeth."

And so he departed from them and betaught [*commended*]

them unto God. And then he mounted upon his horse, and rode into many strange and wild countries and through many waters and valleys, and evil was he lodged. And at the last by fortune him happened against a night to come to a fair curtilage [*enclosure*], and therein he found an old gentlewoman that lodged him with a good will, and there he had good cheer for him and his horse. And when time was, his host brought him into a fair garret over the gate to his bed. There Sir Launcelot unarmed him, and set his harness by him, and went to bed, and anon he fell on sleep. So soon after there came one on horseback, and knocked at the gate in great haste. And when Sir Launcelot heard this he arose up, and looked out at the window, and saw by the moonlight three knights came riding after one man, and all three lashed on him at once with swords, and that one knight turned on them knightly again and defended him.

"Truly," said Sir Launcelot, "yonder one knight shall I help, for it were shame for me to see three knights on one, and if he be slain I am partner of his death."

And therewith he took his harness and went out at a window by a sheet down to the four knights, and then Sir Launcelot said on high [*in a loud voice*], "Turn you knights unto me, and leave your fighting with that knight."

And then they all three left Sir Kay, and turned unto Sir Launcelot, and there began great battle, for they alighted all three, and struck many great strokes at Sir Launcelot, and assailed him on every side. Then Sir Kay dressed him for to have holpen Sir Launcelot.

"Nay, sir," said he, "I will none of your help, therefore as ye will have my help let me alone with them."

Sir Kay for the pleasure of the knight suffered him to do his will, and so stood aside. And then anon within six strokes Sir Launcelot had stricken them to the earth.

And then they all three cried, "Sir knight, we yield us unto you as man of might matchless."

"As to that," said Sir Launcelot, "I will not take your yielding unto me, but so that ye yield you unto Sir Kay the seneschal; on that covenant I will save your lives and else not."

"Fair knight," said they, "that were we loath to do; for as for Sir Kay we chased him hither, and had overcome him had not ye been; therefore to yield us unto him it were no reason."

"Well, as to that," said Sir Launcelot, "advise you well, for ye may choose whether ye will die or live, for and [*if*] ye be yielden it shall be unto Sir Kay."

"Fair knight," then they said, "in saving our lives we will do as thou commandest us."

"Then shall ye," said Sir Launcelot, "on Whitsunday next coming go unto the court of King Arthur, and there shall ye yield you unto Queen Guenever, and put you all three in her grace and mercy, and say that Sir Kay sent you thither to be her prisoners."

"Sir," they said, "it shall be done by the faith of our bodies, and we be living."

And there they swore, every knight upon his sword. And so Sir Launcelot suffered them so to depart. And then Sir Launcelot knocked at the gate with the pommel of his sword, and with that came his host, and in they entered, Sir Kay and he.

"Sir," said his host, "I wend ye had been in your bed."

"So I was," said Sir Launcelot, "but I arose and leaped out at my window for to help an old fellow of mine."

And so when they came nigh the light Sir Kay knew well that it was Sir Launcelot, and therewith he kneeled down and thanked him of all his kindness that he hath holpen him twice from the death.

"Sir," he said, "I have done nothing but that I ought to do, and ye are welcome, and here shall ye repose you and take your rest."

So when Sir Kay was unarmed he asked after meat, so there was meat fetched him, and he ate strongly. And when he had supped they went to their beds, and were lodged together in one bed. On the morn Sir Launcelot arose early, and left Sir Kay sleeping: and Sir Launcelot took Sir Kay's armor and his shield and armed him: and so he went to the stable and took his horse, and took his leave of his host, and so he departed. Then soon after arose Sir Kay and missed Sir Launcelot: and then he espied that he had his armor and his horse.

"Now, by my faith, I know well that he will grieve some of King Arthur's court: for on him knights will be bold, and deem that it is I, and that will beguile them; and because of his armor and shield, I am sure that I shall ride in peace." And then soon after departed Sir Kay, and thanked his host.

Now let us speak of Sir Launcelot, that rode a great while in a deep forest, where he saw a black brachet [*small hound*], seeking in manner as it had been in the fealty [*track*] of an hurt deer, and therewith he rode after the brachet; and he saw lie on the ground a large fealty of blood, and then Sir Launcelot rode after, and ever the brachet looked behind her. And so she went through a great marish [*marsh*], and ever Sir Launcelot followed; and then was he ware of an old manor, and thither ran the brachet, and so over the bridge. So Sir Launcelot rode over the bridge, that was old and feeble. And when he came into the midst of a great hall, there saw he lie a dead knight, that was a seemly man, and that brachet licked his wounds. And therewith came out a lady weeping and wringing her hands, and she said, "O knight, too much sorrow hast thou brought me."

"Why say ye so?" said Sir Launcelot, "I did never this knight no harm, for hither by track of blood this brachet brought me; and therefore, fair lady, be not displeased with me, for I am full sore aggrieved of your grievance."

"Truly, sir," she said, "I trow it be not ye that have slain my husband, for he that did that deed is sore wounded, and he is never likely to recover, that shall I ensure him."

"What was your husband's name?" said Sir Launcelot.

"Sir," said she, "his name was called Sir Gilbert, one of the best knights of the world, and he that hath slain him I know not his name."

"Now God send you better comfort," said Sir Launcelot.

And so he departed and went into the forest again, and there he met with a damsel, the which knew him well, and she said aloud, "Well be ye found, my lord; and now I require thee on thy knighthood help my brother that is sore wounded, and never stinteth bleeding, for this day fought he with Sir Gilbert and slew him in plain battle, and there was my brother sore wounded, and there is a lady a sorceress that dwelleth in a castle here beside, and this day she told me my brother's wounds should never be whole till I could find a knight that would go into the Chapel Perilous, and there he should find a sword and a bloody cloth that the wounded knight was lapped in, and a piece of that cloth and sword should heal my brother's wounds, so that his wounds were searched [*touched*] with the sword and the cloth."

"This is a marvellous thing," said Sir Launcelot, "but what is your brother's name?"

"Sir," said she, "his name is Sir Meliot de Logres."

"That me repenteth," said Sir Launcelot, "for he is a fellow of the Table Round, and to his help I will do my power."

"Then, sir," said she, "follow even this highway, and it will bring you unto the Chapel Perilous, and here I shall abide till God send you here again, and but you speed I know no knight living that may achieve that adventure."

Right so Sir Launcelot departed, and when he came unto the Chapel Perilous he alighted down, and tied his horse to a little gate. And as soon as he was within the churchyard he saw on the front of the chapel many fair rich shields turned up so down [*upside down*], and many of the shields Sir Launcelot had seen knights bear beforehand. With that he saw by him stand there thirty great knights, more by a yard than any man that ever he had seen, and all those grinned and gnashed at Sir Launcelot. And when he saw their countenance he dread him sore, and so put his shield afore him, and took his sword in his hand ready unto battle; and they were all armed in black harness, ready with their shields and their swords drawn. And when Sir Launcelot would have gone throughout them, they scattered on every side of him, and gave him the way, and therewith he waxed all bold and entered into the chapel, and then he saw no light but a dim lamp burning, and then was he ware of a corpse covered with a cloth of silk. Then Sir Launcelot stooped down and cut a piece away of that cloth, and then it fared under him as the earth had quaked a little; therewithal he feared. And then he saw a fair sword lie by the dead knight, and that he gat in his hand and hied him out of the chapel. Anon as ever he was in the chapel-yard all the knights spake to him with a grimly voice, and said, "Knight, Sir Launcelot, lay that sword from thee, or else thou shalt die."

"Whether I live or die," said Sir Launcelot, "will no great word get it again, therefore fight for it and ye list."

Then right so he passed throughout them, and beyond the chapel-yard there met him a fair damsel, and said, "Sir Launcelot, leave that sword behind thee, or thou wilt die for it."

"I leave it not," said Sir Launcelot, "for no entreaties."

"No," said she, "and thou didst leave that sword, Queen Guenever should ye never see."

"Then were I a fool and I would leave this sword," said Launcelot.

"Now, gentle knight," said the damsel, "I require thee to kiss me but once."

"Nay," said Sir Launcelot, "that God me forbid."

"Well, sir," said she, "and thou hadst kissed me thy life days had been done, but now alas," she said, "I have lost all my labor, for I ordained this chapel for thy sake. And, Sir Launcelot, now I tell thee, I have loved thee this seven year. But since I may not have [thee] alive, I had kept no more joy in this world but to have [thee] dead. Then would I have balmed [thee] and preserved [thee], and so have kept [thee] my life days, and daily I should have kissed thee."

"Ye say well," said Sir Launcelot, "God preserve me from your subtle crafts."

And therewithal he took his horse and so departed from her. And when Sir Launcelot was departed she took such sorrow that she died within a fourteen night [*fortnight*], and her name was Hellawes the sorceress, lady of the castle Nigramous. Anon Sir Launcelot met with the damsel, Sir Meliot's sister. And when she saw him she clapped her hands and wept for joy, and then they rode unto a castle thereby, where Sir Meliot lay. And anon as Sir Launcelot saw him he knew him, but he was pale as the earth for bleeding. When Sir Meliot saw Sir Launcelot, he kneeled upon his knees and cried on high: "O lord Sir Launcelot help me!" Anon Sir Launcelot leaped unto him, and touched his wounds with Sir Gilbert's sword, and then he wiped his wounds with a part of the bloody cloth that Sir Gilbert was wrapped in, and anon a wholer man in his life was he never. And then there was great joy between them, and they made Sir Launcelot all the cheer that they might, and so on the morn Sir Launcelot took his leave, and bade Sir Meliot hie him to the court of my lord Arthur, "for it draweth nigh to the feast of Pentecost, and there, by the grace of God, ye shall find me." And therewith they departed.

Sir Launcelot came home two days afore the feast of Pentecost. And King Arthur and all the court were full glad of his coming. And when Sir Gawaine, Sir Ewaine, Sir Sagramour, and Sir Ector de Maris saw Sir Launcelot in Sir Kay's armor, then they wist well it was he that smote them down all with one spear. Then there was laughing and smiling among them. And ever now and then came all the knights home that Sir Turquine had taken prisoners, and they all honored and worshipped Sir Launcelot. When Sir Gaheris heard them speak, he said: "I saw all the battle, from the beginning to the ending."

And there he told King Arthur all how it was, and how Sir Turquine was the strongest knight that ever he saw except Sir Launcelot; there were many knights bare him record, nigh threescore. Then Sir Kay told the king how Sir Launcelot had rescued him when he was in danger to have been slain, and how "he made the knights to yield them to me, and not to him." And there they were, all three, and bare record. "And," said Sir Kay, "because Sir Launcelot took my harness, and left me his, I rode in good peace, and no man would have to do with me." Then anon therewithal came the three knights that fought with Sir Launcelot at the long bridge, and there they yielded them unto Sir Kay, and Sir Kay forsook them, and said he fought never with them; "but I shall ease your hearts," said Sir Kay, "yonder is Sir Launcelot that overcame you." When they understood that, they were glad. And then Sir Meliot de Logres came home, and told King Arthur how Sir Launcelot had saved him from the death. And all his deeds were known, how four queens, sorceresses, had him in prison, and how he was delivered by King Bagdemagus' daughter. Also there were told all the great deeds of arms that Sir Launcelot did betwixt the two kings, that is to say, the King of Northgalis and King Bagdemagus. All the truth Sir Gahalatine did tell, and Sir Mador de la Porte, and Sir Mordred, for they were at that same tournament. Then came in the lady that knew Sir Launcelot when that he wounded Sir Belleus at the pavilion. And there at the request of Sir Launcelot, Sir Belleus was made knight of the Round Table.

And so at that time Sir Launcelot had the greatest name of any knight of the world, and most he was honored of high and low.

[On a day, that might be a matter of two years before that feast of Pentecost whereof it will be told in the Book of Sir Tristram, it happened that Queen Guenever was angered with Sir Launcelot, yet truly for no fault of his, but only because a certain enchantress had wrought that Sir Launcelot seemed to have shamed his knighthood.

Then the queen was nigh out of her wit, and then she writhed and weltered as a mad woman; and at the last the queen met with Sir Launcelot, and thus she said,] "False traitor knight that thou art, look thou never abide in my court, and not so hardy, thou false traitor knight that thou art, that ever thou come in my sight."

"Alas!" said Sir Launcelot: and therewith he took such an heartly sorrow at her words that he fell down to the floor in a swoon. And therewithal Queen Guenever departed. And when Sir Launcelot awoke of his swoon he leaped out at a bay window into a garden, and there with thorns he was all to-scratched in his visage and his body, and so he ran forth he wist not whither, and was wild wood [*insane*] as ever was man.

"Wit ye well," said dame Elaine[1] to Sir Bors, "I would lose my life for him rather than he should be hurt; but alas, I cast me never for to see him; and the chief causer of this is dame Guenever."

"Madam," said dame Brisen, the which had made the enchantment before betwixt Sir Launcelot and her, "I pray you heartily let Sir Bors depart and hie him with all his might, as fast as he may, to seek Sir Launcelot. For I warn you he is clean out of his mind, and yet he shall be well holpen, and but by miracle."

Then wept dame Elaine, and so did Sir Bors de Ganis, and so they departed; and Sir Bors rode straight unto Queen Guenever, and when she saw Sir Bors she wept as she were wood.

"Fie on your weeping," said Sir Bors, "for ye weep never

[1] This is not Elaine, the maid of Astolat—whom we shall meet hereafter—but another Elaine.

but when there is no boot. Alas!" said Sir Bors, "that ever Sir Launcelot's kin saw you. For now have ye lost the best knight of our blood, and he that was all our leader and our succor. And I dare say and make it good, that all kings, Christian nor heathen, may not find such a knight, for to speak of his nobleness and courtesy with his beauty and his gentleness. Alas," said Sir Bors, "what shall we do that be of his blood?"

"Alas!" said Sir Ector de Maris.

"Alas!" said Sir Lionel.

And when the queen heard them say so, she fell to the ground in a deadly sound [*swoon*]; and then Sir Bors took her, and [roused] her, and when she was come to herself again she kneeled afore the three knights, and held up both her hands, and besought them to seek him, and not to spare for no goods but that he be found, "for I wot well he is out of his mind." And Sir Bors, Sir Ector, Sir Lionel, departed from the queen, for they might not abide no longer for sorrow: and then the queen sent them treasure enough for their expenses, and so they took their horses and their armor, and departed. And then they rode from country to country, in forests and in wildernesses and in wastes, and ever they laid watch as well both at forests and at all manner of men as they rode, to hearken and to inquire after him, as he that was a naked man in his shirt, with a sword in his hand. And thus they rode well nigh a quarter of a year, endlong and overthwart,[1] in many places, forests and wildernesses,

[1] "Endlong and overthwart," *lengthways and crossways* of the land.

and oftentimes were evil lodged for his sake, and yet for all their labor and seeking could they never hear word of him. And wit ye well these three knights were passing sorry.

Then Sir Gawaine, Sir Uwaine, Sir Sagramour le Desirous, Sir Agloval, and Sir Percival de Galis, took upon them by the great desire of King Arthur, and in especial by the queen, to seek throughout all England, Wales, and Scotland, to find Sir Launcelot. And with them rode eighteen knights more to bear them fellowship. And wit ye well they lacked no manner of spending: and so were they three and twenty knights.

And thus as these noble knights rode together, they by one assent departed, and then they rode by two, by three, and by four, and by five; and ever they assigned where they should meet.

And now leave we a little of Sir Ector and Sir Percival, and speak we of Sir Launcelot, that suffered and endured many sharp showers, which ever ran wild wood, from place to place, and lived by fruit and such as he might get, and drank water, two years; and other clothing had he but little, save his shirt and his breeches. And thus, as Sir Launcelot wandered here and there, he came into a fair meadow where he found a pavilion, and there upon a tree hung a white shield and two swords hung thereby, and two spears there leaned against a tree; and when Sir Launcelot saw the swords, anon he leaped to the one sword, and took it in his hand, and drew it out, and then he lashed at the shield that all the meadow rang of the dints that he gave with such a noise as ten knights had fought together. Then there came forth a dwarf, and leaped unto Sir Launcelot, and would have had the sword out of his hand; and then Sir Launcelot took him by both the shoulders and threw him to the ground upon his neck, that he had almost broken his neck; and therewithal the dwarf cried for help. Then came forth a likely knight, and well apparelled in scarlet, furred with miniver. And anon as he saw Sir Launcelot, he deemed that he should be out of his wit: and then he said with fair speech, "Good man, lay down that sword, for, as me seemeth, thou hast more need of sleep, and of warm clothes, than to wield that sword."

"As for that," said Sir Launcelot, "come not too nigh; for, and thou do, wit thou well I will slay thee."

And when the knight of the pavilion saw that, he started backward within the pavilion. And then the dwarf armed him lightly, and so the knight thought by force and might to take the sword from Sir Launcelot, and so he came stepping out, and when Sir Launcelot saw him come so all armed with his sword in his hand, then Sir Launcelot flew to him with such a might and hit him upon the helm such a buffet that the stroke troubled his brains, and therewith the sword brake in three. And the knight fell to the earth as he had been dead, the blood bursting out of his mouth, nose, and ears. And then Sir Launcelot ran into the pavilion, and rushed even into the warm bed.

Then the knight awaked out of his swoon, and looked up weakly with his eyes, and then he asked where was that mad man that had given him such a buffet? "for such a buffet had I never of man's hand."

"Sir," said the dwarf, "it is not worship to hurt him, for he is a man out of his wit, and doubt ye not he hath been a man of great worship, and for some heartly sorrow that he hath taken he is fallen mad; and me seemeth he resembleth much unto Sir Launcelot; for him I saw at the great tournament beside Lonazep."

"Jesu defend," said that knight, "that ever that noble knight Sir Launcelot should be in such a plight. But whatsoever he be, harm will I none do him."

And this knight's name was Sir Bliant. Then he said unto the dwarf, "Go thou in all haste on horseback unto my brother Sir Seliaunt, that is at the Castle Blanche, and tell him of mine adventure, and bid him bring with him an horse-litter and then will we bear this knight unto my castle."

So the dwarf rode fast, and came again, and brought Sir Seliaunt with him, and six men with an horse-litter; and so they took up the feather-bed with Sir Launcelot, and so carried all with them to the Castle Blanche, and he never wakened until he was within the castle; and then they bound his hands and his feet, and gave him good meats and good drinks, and brought him again to his strength and his fairness; but in his wit they could not bring him again, nor to know himself. Thus Sir Launcelot was there more than a year and a half.

Then upon a day this lord of that castle, Sir Bliant, took his arms on horseback with a spear to seek adventures, and as he rode in a forest there met him two knights adventurous; the one was Sir Breuse sans Pitie, and his brother Sir

Bertlot. And these two ran both at once upon Sir Bliant, and brake both their spears upon his body, and then they drew out their swords and made a great battle and fought long together; but at the last Sir Bliant was sore wounded, and felt himself faint, and then he fled on horseback towards his castle. And as they came hurling under the castle, where Sir Launcelot lay in a window and saw two knights laid upon Sir Bliant with their swords, and when Sir Launcelot saw that, yet as wood [*crazy*] as he was, he was sorry for his lord Sir Bliant; and then Sir Launcelot brake his chains from his legs.

And so Sir Launcelot ran out at a postern, and there he met with the two knights that chased Sir Bliant, and there he pulled down Bertlot with his bare hands from his horse, and therewithal he writhed his sword out of his hands, and so he leaped unto Sir Breuse, and gave him such a buffet upon the head that he tumbled backward over his horse's crupper. And when Sir Bertlot saw his brother have such a fall, he gat a spear in his hand, and would have run Sir Launcelot through. That saw Sir Bliant, and struck off the hand of Sir Bertlot; and then Sir Breuse and Sir Bertlot gat their horses and fled away. When Sir Seliaunt came, and saw what Sir Launcelot had done for his brother, then he thanked God, and so did his brother, that ever they did him any good. But when Sir Bliant saw that Sir Launcelot was hurt with the breaking of his chains, then he was sorry that he had bound him. "Bind him no more," said Sir Seliaunt, "for he is happy and gracious." Then they made great joy of Sir Launcelot, and they bound him no more;

and so he abode there half a year and more. And in a morning early Sir Launcelot was ware where came a great boar, with many hounds nigh him; but the boar was so big that there might no hounds tear him, and the hunters came after blowing their horns both on horseback and on foot; and at the last Sir Launcelot was ware where one of them alighted and tied his horse to a tree, and leaned his spear against the tree.

So came Sir Launcelot and found the horse bound to a tree, and a spear leaning against a tree, and a sword tied unto the saddle bow. And then Sir Launcelot leaped into the saddle, and gat that spear in his hand, and then he rode after the boar; and then Sir Launcelot was ware where the boar set his back to a tree, fast by an hermitage. Then Sir Launcelot ran at the boar with his spear. And therewith the boar turned him nimbly, and rove [*gashed*] out the lungs and the heart of the horse, so that Sir Launcelot fell to the earth, and or ever Sir Launcelot might get from the horse, the boar rove him on the brawn of the thigh, up to the hough bone. And then Sir Launcelot was wroth, and up he gat upon his feet, and drew his sword, and he smote off the boar's head at one stroke. And therewithal came out the hermit, and saw him have such a wound; then the hermit came to Sir Launcelot and bemoaned him, and would have had him home unto his hermitage. But when Sir Launcelot heard him speak, he was so wroth with his wound that he ran upon the hermit to have slain him, and the hermit ran away, and when Sir Launcelot might not overget him he threw his sword after him, for Sir Launcelot might go no farther for bleeding. Then the hermit turned again, and asked Sir Launcelot how he was hurt.

"Fellow," said Sir Launcelot, "this boar hath bitten me sore."

"Then come with me," said the hermit, "and I shall heal you."

"Go thy way," said Sir Launcelot, "and deal not with me."

Then the hermit ran his way, and there he met with a good knight with many men.

"Sir," said the hermit, "here is fast by my place the goodliest man that ever I saw, and he is sore wounded with a boar, and yet he hath slain the boar. But well I wot and he be not holpen, that goodly man shall die of that wound, and that were great pity."

Then that knight, at the desire of the hermit, gat a cart, and in that cart that knight put the boar and Sir Launcelot, for Sir Launcelot was so feeble that they might right easily deal with him. And so Sir Launcelot was brought unto the hermitage, and there the hermit healed him of his wound. But the hermit might not find Sir Launcelot's sustenance, and so he impaired and waxed feeble, both of his body and of his wit, for the default of his sustenance, and waxed more wood than he was aforehand. And then, upon a day, Sir Launcelot ran his way into the forest; and by adventure came into the city of Corbin, where dame Elaine was.

And so when he was entered into the town, he ran through the town to the castle; and then all the young men of the city ran after Sir Launcelot, and there they threw turfs at him, and gave him many sad strokes; and as Sir Launcelot might reach any of them, he threw them so that they would never more come in his hands, for of some he brake their legs, and some their arms, and so fled into the castle. And then came out knights and squires for to rescue Sir Launcelot, and when they beheld him and looked upon his person, they thought they saw never so goodly a man; and when they saw so many wounds upon him, they all deemed that he had been a man of worship. And then they ordained clothes unto his body, and straw underneath him, and a little house, and then every day they would throw him meat, and set him drink, but there were few or none that would bring meat to his hands.

So it befell that King Pelles had a nephew whose name was Castor, and he desired of the king his uncle for to be made knight; and so at the request of this Castor, the king made him knight at the feast of Candlemas. And when Castor was made knight, that same day he gave many gowns; and so Sir Castor sent for the fool, that was Sir Launcelot, and when [Sir Launcelot] saw his time, he went into the garden and there laid him down by a well and slept. And in the afternoon dame Elaine and her maidens went into the garden for to play them; and as they roamed up and down, one of dame Elaine's maidens espied where lay a goodly man by the well sleeping, and anon showed him to dame Elaine.

"Peace," said dame Elaine, "and say no word."

And then she brought dame Elaine where he lay. And

when that she beheld him, anon she fell in remembrance of him, and knew him verily for Sir Launcelot, and therewithal she fell on weeping so heartily that she sank even to the earth. And when she had thus wept a great while, then she arose and called her maidens, and said she was sick. And so she went out of the garden, and she went straight to her father, and there she took him apart by himself, and then she said, "O father, now have I need of your help, and but if that ye help me, farewell my good days for ever."

"What is that, daughter?" said King Pelles.

"Sir," she said, "thus is it: in your garden I went for to sport, and there by the well I found Sir Launcelot du Lake sleeping."

"I may not believe that," said King Pelles.

"Sir," she said, "truly he is there, and me seemeth he should be distract out of his wit."

"Then hold you still," said the king, "and let me deal."

Then the king called to him such as he most trusted, four persons, and dame Elaine his daughter. And when they came to the well and beheld Sir Launcelot, anon dame Brisen knew him.

"Sir," said dame Brisen, "we must be wise how we deal with him, for this knight is out of his mind, and if we awake him rudely, what he will do we all know not. But ye shall abide, and I shall throw such an enchantment upon him that he shall not awake within the space of an hour."

And so she did. Then within a little while after King Pelles commanded that all people should avoid [*leave*], that none should be in that way there as the king would come. And so when this was done, these four men and these ladies laid hand on Sir Launcelot. And so they bare him into a tower, and so into the chamber where as was the [Holy Grail], and by force Sir Launcelot was laid by that holy vessel; and then there came an holy man and uncovered the vessel, and so by miracle, and by virtue of that holy vessel, Sir Launcelot was all healed and recovered. And when he was awaked, he groaned, and sighed sore, and complained greatly that he was passing sore.

And when Sir Launcelot saw King Pelles and dame Elaine, he waxed ashamed, and thus he said, "O good Lord Jesu, how came I here? for God's sake, my lord, let me wit how I came here."

"Sir," said dame Elaine, "into this country ye came like a mad man all out of your wit, and here ye have been kept as a fool, and no creature here knew what ye were till that by fortune a maid of mine brought me unto you where as ye lay sleeping by a well side, and anon as I verily beheld you I knew you; and then I told my father, and so ye were brought before this holy vessel, and by the virtue of it thus were ye healed."

"O Jesu, mercy!" said Sir Launcelot, "if this be sooth, how many be there that know of my woodness?"

"So God me help," said dame Elaine, "no moe [*more*] but my father and I and dame Brisen."

"Now for Christ's love," said Sir Launcelot, "keep it secret, and let no man know it in the world, for I am sore ashamed that I have been thus miscarried, for I am banished out of the country of Logris for ever, that is for to say the country of England."

And so Sir Launcelot lay more than a fortnight, or ever that he might stir for soreness.

And then after this King Pelles with ten knights, and dame Elaine and twenty ladies, rode unto the castle of Bliant, that stood in an island enclosed in iron, with a fair water, deep and large. And when they were there Sir Launcelot let call it the Joyous Isle, and there was he called none otherwise but Le Chevalier Mal Fait, *the knight that hath trespassed.* Then Sir Launcelot let make him a shield all of sable, and a queen crowned in the midst all of silver, and a knight, clean armed, kneeling before her; and every day once, for any mirths that all the ladies might make him, he would once every day look towards the realm of Logris where King Arthur and Queen Guenever were, and then would he fall upon weeping as though his heart should to-brast [*burst to pieces*]. So it fell that time that Sir Launcelot heard of a jousting fast by his castle, within three leagues. Then he called unto him a dwarf, and he bade him go unto that jousting, "and, or ever the knights depart, look thou make there a cry in the hearing of all the knights, that there is one knight in the Joyous Isle, that is the castle Bliant, and say that his name is Le Chevalier Mal Fait, that will joust against knights that will come; and who that putteth that knight to the worst shall have a fair maid and a gerfalcon."

So when this cry was made, unto Joyous Isle drew knights to the number of five hundred. And wit ye well there was never seen in Arthur's days one knight that did so much deeds of arms as Sir Launcelot did three days together. For he had the better of all the five hundred knights, and there was not one slain of them. And after that Sir Launcelot made them all a great feast. And in the meanwhile came Sir Percival de Galis and Sir Ector de Maris under that castle that was called the Joyous Isle. And as they beheld that gay castle they would have gone to that castle, but they might not for the broad water, and bridge could they find none. Then they saw on the other side a lady with a sperhawk in her hand, and Sir Percival called unto her, and asked that lady who was in that castle.

"Fair knight," she said, "here within this castle is the fairest lady in this land, and her name is Elaine. Also we have in this castle the fairest knight and the mightiest man that is, I dare say, living, and he calleth himself Le Chevalier Mal Fait."

"How came he into these marches?" said Sir Percival.

"Truly," said the damsel, "he came into this country like a mad man, with dogs and boys chasing him through the city of Corbin; and by the Holy Grail he was brought into his wit again, but he will not do battle with no knight but by underne [*nine in the morning*] or by noon. And if ye list to come into the castle, ye must ride unto the farther side of the castle, and there shall ye find a vessel that will bear you and your horse."

Then they departed and came unto the vessel. And then Sir Percival alighted and said unto Sir Ector de Maris, "Ye shall abide me here, until I know what manner of knight he is, for it were a great shame unto us, inasmuch as he is but one knight, and we should both do battle with him."

"Do as ye list," said Sir Ector de Maris, "here shall I abide you until that I hear of you again."

Then Sir Percival passed the water; and when he came unto the castle gate, he said to the porter, "Go thou unto the good knight within the castle, and tell him that here is come an errant knight to joust with him."

"Sir," said the porter, "ride ye within the castle, and there shall ye find a common place for jousting, that lords and ladies may behold you."

So anon as Sir Launcelot had warning, he was soon ready. And there Sir Percival and Sir Launcelot encountered with such a might, and their spears were so rude, that both the horses and the knights fell to the ground. And then they avoided their horses, and drew out their swords, and hewed away cantels [*pieces*] of their shields, and hurled together with their shields like two wild boars, and either wounded other passing sore. And at the last Sir Percival spake first, when they had fought more than two hours.

"Fair knight," said Sir Percival, "I require thee tell me thy name, for I met never with such a knight as ye are."

"Sir," said Sir Launcelot, "my name is Le Chevalier Mal Fait. Now tell me your name," said Sir Launcelot, "I require you, as ye are a gentle knight."

"Truly," said Sir Percival, "my name is Sir Percival de Galis, which is brother unto the good knight Sir Lamorack de Galis, and King Pellinore was our father, and Sir Aglo-val is my brother."

"Alas!" said Sir Launcelot, "what have I done, to fight with you that are a knight of the Round Table, that some time was your fellow in King Arthur's court?"

And therewithal Sir Launcelot kneeled down upon his knees, and threw away his shield and his sword from him. When Sir Percival saw him do so, he marvelled what he meant. And then thus he said, "Sir knight, whatsoever thou be, I require thee upon the high order of knighthood, tell me thy true name."

Then he said, "Truly my name is Sir Launcelot du Lake, King Ban's son of Benoy."

"Alas!" said Sir Percival, "what have I done! I was sent by the queen for to seek you, and so I have sought you nigh this two year; and yonder is Sir Ector de Maris your brother abideth me on the other side of the yonder water. Now I pray you forgive me mine offence that I have here done."

"It is soon forgiven," said Sir Launcelot.

Then Sir Percival sent for Sir Ector de Maris. And when Sir Launcelot had a sight of him, he ran unto him and took him in his arms, and then Sir Ector kneeled down and either wept upon other, that all had pity to behold them. Then came dame Elaine, and she there made them great cheer as might lie in her power; and there she told Sir Ector and Sir Percival how and in what manner Sir Launcelot came into that country, and how he was healed. And there it was known how long Sir Launcelot was with Sir Bliant and with Sir Seliaunt, and how he first met with them, and how he departed from them because of a boar;

and how the hermit healed Sir Launcelot of his great wound, and how that he came to Corbin.

"Sir," said Sir Ector, "I am your own brother, and ye are the man in the world that I love most, and, if I understood that it were your disworship, ye may right well understand that I would never counsel you thereto; but King Arthur and all his knights, and in especial Queen Guenever, made such dole and sorrow that it was marvel to hear and see. And ye must remember the great worship and renown that ye be of, how that ye have been more spoken of than any other knight that is now living, for there is none that beareth the name now but ye and Sir Tristram. Therefore, brother," said Sir Ector, "make you ready to ride unto the court with us, and I dare well say there was never knight better welcome unto the court than ye. And I wot well and can make it good," said Sir Ector, "it hath cost my lady the queen twenty thousand pound the seeking of you."

"Well, brother," said Sir Launcelot, "I will do after your counsel and ride with you."

So then they took their horses, and made them ready, and took their leave of King Pelles and of dame Elaine; and when Sir Launcelot should depart, dame Elaine made great sorrow.

Then they departed, and within five days' journey they came to Camelot, which is called, in English, Winchester. And when Sir Launcelot was come among them, the king and all the knights made great joy of him; and there Sir Percival de Galis and Sir Ector de Maris began to tell of all the adventures, how Sir Launcelot had been out of his mind all the time of his absence, how he called himself Le Chevalier Mal Fait, as much as to say the knight that had trespassed, and in three days Sir Launcelot smote down five hundred knights. And ever as Sir Ector and Sir Percival told these tales of Sir Launcelot, Queen Guenever wept as she would have died; then afterward the queen made great joy.

"O Jesu!" said King Arthur, "I marvel for what cause ye, Sir Launcelot, went out of your mind?"

"My lord," said Sir Launcelot, "if I did any folly, I have found that I sought."

And so the king held him still, and spake no more; but all Sir Launcelot's kin knew for whom he went out of his mind. And then there were great feasts made and great joy, and many great lords and ladies, when they heard that Sir Launcelot was come to the court again, made great joy.

BOOK III

OF SIR GARETH OF ORKNEY

BOOK III

OF SIR GARETH OF ORKNEY

WHEN Arthur held his Round Table most fully, it fortuned that he commanded that the high feast of Pentecost should be holden at a city and a castle, the which in those days was called King-Kenadon, upon the sands that marched [*bordered*] nigh Wales. So ever the king had a custom that at the feast of Pentecost, in especial afore other feasts in the year, he would not go that day to meat until he had heard or seen of a great marvel. And for that custom all manner of strange adventures came before Arthur as at that feast before all other feasts. And so Sir Gawaine, a little tofore noon of the day of Pentecost, espied at a window three men upon horseback and a dwarf on foot. And so the three men alighted, and the dwarf kept their horses, and one of the three men was higher than the other twain by a foot and a half. Then Sir Gawaine went unto the king and said, "Sir, go to your meat, for here at hand come strange adventures."

So Arthur went unto his meat with many other kings. And there were all the knights of the Round Table, save those that were prisoners or slain at a rencounter. Then at the high feast evermore they should be fulfilled the whole number of an hundred and fifty, for then was the Round Table fully accomplished. Right so came into the hall two men well beseen and richly, and upon their shoulders there leaned the goodliest young man and the fairest that ever they all saw, and he was large and long, and broad in the shoulders, and well visaged, and the fairest and the largest handed that ever man saw, but he fared as though he might not go nor bear himself but if he leaned upon their shoulders. Anon as Arthur saw him, there was made peace [*silence*] and room, and right so they went with him unto the high dais, without saying of any words. Then this big young man pulled him aback, and easily stretched up straight, saying, "King Arthur, God you bless, and all your fair fellowship, and in especial the fellowship of the Table Round. And for this cause I am come hither, to pray you and require you to give me three gifts, and they shall not be unreasonably asked, but that ye may worshipfully and honorably grant them me, and to you no great hurt nor loss. And as for the first gift I will ask now, and the other two gifts I will ask this day twelvemonth wheresoever ye hold your high feast."

"Now ask," said Arthur, "and ye shall have your asking."

"Now, sir, this is my petition for this feast, that ye will give me meat and drink sufficiently for this twelvemonth, and at that day I will ask mine other two gifts."

"My fair son," said Arthur, "ask better, I counsel thee, for this is but a simple asking, for my heart giveth me to thee greatly that thou art come of men of worship, and greatly my conceit faileth me but thou shalt prove a man of right great worship."

"Sir," said he, "thereof be as it may, I have asked that I will ask."

"Well," said the king, "ye shall have meat and drink enough, I never defended that none, neither my friend nor my foe. But what is thy name I would wit?"

"I cannot tell you," said he.

"That is marvel," said the king, "that thou knowest not thy name, and thou art the goodliest young man that ever I saw."

Then the king betook him to Sir Kay, the steward, and charged him that he should give him of all manner of meats and drinks of the best, and also that he had all manner of finding as though he were a lord's son.

"That shall little need," said Sir Kay, "to do such cost upon him; for I dare undertake he is a villain born, and never will make man, for and he had come of gentlemen he would have asked of you horse and armor, but such as he is, so he asketh. And since he hath no name, I shall give him a name: that shall be Beaumains, that is Fairhands, and into the kitchen I shall bring him, and there he shall have fat browis [*broth*] every day, that he shall be as fat by the twelvemonth's end as a pork hog."

Right so the two men departed, and left him to Sir Kay, that scorned him and mocked him.

Thereat was Sir Gawaine wroth, and in especial Sir Launcelot bade Sir Kay leave his mocking, "for I dare lay my head he shall prove a man of great worship."

"Let be," said Sir Kay, "it may not be, by no reason, for as he is, so hath he asked."

"Beware," said Sir Launcelot; "so ye gave the good

knight Brewnor, Sir Dinadan's brother, a name, and ye called him La Cote Mal Taile, and that turned you to anger afterward."

"As for that," said Sir Kay, "this shall never prove none such; for Sir Brewnor desired ever worship, and this desireth bread and drink, and broth; upon pain of my life he was fostered up in some abbey, and, howsoever it was, they failed meat and drink, and so hither he is come for his sustenance."

And so Sir Kay bade get him a place and sit down to meat, so Beaumains went to the hall door, and set him down among boys and lads, and there he eat sadly. And then Sir Launcelot after meat bade him come to his chamber, and there he should have meat and drink enough. And so did Sir Gawaine, but he refused them all; he would do none other but as Sir Kay commanded him, for no proffer. But as touching Sir Gawaine, he had reason to proffer him lodging, meat, and drink, for that proffer came of his blood, for he was nearer kin to him than he wist. But that Sir Launcelot did was of his great gentleness and courtesy. So thus he was put into the kitchen, and lay nightly as the boys of the kitchen did. And so he endured all that twelvemonth, and never displeased man nor child, but always he was meek and mild. But ever when he saw any jousting of knights, that would he see and he might. And ever Sir Launcelot would give him gold to spend, and clothes, and so did Sir Gawaine. And where were any masteries done thereat would he be, and there might none cast the bar or stone to him by two yards. Then would Sir Kay say, "How like you my boy of the kitchen?" So it passed on till the feast of Pentecost, and at that time the king held it at Caerleon, in the most royallest wise that might be, like as yearly he did. But the king would eat no meat on the Whitsunday till he had heard of some adventure. And then came there a squire to the king, and said, "Sir, ye may go to your meat, for here cometh a damsel with some strange adventure." Then was the king glad, and set him down. Right so there came in a damsel, and saluted the king, and prayed him for succor.

"For whom?" said the king: "what is the adventure?"

"Sir," said she, "I have a lady of great worship and renown, and she is besieged with a tyrant, so that she may not go out of her castle, and because that here in your court are called the noblest knights of the world, I come unto you and pray you for succor."

"What call ye your lady, and where dwelleth she, and who is he and what is his name that hath besieged her?"

"Sir king," said she, "as for my lady's name, that shall not be known for me as at this time; but I let you wit she is a lady of great worship, and of great lands. And as for the tyrant that besiegeth her and destroyeth her land, he is called the Red Knight of the Red Lawns."

"I know him not," said the king.

"Sir," said Sir Gawaine, "I know him well, for he is one of the perilous knights of the world; men say that he hath seven men's strength, and from him I escaped once full hard with my life."

"Fair damsel," said the king, "there be knights here

that would do their power to rescue your lady, but because ye will not tell her name nor where she dwelleth, therefore none of my knights that be here now shall go with you by my will."

"Then must I speak further," said the damsel.

Then with these words came before the king Beaumains, while the damsel was there; and thus he said: "Sir king, God thank you, I have been this twelve months in your kitchen, and have had my full sustenance, and now I will ask my two gifts that be behind."

"Ask upon my peril," said the king.

"Sir, these shall be my two gifts: first, that ye will grant me to have this adventure of the damsel, for it belongeth to me."

"Thou shalt have it," said the king; "I grant it thee."

"Then, sir, this is now the other gift: that ye shall bid Sir Launcelot du Lake to make me a knight, for of him I will be made knight, and else of none; and when I am passed, I pray you let him ride after me, and make me knight when I require him."

"All this shall be done," said the king.

"Fie on thee," said the damsel; "shall I have none but one that is your kitchen page?"

Then was she wroth, and took her horse and departed. And with that there came one to Beaumains, and told him that his horse and armor was come for him, and there was a dwarf come with all things that him needed in the richest manner. Thereat all the court had much marvel from whence came all that gear. So when he was armed, there was none but few so goodly a man as he was. And right so he came into the hall, and took his leave of King Arthur and of Sir Gawaine, and of Sir Launcelot, and prayed him that he would hie after him; and so departed and rode after the damsel.

But there went many after to behold how well he was horsed and trapped in cloth of gold, but he had neither shield nor spear. Then Sir Kay said openly in the hall: "I will ride after my boy of the kitchen, for to wit [*know*] whether he will know me for his better."

Sir Launcelot and Sir Gawaine said, "Yet abide at home."

So Sir Kay made him ready, and took his horse and his spear, and rode after him. And right as Beaumains overtook the damsel, right so came Sir Kay, and said, "Beaumains, what sir, know ye not me?"

Then he turned his horse, and knew it was Sir Kay, that had done him all the despite as ye have heard afore.

"Yea," said Beaumains, "I know you for an ungentle knight of the court, and therefore beware of me."

Therewith Sir Kay put his spear in the rest and ran straight upon him, and Beaumains came as fast upon him with his sword in his hand; and so he put away his spear with his sword, and with a foin [*feint*] thrust him through the side, that Sir Kay fell down as he had been dead, and he alighted down and took Sir Kay's shield and his spear, and started upon his own horse, and rode his way. All that saw Sir Launcelot, and so did the damsel. And then he bade his dwarf start upon Sir Kay's horse, and so he did. By that Sir Launcelot was come. Then he proffered Sir Launcelot to joust, and either made them ready, and came together so fiercely that either bare down other to the earth, and sore were they bruised. Then Sir Launcelot arose and helped him from his horse. And then Beaumains threw his shield from him, and proffered to fight with Sir Launcelot on foot, and so they rushed together like boars, tracing, racing, and foining, to the mountenance [*amount*] of an hour, and Sir Launcelot felt him so big that he marvelled of his strength, for he fought more like a giant than a knight, and that his fighting was durable and passing perilous. For Sir Launcelot had so much ado with him that he dreaded himself to be shamed, and said, "Beaumains, fight not so sore, your quarrel and mine is not so great but we may leave off."

"Truly, that is truth," said Beaumains, "but it doth me good to feel your might, and yet, my lord, I showed not the uttermost."

"Well," said Sir Launcelot, "for I promise you by the faith of my body I had as much to do as I might to save myself from you unshamed, and therefore have ye no doubt of none earthly knight."

"Hope ye so that I may any while stand a proved knight?" said Beaumains.

"Yea," said Launcelot, "do ye as ye have done, and I shall be your warrant."

"Then, I pray you," said Beaumains, "give me the order of knighthood."

"Then must ye tell me your name," said Launcelot, "and of what kin ye be born."

"Sir, so that ye will not discover me I shall," said Beaumains.

"Nay," said Sir Launcelot, "and that I promise you by the faith of my body, until it be openly known."

"Then, Sir," he said, "my name is Gareth, and brother unto Sir Gawaine, of father and mother."

"Ah! Sir," said Launcelot, "I am more gladder of you than I was, for ever me thought ye should be of great blood, and that ye came not to the court neither for meat nor for drink."

And then Sir Launcelot gave him the order of knighthood. And then Sir Gareth prayed him for to depart, and let him go. So Sir Launcelot departed from him and came to Sir Kay, and made him to be borne home upon his shield, and so he was healed hard with the life, and all men scorned Sir Kay, and in especial Sir Gawaine and Sir Launcelot said it was not his part to rebuke [any] young man, for full little knew he of what birth he is come, and for what cause he came to this court. And so we leave off Sir Kay and turn we unto Beaumains. When he had overtaken the damsel anon she said, "What dost thou here? thou stinkest all of the kitchen, thy clothes be foul of the grease and tallow that thou gainedst in King Arthur's kitchen; weenest thou," said she, "that I allow thee for yonder knight that thou killedst? Nay truly, for thou slewest him unhappily and cowardly, therefore return again, kitchen page. I know thee well, for Sir Kay named thee Beaumains. What art thou but a turner of broaches and a washer of dishes!"

"Damsel," said Sir Beaumains, "say to me what ye list, I will not go from you whatsoever ye say, for I have undertaken of King Arthur for to achieve your adventure, and I shall finish it to the end, or I shall die therefor."

"Fie on thee, kitchen knave. Wilt thou finish mine adventure? thou shalt anon be met withal, that thou wouldest not, for all the broth that ever thou suppest, once look him in the face."

"I shall assay," said Beaumains. So as they thus rode in the wood, there came a man flying all that he might.

"Whither wilt thou?" said Beaumains.

"O lord," said he, "help me, for hereby in a slade are six thieves which have taken my lord and bound him, and I am afraid lest they will slay him."

"Bring me thither," said Sir Beaumains.

And so they rode together till they came there as the knight was bound; and then he rode unto the thieves, and struck one at the first stroke to death, and then another, and at the third stroke he slew the third thief; and then the other three fled, and he rode after and overtook them, and then those three thieves turned again and hard assailed Sir Beaumains; but at the last he slew them; and then returned and unbound the knight. And the knight thanked him, and prayed him to ride with him to his castle there a little beside, and he should worshipfully reward him for his good deeds.

"Sir," said Sir Beaumains, "I will no reward have; I was this day made knight of the noble Sir Launcelot, and therefore I will have no reward, but God reward me. And also I must follow this damsel."

And when he came nigh her, she bade him ride from her, "for thou smellest all of the kitchen. Weenest thou that I have joy of thee? for all this deed that thou hast done is but mishappened thee. But thou shalt see a sight that shall make thee to turn again, and that lightly."

[Then all the next day] this Beaumains rode with that lady till even-song time, and ever she chid him and would not rest. And then they came to a black lawn, and there was a black hawthorn, and thereon hung a black banner, and on the other side there hung a black shield, and by it stood a black spear and a long, and a great black horse covered with silk, and a black stone fast by it.

There sat a knight all armed in black harness, and his name was the Knight of the Black Lawns. When the damsel saw the black knight, she bade Sir Beaumains flee down the valley, for his horse was not saddled.

"I thank you," said Sir Beaumains, "for always ye will have me a coward."

With that the black knight came to the damsel, and said, "Fair damsel, have ye brought this knight from King Arthur's court to be your champion?"

"Nay, fair knight," said she, "this is but a kitchen knave, that hath been fed in King Arthur's kitchen for alms."

"Wherefore cometh he in such array?" said the knight: "it is great shame that he beareth you company."

"Sir, I cannot be delivered of him," said the damsel, "for with me he rideth maugre [*in spite of*] mine head; would to God ye would put him from me, or else to slay him if ye may, for he is an unhappy knave, and unhappy hath he done to-day through misadventure; for I saw him slay two knights at the passage of the water, and other deeds he did before right marvellous, and all through unhappiness."

"That marvelleth me," said the black knight, "that any man the which is of worship will have to do with him."

"Sir, they know him not," said the damsel, "and because he rideth with me they think he is some man of worship born."

"That may be," said the black knight, "howbeit, as ye say that he be no man of worship, he is a full likely person, and full like to be a strong man; but thus much shall I grant you," said the black knight, "I shall put him down upon his feet, and his horse and his harness he shall leave with me, for it were shame to me to do him any more harm."

When Sir Beaumains heard him say thus, he said, "Sir knight, thou art full liberal of my horse and my harness. I let thee wit it cost thee nought, and whether it liketh thee or not this lawn will I pass, maugre thine head, and horse nor harness gettest thou none of me, but if thou win them with thy hands; and therefore let see what thou canst do."

"Sayst thou that?" said the black knight, "now yield thy lady from thee, for it beseemeth never a kitchen page to ride with such a lady."

"Thou liest," said Beaumains, "I am a gentleman born, and of more high lineage than thou, and that will I prove on thy body."

Then in great wrath they departed with their horses, and came together as it had been the thunder; and the black knight's spear brake, and Beaumains thrust him through both his sides, and therewith his spear brake, and the truncheon left still in his side. But nevertheless the black knight drew his sword, and smote many eager strokes and of great might, and hurt Beaumains full sore. But at the last the black knight within an hour and a half he fell down off his horse in a swoon, and there he died. And then Beaumains saw him so well horsed and armed, then he alighted down, and armed him in his armor, and so took his horse, and rode after the damsel. When she saw him come nigh, she said, "Away, kitchen knave, out of the wind, for the smell of thy foul clothes grieveth me. Alas," she said, "that ever such a knave as thou art should by mishap slay so good a knight as thou hast done, but all this is thine unhappiness. But hereby is one shall pay thee all thy payment, and therefore yet I counsel thee, flee."

"It may happen me," said Beaumains, "to be beaten or slain, but I warn you, fair damsel, I will not flee away for him, nor leave your company for all that ye can say; for ever ye say that they slay me or beat me, but how soever it happeneth I escape, and they lie on the ground, and therefore it were as good for you to hold you still, than thus to rebuke me all day, for away will I not till I feel the uttermost of this journey, or else I will be slain or truly beaten;

therefore ride on your way, for follow you I will, whatsoever happen."

Thus as they rode together they saw a knight come driving by them all in green, both his horse and his harness, and when he came nigh the damsel he asked of her, "Is that my brother, the black knight, that ye have brought with you?"

"Nay, nay," said she, "this unhappy kitchen knave hath slain your brother through unhappiness."

"Alas!" said the green knight, "that is great pity that so noble a knight as he was should so unhappily be slain, and namely of a knave's hand, as ye say he is. Ah, traitor!" said the green knight, "thou shalt die for slaying of my brother; he was a full noble knight, and his name was Sir Periard."

"I defy thee," said Sir Beaumains, "for I let thee to wit I slew him knightly, and not shamefully."

Therewithal the green knight rode unto an horn that was green, and it hung upon a thorn, and there he blew three deadly notes, and there came three damsels that lightly armed him. And then took he a great horse, and a green shield and a green spear. And then they ran together with all their mights, and brake their spears unto their hands. And then they drew their swords, and gave many sad strokes, and either of them wounded other full ill. And at the last at an overthwart Beaumains' horse struck the green knight's horse upon the side [that] he fell to the earth. And then the green knight avoided his horse lightly, and dressed him upon foot. That saw Beaumains, and therewithal he alighted, and they rushed together like two mighty champions a long while, and sore they bled both. With that came the damsel and said, "My lord the green knight, why for shame stand ye so long fighting with the kitchen knave? Alas, it is shame that ever ye were made knight, to see such a lad match such a knight as the weed overgrew the corn."

Therewith the green knight was ashamed, and therewithal he gave a great stroke of might, and clave his shield through. When Beaumains saw his shield cloven asunder he was a little ashamed of that stroke, and of her language; and then he gave him such a buffet upon the helm that he fell on his knees; and so suddenly Beaumains pulled him upon the ground grovelling. And then the green knight cried him mercy, and yielded him unto Sir Beaumains, and prayed him to slay him not.

"All is in vain," said Beaumains, "for thou shalt die, but if this damsel that came with me pray me to save thy life."

And therewithal he unlaced his helm, like as he would slay him.

"Fie upon thee, false kitchen page, I will never pray thee to save his life, for I never will be so much in thy danger."

"Then shall he die," said Beaumains.

"Not so hardy, thou foul knave," said the damsel, "that thou slay him."

"Alas," said the green knight, "suffer me not to die, for a fair word may save my life. O fair knight," said the green knight, "save my life, and I will forgive the death of my brother, and for ever to become thy man, and thirty knights that hold of me for ever shall do you service."

Said the damsel, "That such a kitchen knave should have thee and thirty knights' service!"

"Sir knight," said Sir Beaumains, "all this availeth not, but if my damsel speak with me for thy life."

And therewithal he made resemblance to slay him.

"Let be," said the damsel, "thou knave, slay him not, for if thou do, thou shalt repent it."

"Damsel," said Sir Beaumains, "your charge is to me a pleasure, and at your commandment his life shall be saved, and else not."

Then he said, "Sir knight with the green arms, I release thee quit [*acquitted*] at this damsel's request, for I will not make her wroth, I will fulfil all that she chargeth me."

And then the green knight kneeled down and did him homage with his sword.

And always the damsel rebuked Sir Beaumains. And so that night they went unto rest, and all that night the green knight commanded thirty knights privily to watch Beaumains, for to keep him from all treason. And so on the morn they all arose, and heard their mass and brake their fast, and then they took their horses and rode on their way, and the green knight conveyed them through the forest, and there the green knight said, "My lord Beaumains, I and these thirty knights shall be alway at your summons, both early and late, at your calling, and where that ever ye will send us."

"It is well said," said Beaumains; "when that I call upon you ye must yield you unto King Arthur and all your knights."

"If that ye so command us, we shall be ready at all times," said the green knight.

"Fie, fie upon thee," said the damsel, "that any good knights should be obedient unto a kitchen knave."

So then departed the green knight and the damsel. And then she said unto Beaumains, "Why followest thou me, thou kitchen boy, cast away thy shield and thy spear and flee away, yet I counsel thee betimes, or thou shalt say right soon, Alas!"

"Damsel," said Sir Beaumains, "ye are uncourteous so to rebuke me as ye do, for meseemeth I have done you great service, and ever ye threaten me for I shall be beaten with knights that we meet, but ever for all your boast they lie in the dust or in the mire, and therefore I pray you rebuke me no more; and when ye see me beaten or yielden as recreant, then may ye bid me go from you shamefully, but first I let you wit I will not depart from you, for I were worse than a fool and I would depart from you all the while that I win worship."

"Well," said she, "right soon there shall meet a knight shall pay thee all thy wages, for he is the most man of worship of the world, except King Arthur."

"I will well," said Beaumains; "the more he is of worship the more shall be my worship to have ado with him."

Then anon they were ware where was before them a city

rich and fair. And betwixt them and the city a mile and a half there was a fair meadow that seemed new mown, and therein were many pavilions fair to behold.

"Lo," said the damsel, "yonder is a lord that owneth yonder city, and his custom is when the weather is fair to lie in this meadow to joust and tourney; and ever there be about him five hundred knights and gentlemen of arms, and there be all manner of games that any gentleman can devise."

"That goodly lord," said Beaumains, "would I fain see."

"Thou shalt see him time enough," said the damsel.

And so as she rode near she espied the pavilion where he was.

"Lo," said she, "seest thou yonder pavilion, that is all of the color of Inde, and all manner of thing that there is about, men and women, and horses trapped, shields and spears, all of the color of Inde, and his name is Sir Persant of Inde, the most lordliest knight that ever thou lookedst on."

"It may well be," said Beaumains, "but be he never so stout a knight, in this field I shall abide till that I see him under his shield."

"Ah, fool," said she, "thou wert better flee betimes."

"Why," said Beaumains, "and he be such a knight as ye make him, he will not set upon me with all his men, or with his five hundred knights. For and there come no more but one at once, I shall him not fail whilst my life lasteth."

"Fie, fie," said the damsel, "that ever such a dirty knave should blow such a boast."

"Damsel," he said, "ye are to blame so to rebuke me, for I had liever do five battles than so to be rebuked; let him come, and then let him do his worst."

"Sir," she said, "I marvel what thou art, and of what kin thou art come: boldly thou speakest, and boldly thou hast done, that have I seen: therefore I pray thee save thyself and thou mayest, for thy horse and thou have had great travail, and I dread we dwell over long from the siege, for it is but hence seven mile, and all perilous passages we are past, save all only this passage, and here I dread me sore lest ye shall catch some hurt, therefore I would ye were hence, that ye were not bruised nor hurt with this strong knight. But I let you wit this Sir Persant of Inde is nothing of might nor strength unto the knight that laid the siege about my lady."

"As for that," said Sir Beaumains, "be it as it may; for since I am come so nigh this knight I will prove his might or [*ere*] I depart from him, and else I shall be shamed and [*if*] I now withdraw me from him. And therefore, damsel, have ye no doubt by the grace of God I shall so deal with this knight, that within two hours after noon I shall deliver him, and then shall we come to the siege by daylight."

"Oh, mercy, marvel have I," said the damsel, "what manner a man ye be, for it may never be otherwise but that ye be come of a noble blood, for so foul and shamefully did never woman rule a knight as I have done you, and ever courteously ye have suffered me, and that came never but of a gentle blood."

"Damsel," said Beaumains, "a knight may little do that

may not suffer a damsel; for whatsoever ye said unto me I took none heed to your words, for the more ye said the more ye angered me, and my wrath I wreaked upon them that I had ado withal. And therefore all the missaying that ye missayed me furthered me in my battle, and caused me to think to show and prove myself at the end what I was; for peradventure though I had meat in King Arthur's kitchen, yet I might have had meat enough in other places; but all that I did for to prove my friends; and whether I be a gentleman born or no, fair damsel, I have done you gentleman's service, and peradventure better service yet will I do you or [*before*] I depart from you."

"Alas," said she, "fair Beaumains, forgive me all that I have missaid and misdone against you."

"With all my heart," said Sir Beaumains, "I forgive it you, for ye did nothing but as ye ought to do, for all your evil words pleased me; and, damsel," said Sir Beaumains, "sith [*since*] it liketh you to speak thus fair to me, wit ye well it gladdeth greatly mine heart; and now meseemeth there is no knight living but I am able enough for him."

With this Sir Persant of Inde had espied them, as they hoved [*hovered*] in the field, and knightly he sent to them to know whether he came in war or in peace.

"Say unto thy lord," said Sir Beaumains, "I take no force,[1] but whether as him list[2] himself."

So the messenger went again unto Sir Persant, and told him all his answer.

[1] "I take no force," *I care not.*

[2] "Him list," *he wishes, he pleases.*

"Well," said he, "then will I have ado with him to the uttermost;" and so he purveyed him [*prepared himself*], and rode against him. And when Sir Beaumains saw him, he made him ready, and there they met with all the might that their horses might run, and brake their spears either in three pieces, and their horses rashed so together that both their horses fell dead to the earth; and lightly they avoided their horses, and put their shields before them, and drew their swords, and gave each other many great strokes, that sometime they so hurled together that they fell both grovelling on the ground. Thus they fought two hours and more, that their shields and their hauberks were all forhewen [*hewn to pieces*] and in many places they were sore wounded. So at the last Sir Beaumains smote him through the cost [*rib part*] of the body, and then he retrayed him [*drew back*] here and there, and knightly maintained his battle long time. And at the last Sir Beaumains smote Sir Persant on the helm that he fell grovelling to the earth, and then he leaped overthwart [*across*] upon him, and unlaced his helm for to have slain him. Then Sir Persant yielded him, and asked him mercy. With that came the damsel and prayed him to save his life.

"I will well," said Sir Beaumains, "for it were pity that this noble knight should die."

"Gramercy," said Sir Persant, "gentle knight and damsel, for certainly now I know well it was you that slew the black knight my brother at the blackthorn; he was a full noble knight, his name was Sir Periard. Also I am sure that ye are he that won mine other brother the green knight:

his name was Sir Pertolope. Also ye won the red knight, my brother, Sir Perimones. And now, sir, sith ye have won these knights, this shall I do for to please you: ye shall have homage and fealty of me, and an hundred knights to be always at your command, to go and ride where ye will command us."

And so they went unto Sir Persant's pavilion, and there he drank wine and eat spices. And afterward Sir Persant made him to rest upon a bed till it was supper time, and after supper to bed again. And so we leave him there till on the morrow.

Now leave we the knight and the dwarf, and speak we of Beaumains, that all night lay in the hermitage, and upon the morn he and the damsel Linet heard their mass, and brake their fast. And then they took their horses and rode throughout a fair forest, and then they came to a plain, and saw where were many pavilions and tents, and a fair castle, and there was much smoke and great noise. And when they came near the siege Sir Beaumains espied upon great trees, as he rode, how there hung full goodly armed knights by the neck, and their shields about their necks with their swords, and gilt spurs upon their heels, and so there hung shamefully nigh forty knights with rich arms. Then Sir Beaumains abated his countenance, and said, "What thing meaneth this?"

"Fair sir," saith the damsel, "abate not your cheer for all this sight, for ye must encourage yourself, or else ye be all shent [*ruined*], for all these knights came hither unto this siege to rescue my sister dame Lyoness, and when the red knight of the red lawns had overcome them, he put them to this shameful death, without mercy and pity, and in the same wise he will serve you, but if ye quit [*acquit*] you the better."

"Now Jesu defend me," said Sir Beaumains, "from such a villanous death and shenship [*disgrace*] of arms! for rather than thus I should fare withal, I would rather be slain manfully in plain battle."

"So were ye better," said the damsel, "trust not in him, for in him is no courtesy, but all goeth to the death or shameful murder, and that is great pity, for he is a full likely man and well made of body, and a full noble knight of prowess, and a lord of great lands and possessions."

"Truly," said Sir Beaumains, "he may well be a good knight, but he useth shameful customs, and it is great marvel that he endureth so long, that none of the noble knights of my lord King Arthur's court have not dealt with him."

And then they rode unto the ditches, and saw them double ditched with full strong walls, and there were lodged many great estates and lords nigh the walls, and there was great noise of minstrels, and the sea beat upon the one side of the walls, where as were many ships and mariners' noise with hale and how.[1] And also there was fast by a sycamore tree, and thereon hung an horn, the greatest that ever they saw, of an elephant's bone.

"And this knight of the red lawns hath hanged it up there, that if there come any errant knight, he must blow

[1] "Hale and how," *haul and ho:* the sailors' cries in hoisting away, &c.

that horn, and then will he make him ready, and come to him to do battle. But sir, I pray you," said the damsel Linet, "blow ye not the horn till it be high noon, for now it is about prime, and now increaseth his might, that, as men say, he hath seven men's strength."

"Ah, fie for shame, fair damsel, say ye never so more to me, for, and he were as good a knight as ever was, I shall never fail him in his most might, for either I will win worship worshipfully, or die knightly in the field."

And therewith he spurred his horse straight to the sycamore tree and blew the horn so eagerly that all the siege and the castle rang thereof. And then there leaped our knights out of their tents and pavilions, and they within the castle looked over the walls and out at windows. Then the red knight of the red lawns armed him hastily, and two barons set on his spurs upon his heels, and all was blood-red, his armor, spear, and shield. And an earl buckled his helm upon his head, and then they brought him a red spear and a red steed, and so he rode into a little vale under the castle, that all that were in the castle and at the siege might behold the battle.

"Sir," said the damsel Linet unto Sir Beaumains, "look ye be glad and light, for yonder is your deadly enemy, and at yonder window is my lady my sister, dame Lyoness."

"Where?" said Beaumains.

"Yonder," said the damsel, and pointed with her finger.

"That is truth," said Beaumains. "She seemeth afar the fairest lady that ever I looked upon, and truly," he said,

"I ask no better quarrel than now for to do battle, for truly she shall be my lady, and for her I will fight."

And ever he looked up to the window with glad countenance. And the lady Lyoness made courtesy to him down to the earth, with holding up both her hands. With that the red knight of the red lawns called to Sir Beaumains, "Leave, sir knight, thy looking, and behold me, I counsel thee, for I warn thee well she is my lady, and for her I have done many strong battles."

"If thou have so done," said Beaumains, "meseemeth it was but waste labor, for she loveth none of thy fellowship, and thou to love that loveth not thee, is a great folly. For if I understood that she were not glad of my coming, I would be advised or I did battle for her, but I understand by the besieging of this castle she may forbear thy company. And therefore wit thou well, thou red knight of the red lawns, I love her and will rescue her, or else die in the quarrel."

"Sayest thou that?" said the red knight; "me seemeth thou ought of reason to beware by yonder knights that thou sawest hang upon yonder great elms."

"Fie, fie, for shame," said Sir Beaumains, "that ever thou shouldest say or do so evil and such shamefulness, for in that thou shamest thyself and the order of knighthood, and thou mayst be sure there will no lady love thee that knoweth thy detestable customs. And now thou weenest [*thinkest*] that the sight of these hanged knights should fear [*scare*] me and make me aghast, nay truly not so, that shameful sight causeth me to have courage and hardiness against thee, more than I would have had against thee and if thou be a well ruled knight."

"Make thee ready," said the red knight of the red lawns, "and talk no longer with me."

Then Sir Beaumains bade the damsel go from him, and then they put their spears in their rests, and came together with all the might they had, and either smote other in the midst of their shields, that the paytrels [*breast-plates*], surcingles, and cruppers burst, and fell both to the ground with the reins of their bridles in their hands, and so they lay a great while sore astonied, and all they that were in the castle and at the siege wend [*thought*] their necks had been broken, and then many a stranger and other said that the strange knight was a big man and a noble jouster, "for or [*ere*] now we saw never no knight match the red knight of the red lawns;" thus they said both within the castle and without. Then they lightly avoided their horses and put their shields afore them, and drew their swords and ran together like two fierce lions, and either gave other such buffets upon their helms that they reeled both backward two strides; and then they recovered both, and hewed great pieces from their harness and their shields that a great part fell in the fields.

And then thus they fought till it was past noon and never would stint till at last they lacked wind both, and then they stood wagging and scattering, panting, blowing and bleeding, that all that beheld them for the most part wept for pity. So when they had rested them a while they went to battle again, tracing, racing, foining [*feinting*], as two boars. And at some time they took their run as it had been two rams, and hurtled together that sometimes they fell grovelling to the earth; and at some time they were so amazed that either took other's sword instead of his own.

Thus they endured till even-song time [*vespers*], that there was none that beheld them might know whether was like to win the battle; and their armor was so far hewn that men might see their naked sides, and in other places they were naked, but ever the naked places they did defend. And the red knight was a wily knight of war, and his wily fighting taught Sir Beaumains to be wise; but he abought [*paid for*] it full sore ere he did espy his fighting. And thus by assent of them both, they granted either other to rest; and so they set them down upon two mole-hills there beside the fighting place, and either of them unlaced his helm, and took the cold wind, for either of their pages was fast by them, to come when they called to unlace their harness and to set it on again at their command. And then when Sir Beaumains' helm was off, he looked up unto the window, and there he saw the fair lady dame Lyoness. And she made to him such countenance that his heart was light and joyful. And therewith he started up suddenly, and bade the red knight make him ready to do the battle to the uttermost.

"I will well," said the red knight.

And then they laced up their helms, and their pages avoided [*got out of the way*], and they stepped together and fought freshly. But the red knight of the red lawns awaited him, and at an overthwart [*crosswise*] smote him within the hand, that his sword fell out of his hand; and yet he gave him another buffet on the helm that he fell grovelling to the earth, and the red knight fell over him for to hold him down.

Then cried the maiden Linet on high, "O Sir Beaumains, where is thy courage become! Alas, my lady my sister beholdeth thee, and she sobbeth and weepeth, that maketh mine heart heavy."

When Sir Beaumains heard her say so, he started up with a great might and gat him upon his feet, and lightly he leaped to his sword and griped it in his hand, and doubled his pace unto the red knight, and there they fought a new battle together. But Sir Beaumains then doubled his strokes, and smote so thick that he smote the sword out of his hand, and then he smote him upon the helm that he fell to the earth, and Sir Beaumains fell upon him, and unlaced his helm to have slain him; and then he yielded him and asked mercy, and said with a loud voice, "O noble knight, I yield me to thy mercy."

Then Sir Beaumains bethought him upon the knights that he had made to be hanged shamefully, and then he said, "I may not with my worship save thy life, for the shameful deaths thou hast caused many full good knights to die."

"Sir," said the red knight of the red lawns, "hold your hand, and ye shall know the causes why I put them to so shameful a death."

"Say on," said Sir Beaumains.

"Sir, I loved once a lady, a fair damsel, and she had her brother slain, and she said it was Sir Launcelot du Lake, or else Sir Gawaine, and she prayed me as that I loved her heartily that I would make her a promise by the faith of my knighthood for to labor daily in arms until I met with one of them, and all that I might overcome I should put them unto a villanous death; and this is the cause that I have put all these knights to death, and so I ensured her to do all the villany unto King Arthur's knights, and that I should take vengeance upon all these knights. And, sir, now I will thee tell that every day my strength increaseth till noon, and all this time have I seven men's strength."

Then came there many earls, and barons, and noble knights, and prayed that knight to save his life, and take him to your prisoner: and all they fell upon their knees and prayed him of mercy, and that he would save his life, and, "Sir," they all said, "it were fairer of him to take homage and fealty, and let him hold his lands of you, than for to slay him: by his death ye shall have none advantage, and his misdeeds that be done may not be undone; and therefore he shall make amends to all parties, and we all will become your men, and do you homage and fealty."

"Fair lords," said Beaumains, "wit you well I am full loth to slay this knight, nevertheless he hath done passing ill and shamefully. But insomuch all that he did was at a lady's request, I blame him the less, and so for your sake I will release him, that he shall have his life upon this covenant, that he go within the castle and yield him there to the lady, and if she will forgive and quit [*acquit*] him, I will well; with this that he make her amends of all the trespass he hath done against her and her lands. And also, when that is done, that ye go unto the court of King Arthur, and there that ye ask Sir Launcelot mercy, and Sir Gawaine, for the evil will ye have had against them."

"Sir," said the red knight of the red lawns, "all this will I do as ye command, and certain assurance and sureties ye shall have."

And so then when the assurance was made, he made his homage and fealty, and all those earls and barons with him. And then the maiden Linet came to Sir Beaumains and unarmed him, and searched his wounds, and stinted his blood, and in likewise she did to the red knight of the red lawns. And so they sojourned ten days in their tents. And the red knight made his lords and servants to do all the pleasure that they might unto Sir Beaumains.

And within a while after, the red knight of the red lawns went unto the castle and put him in the lady Lyoness' grace, and so she received him upon sufficient sureties, and all her hurts were well restored of all that she could complain. And then he departed and went unto the court of King Arthur, and there openly the red knight of the red lawns put him in the mercy of Sir Launcelot and Sir Gawaine, and there he told openly how he was overcome, and by whom, and also he told of all the battles, from the beginning to the ending.

"Jesus, mercy," said King Arthur and Sir Gawaine, "we marvel much of what blood he is come, for he is a full noble knight."

"Have ye no marvel," said Sir Launcelot, "for ye shall

right well wit that he is come of a full noble blood, and, as for his might and hardiness, there be but few now living that is so mighty as he is and so noble of prowess."

"It seemeth by you," said King Arthur, "that ye know his name, and from whence he is come, and of what blood he is."

"I suppose I do so," said Sir Launcelot, "or else I would not have given him the order of knighthood; but he gave me at that time such charge that I should never discover him until he required me, or else it be known openly by some other."

Now return we unto Sir Beaumains, which desired of the damsel Linet that he might see her sister his lady.

"Sir," said she, "I would fain ye saw her."

Then Sir Beaumains armed him at all points, and took his horse and his spear, and rode straight to the castle. And when he came to the gate, he found there many men armed, that pulled up the drawbridge and drew the port close. Then marvelled he why they would not suffer him to enter in. And then he looked up to the window, and there he saw the fair lady dame Lyoness, that said on high: "Go thy way, Sir Beaumains, for as yet thou shalt not wholly have my love, until the time thou be called one of the number of the worthy knights; and therefore go and labor in arms worshipfully these twelve months, and then ye shall hear new tidings; and perdé [*per dieu, truly*] a twelvemonth will be soon gone, and trust you me, fair knight, I shall be true unto you, and shall never betray you, but unto my death I shall love you and none other."

And therewithal she turned her from the window. And Sir Beaumains rode away from the castle in making great moan and sorrow; and so he rode here and there, and wist not whither he rode, till it was dark night; and then it happened him to come to a poor man's house, and there he was harbored all that night. But Sir Beaumains could have no rest, but wallowed and writhed for the love of the lady of the castle. And so on the morrow he took his horse and his armor, and rode till it was noon; and then he came unto a broad water, and thereby was a great lodge, and there he alighted to sleep, and laid his head upon his shield, and betook his horse to the dwarf, and commanded him to watch all night.

Now turn we to the lady of the castle, that thought much upon Sir Beaumains; and then she called unto her Sir Gringamor her brother, and prayed him in all manner, as he loved her heartily, that he would ride after Sir Beaumains, "and ever have him in a wait [*look after him*] till that ye may find him sleeping, for I am sure in his heaviness he will alight down in some place and lie down to sleep, and therefore have your watch upon him, and, in the priviest wise [*softest way*] that ye can, take his dwarf from him, and go your way with him as fast as ever ye may or Sir Beaumains awake; for my sister Linet hath showed me that the dwarf can tell of what kindred he is come, and what his right name is; and in the meanwhile I and my sister will ride to your castle to await when ye shall bring with you this dwarf, and then when ye have brought him to your castle, I will have him in examination myself; unto the time I know what his right name is, and of what kindred he is come, shall I never be merry at my heart."

"Sister," said Sir Gringamor, "all this shall be done after your intent." And so he rode all the other day and the night till that he found Sir Beaumains lying by a water, and his head upon his shield, for to sleep. And then when he saw Sir Beaumains fast on sleep, he came stilly stalking behind the dwarf, and plucked him fast under his arm, and so he rode away with him as fast as ever he might unto his own castle. But ever as he rode with the dwarf towards his castle, he cried unto his lord and prayed him of help. And therewith awoke Sir Beaumains, and up he leaped lightly, and saw where Sir Gringamor rode his way with the dwarf, and so Sir Gringamor rode out of his sight.

Then Sir Beaumains put on his helm anon, and buckled his shield, and took his horse and rode after him all that ever he might ride, through marshes and fields and great dales, that many times his horse and he plunged over the head in deep mires, for he knew not the way, but he took the next [*nearest*] way in that woodness [*madness*] that many times he was like to perish. [And so he came following his dwarf to Sir Gringamor's castle. But aforetime the lady Lyoness had come and had the dwarf in examination; and the dwarf had told the lady how that Sir Beaumains was the son of a king, and how his mother was sister to King Arthur, and how his right name was Sir Gareth of Orkney.]

And as they sat thus talking, there came Sir Beaumains at the gate with an angry countenance, and his sword drawn in his hand, and cried aloud that all the castle might hear it, saying, "Thou traitor, Sir Gringamor, deliver me my dwarf again, or by the faith that I owe to the order of knighthood, I shall do thee all the harm that I can."

Then Sir Gringamor looked out at a window, and said, "Sir Gareth of Orkney, leave thy boasting words, for thou gettest not thy dwarf again."

"Thou coward knight," said Sir Gareth, "bring him with thee, and come and do battle with me, and win him, and take him."

"So will I do," said Sir Gringamor, "and me list [*if it please me*], but for all thy great words thou gettest him not."

"Ah, fair brother," said dame Lyoness, "I would he had his dwarf again, for I would not he were wroth, for now he hath told me all my desire I will no longer keep the dwarf. And also, brother, he hath done much for me, and delivered me from the red knight of the red lawns, and therefore, brother, I owe him my service afore all knights living; and wit ye well I love him above all other knights, and full fain would I speak with him, but in no wise I would he wist what I were, but that I were another strange lady."

"Well," said Sir Gringamor, "sith [*since*] that I know your will, I will now obey unto him."

And therewithal he went down unto Sir Gareth, and said, "Sir, I cry you mercy, and all that I have misdone against your person I will amend it at your own will, and therefore I pray you that you will alight, and take such cheer as I can make you here in this castle."

"Shall I then have my dwarf again?" said Sir Gareth.

"Yea, sir, and all the pleasure that I can make you, for as soon as your dwarf told me what ye were and of what blood that ye are come, and what noble deeds ye have done in these marches [*borders*], then I repent me of my deeds."

And then Sir Gareth alighted down from his horse, and therewith came his dwarf and took his horse.

"O my fellow," said Sir Gareth, "I have had many evil adventures for thy sake."

And so Sir Gringamor took him by the hand, and led him into the hall, and there was Sir Gringamor's wife.

And then there came forth into the hall dame Lyoness arrayed like a princess, and there she made him passing good cheer, and he her again. And they had goodly language and lovely countenance together. And Sir Gareth many times thought in himself, "Would to God that the lady of the Castle Perilous were so fair as she is!" There were all manner of games and plays, both of dancing and leaping; and ever the more Sir Gareth beheld the lady, the more he loved her, and so he burned in love that he was past himself in his understanding. And forth towards night they went to supper, and Sir Gareth might not eat, for his love was so hot that he wist not where he was. All these looks Sir Gringamor espied, and after supper he called his sister dame Lyoness unto a chamber, and said: "Fair sister, I have well espied your countenance between you and this knight, and I will, sister, that ye wit that he is a full noble knight, and if ye can make him to abide here, I will do to him all the pleasure that I can, for and ye were better than ye be, ye were well bestowed upon him."

"Fair brother," said dame Lyoness, "I understand well that the knight is good, and come he is of a noble house; notwithstanding I will assay him better, for he hath had great labor for my love, and hath passed many a dangerous passage."

Right so Sir Gringamor went unto Sir Gareth, and said: "Sir, make ye good cheer; for wist [*know*] ye well that she loveth you as well as ye do her, and better if better may be."

"And I wist that," said Sir Gareth, "there lived not a gladder man than I would be."

"Upon my worship," said Sir Gringamor, "trust unto my promise; and as long as it liketh you ye shall sojourn with me, and this lady shall be with us daily and nightly to make you all the cheer that she can."

"I will well," said Sir Gareth, "for I have promised to be nigh this country this twelvemonth. And well I am sure King Arthur and other noble knights will find me where that I am within this twelvemonth. For I shall be sought and found, if that I be on live."

And then the noble knight Sir Gareth went unto the dame Lyoness, which he then much loved, and kissed her many times, and either made great joy of other. And there she promised him her love, certainly to love him and none other the days of her life. Then this lady, dame Lyoness, by the assent of her brother, told Sir Gareth all the truth what she was, and how she was the same lady that he did battle for, and how she was lady of the Castle Perilous. And there she told him how she caused her brother to take away his dwarf, "For this cause, to know the certainty what was your name, and of what kin ye were come."

And then she let fetch before him Linet the damsel, which had ridden with him many dreary ways. Then was Sir Gareth more gladder than he was tofore. And then they troth plight[1] each other to love, and never to fail while their life lasted.

[1] "Troth," *truth,* and "plight," *wove:* "troth plight," *wove their truth together.*

BOOK IV

OF SIR TRISTRAM

BOOK IV

OF SIR TRISTRAM

THERE was a knight that hight Meliodas, and he was lord and king of the country of Lyonesse, and this King Meliodas was as likely a man as any was at that time living. And by fortune he wedded King Mark's sister of Cornwall, whose name was Elizabeth, and she was a right fair lady and a good.

[And it befell on a day that a certain enchantress wrought as he rode on hunting, for he was a great hunter, and made him chase an hart by himself till that he came to an old castle, and there she took him prisoner. Now when Queen Elizabeth missed her husband King Meliodas, she was nigh out of her wit; and she took a gentlewoman with her and ran far into the forest and took such cold that she might not recover. And when she saw] that the deep draughts of death took her, that needs she must die and depart out of this world [and] there was none other boot [*aid, or hope*], she made great moan and sorrow, and said unto her gentlewoman: "When ye see my lord King Meliodas, recommend me unto him, and tell him what pains I endure for his love, and how I must die here for his sake, and for default of good help, and let him wit that I am full sorry to depart out of this world from him, therefore pray him to be good friend unto my soul. And I charge thee, gentlewoman, that thou beseech my lord King Meliodas, that when my son shall be christened let him be named Tristram, that is as much to say as sorrowful birth."

And therewithal this Queen Elizabeth gave up her ghost, and died in the same place. Then the gentlewoman laid her under the shadow of a great tree.

[And it so happened that after seven years King Melliodas took him a second wife, and wedded King Howell's daughter of Brittany. And the new queen was jealous of young Tristram in the behalf of her own children, and put poison for Tristram to drink. But by strange hap her own son drank the poison and died. Then again she put poison in some drink for Tristram; and] by fortune the King Meliodas her husband found the piece [*cup*] with the wine whereas the poison was in, and he, that was most thirsty, took the piece for to drink thereof, and as he would have drunken thereof the queen espied him, and then she ran unto him and pulled the piece from him suddenly. The king marvelled why she did so, and remembered him how her son was suddenly slain with poison. And then he took her by the hand, and thus said to her: "Thou false traitress, thou shalt tell me what manner of drink this is, or else I shall slay thee." And therewith he pulled out his sword, and swore a great oath that he would slay her but if she told him truth.

"Ah! mercy, my lord," said she, "and I shall tell you all."

And then she told him why that she would have slain Tristram, because her children should rejoice the land.

"Well," said King Meliodas, "therefore shall ye have the law."

And so she was damned [*condemned*] by the assent of the barons to be burnt; and then there was made a great fire, and right as she was at the fire for to take her execution, young Tristram kneeled down before King Meliodas, his father, and besought him to give him a boon.

"I will well," said the king.

Then said young Tristram, "Give me the life of your queen, my stepmother."

"That is unrightfully asked," said his father, King Meliodas, "for she would have slain thee with that poison and she might have had her will, and for thy sake most is my cause that she should die."

"Sir," said Tristram, "as for that I beseech you of your mercy that ye will forgive it her, and as for my part, God forgive it her, and I do, and so much it liketh your highness to grant me my boon, for God's love I pray you hold your promise."

"Sith it is so," said the king, "I will that ye have her life and give her to you, and go ye to the fire and take her, and do with her what ye will."

So young Tristram went to the fire, and, by the command of the king, delivered her from the death.

And by the good means of young Tristram he made the king and her accord.

And then [King Meliodas] let ordain a gentleman that was well learned and taught; his name was Gouvernail;

and he sent young Tristram with Gouvernail into France, to learn the language, and nurture, and deeds of arms. And there was Tristram more than seven years. And then when he well could speak the language, and had learned all that he might learn in that country, then he came home to his father King Meliodas again. And so Tristram learned to be an harper passing all other, that there was none such called in no country, and so in harping and on instruments of music he applied him in his youth for to learn. And after as he grew in might and strength he laboured ever in hunting and in hawking, so that never gentleman more, that ever we heard tell of.

Then it befell that King Anguish of Ireland sent to King Mark of Cornwall for his truage [*tribute*], which Cornwall had paid many winters afore time, and all that time King Mark was behind of the truage for seven years. And King Mark and his barons gave unto the messenger of Ireland this answer, and said that they would none pay, and bade the messenger go unto his King Anguish and tell him, "that we will pay him no truage; but tell your lord, and he will always have truage of us of Cornwall, bid him send a trusty knight of his land that will fight for his right, and we shall find another to defend our right." With this answer the messenger departed into Ireland. And when King Anguish understood the answer of the messenger, he was wondrous wroth; and then he called unto him Sir Marhaus the good knight that was nobly proved, and a knight of the Round Table. And this Sir Marhaus was brother unto the Queen of Ireland.

Then the king [prayed Sir Marhaus that he would go and fight for his truage of Cornwall].

"Sir," said Sir Marhaus, "wit [*know*] ye well that I shall not be loth to do battle in the right of you and your land with the best knight of the Round Table, for I know what their deeds be, and for to increase my worship [*worthship*] I will right gladly go to this journey for our right."

So in all haste there was made purveyance for Sir Marhaus, and so he departed out of Ireland, and arrived up in Cornwall, even fast by the castle of Tintagil. And when King Mark understood that he was there arrived to fight for Ireland, then made King Mark great sorrow. For they knew no knight that durst have ado with him. For at that time Sir Marhaus was called one of the famousest and renowned knights of the world.

And thus Sir Marhaus abode in the sea, and every day he sent unto King Mark for to pay the truage that was behind of seven year, or else to find a knight to fight with him for the truage. Then they of Cornwall let make cries in every place, that what knight would fight for to save the truage of Cornwall he should be rewarded so that he should fare the better the term of his life. Then some of the barons said to King Mark, and counselled him to send to the court of King Arthur for to seek Sir Launcelot du Lake. Then there were some other barons that counselled the king not to do so, and said that it was labour in vain, because Sir Marhaus was a knight of the Round Table, therefore any of them will be loth to have ado with other. So the king and all his barons assented that it was no boot [*help*] to seek any knight of the Round Table. When young Tristram heard of this he was wroth and sore ashamed that there durst no knight in Cornwall have ado with Sir Marhaus of Ireland.

Therewithal Sir Tristram went unto his father King Meliodas, and asked him counsel what was best to do for to recover the country of Cornwall for truage. "For as me seemeth," said Sir Tristram, "it were shame that Sir Marhaus, the queen's brother of Ireland, should go away, unless that he were not fought withal."

"As for that," said King Meliodas, "wit ye well, my son Tristram, that Sir Marhaus is called one of the best knights of the world, and knight of the Round Table, and therefore I know no knight in this country that is able to match with him."

"Alas!" said Sir Tristram, "that I am not made knight, and if Sir Marhaus should thus depart into Ireland, God let me never have worship; and I were made knight I should match him; and sir," said Sir Tristram, "I pray you to give me leave to ride unto mine uncle King Mark, and so ye be not displeased, of King Mark will I be made knight."

"I will well," said King Meliodas, "that ye be ruled as your courage will rule you."

And then Sir Tristram thanked his father much, and so made him ready to ride into Cornwall. And in the mean while there came a messenger with letters of love from the daughter of King Faramon of France, unto Sir Tristram, that were full piteous letters, and in them were written many complaints of love. But Sir Tristram had no joy of her letters, nor regard unto her. Also she sent him a little brachet [*hunting hound*] that was passing fair. But when the king's daughter understood that Tristram would not love her, she died for sorrow. So this young Sir Tristram rode unto his uncle King Mark of Cornwall. And when he came there he heard say that there would no knight fight with Sir Marhaus. Then went Sir Tristram unto his uncle and said, —

"Sir, if ye will give me the order of knighthood I will do battle with Sir Marhaus."

"What are ye?" said the king, "and from whence be ye come?"

"Sir," said Tristram, "I come from King Meliodas that wedded your sister, and a gentleman wit ye well I am."

King Mark beheld Sir Tristram, and saw that he was but a young man of age, but he was passingly well made and big.

"Fair sir," said the king, "what is your name, and where were ye born?"

"Sir," said he again, "my name is Tristram, and in the country of Lyonesse was I born."

"Ye say well," said the king, "and if ye will do this battle I shall make you knight."

"Therefore I come to you," said Sir Tristram, "and for none other cause."

But then King Mark made him knight. And therewithal anon as he had made him knight, he sent a messenger unto Sir Marhaus with letters that said that he had found a young knight ready for to take the battle to the uttermost.

"It may well be," said Sir Marhaus; "but tell unto

King Mark that I will not fight with no knight but if he be of blood royal, that is to say either king's son or queen's son, born of a prince or princess."

When King Mark understood that, he sent for Sir Tristram de Lyonesse, and told him what was the answer of Sir Marhaus. Then said Sir Tristram, —

"Since he sayeth so, let him wit that I am come of father's side and mother's side of as noble blood as he is. For, sir, now shall ye know that I am King Meliodas' son, born of your own sister dame Elizabeth, that died in the forest in the birth of me."

"Yea!" said King Mark, "ye are welcome fair nephew to me."

Then in all the haste the king let horse Sir Tristram and arm him in the best manner that might be had or gotten for gold or silver. And then King Mark sent unto Sir Marhaus, and did him to wit [*let him know*] that a better born man than he was himself should fight with him, and his name is Sir Tristram de Lyonesse, [son of] King Meliodas, and born of King Mark's sister. Then was Sir Marhaus glad and blithe that he should fight with such a gentleman. And so by the assent of King Mark and Sir Marhaus they let ordain that they should fight within an island nigh Sir Marhaus' ships; and so was young Sir Tristram put into a little vessel, both his horse and he, and all that to him belonged both for his body and for his horse, so that Sir Tristram lacked no manner thing. And when King Mark and his barons of Cornwall beheld how young Sir Tristram departed with such a carriage [*that is, carrying himself so bravely*] to fight for the right of Cornwall, wit ye well there was neither man nor woman of worship but they wept for to see so young a knight jeopard himself for their right.

For to make short this tale, that when Sir Tristram was arrived within the island, then he looked to the further side, and there he saw at an anchor six ships nigh to the land, and under the shadow of the ships, upon the land, there hoved [*hovered*] the noble knight Sir Marhaus of Ireland. And then Sir Tristram commanded his servant Gouvernail for to bring his horse to the land, and dress his harness at all manner of rights. And when he had so done, he mounted upon his horse. And when he was in his saddle well apparelled, and his shield dressed upon his shoulder, Sir Tristram asked Gouvernail, "Where is this knight that I shall have to do withal?"

"Sir," said his servant Gouvernail, "see ye him not? I wend ye had seen him, yonder he hoveth under the shadow of his ships upon horseback, and his spear in his hand, and his shield upon his shoulder."

"It is truth," said Sir Tristram, "now I see him well enough."

And then he commanded his servant Gouvernail to go again unto his vessel, and commend him "unto mine uncle King Mark, and pray him that if I be slain in this battle, for to bury my body as him seemeth best, and, as for me, let him wit that I will never yield me for no cowardice, and if I be slain and flee not, then have they lost no truage for me. And if so be that I flee or yield me as recreant, bid mine uncle never bury me in Christian burials. And upon my life," said Sir Tristram to Gouvernail, "come thou not nigh this island till thou see me overcome or slain, or else that I win yonder knight."

And so either departed from other weeping.

And then Sir Marhaus perceived Sir Tristram, and thus said unto him: "Young knight Sir Tristram, what doest thou here? Me sore repenteth of thy courage, for wit thou well I have matched with the best knights of the world, and therefore by my counsel return again to thy ship."

"Fair knight and well proved knight," said Sir Tristram, "thou shalt well wit that I may not forsake thee in this quarrel, for I am for thy sake made knight, and thou shalt well wit that I am a king's son born, and such promise have I made at mine uncle's request and mine own seeking, that I shall fight with thee unto the uttermost, to deliver Cornwall from the old truage. Also wit ye well, Sir Marhaus, that for ye are called one of the best renowned knights of the world, and because of that noise and fame that ye have, it will do me good to have to do with you, for never yet sith [*since*] that I was born of my mother was I proved with a good knight, and also sith I have taken the high order of knighthood this day, I am right well pleased that I may have to do with so good a knight as ye are. And now wit ye well, Sir Marhaus of Ireland, that I cast me to win worship on thy body, I trust to God I shall be worshipfully proved upon thy body and for to deliver the country of Cornwall forever from all manner of truage from Ireland."

And when the good knight Sir Marhaus had heard him say what him list, then said he thus again: "Fair knight, sith it is so that thou castest thee to win worship on me, I let thee wit that no worship maist thou leese [*lose*] by me, if thou mayst stand me three strokes, for I let you wit that for my noble deeds, proved and seen, King Arthur made me knight of the Table Round." Then they began to feuter [*place in rest*] their spears, and they met so fiercely together that they smote either other down both horse and all. But Sir Marhaus smote Sir Tristram a great wound in the side with his spear, and then they avoided their horses, and pulled out their swords, and threw their shields afore them, and then they lashed together as men than were wild and courageous. And when they had stricken so together long, then they left their strokes, and foined [*thrust, in feinting*]; and when they saw that that might not prevail them, then they hurtled together like rams to bear either other down. Thus they fought still more than half a day, and either were wounded passing sore, that the blood ran down freshly from them upon the ground. By then Sir Tristram waxed more fresher than Sir Marhaus, and better winded and bigger, and with a mighty stroke he smote Sir Marhaus upon the helm such a buffet, that it went through his helm, and through the coif of steel, and through the brain-pan, and the sword stuck so fast in the helm and in his brain-pan that Sir Tristram pulled thrice at his sword or ever he might pull it out from his head, and there Marhaus fell down on his knees, [and a piece of] the edge of Tristram's sword [was] left in his brain-pan. And suddenly Sir Marhaus rose grovelling, and threw his sword and his shield from him, and so ran to his ships and fled his way, and Sir Tristram had ever his shield and his sword. And when Sir Tristram saw Sir Marhaus withdraw him, he said, "Ah, sir knight of the Round Table, why withdrawest thou thee; thou doest thyself and thy kin great shame, for I am but a young knight, or now I was never proved, and rather than I should withdraw me from thee, I had rather be hewn in an hundred pieces." Sir Marhaus answered no word, but went his way sore groaning.

Anon Sir Marhaus and his fellowship departed into Ireland. And as soon as he came to the king his brother he let search his wounds. And when his head was searched, a piece of Sir Tristram's sword was found therein, and might never be had out of his head for no surgeons, and so he died of Sir Tristram's sword, and that piece of the sword the queen his sister kept it for ever with her, for she thought to be revenged and she might.

Now turn we again unto Sir Tristram, that was sore wounded, and full sore bled, that he might not within a little while when he had taken cold scarcely stir him of his limbs. And then he set him down softly upon a little hill, and bled fast. Then anon came Gouvernail his man with his vessel, and the king and his barons came with procession, and when he was come to the land, King Mark took him in both his arms, and the king and Sir Dinas the seneschal led Sir Tristram into the castle of Tintagil, and then were his wounds searched in the best manner, and laid in bed. And when King Mark saw all his wounds, he wept right heartily, and so did all his lords.

"So God me help," said King Mark, "I would not for all my lands that my nephew died."

So Sir Tristram lay there a month and more, and was like to have died of the stroke that Sir Marhaus had given him first with his spear. For, as the French book saith, that spear's head was envenomed, that Sir Tristram might not be whole thereof. Then was King Mark and all his barons passing heavy, for they deemed none other but that Sir Tristram should not recover. So the king let send after all manner of leeches and surgeons, both men and women, and there was none that would warrant him his life. Then came there a lady, which was a full wise lady, and she said plainly unto King Mark and unto Sir Tristram and unto all the barons, that he should never be whole, but if Sir Tristram went into the same country that the venom came from, and in that country should he be holpen or else never. When King Mark had well heard what the lady said, forthwith he let purvey for Sir Tristram a fair vessel, and well victualled it, and therein was put Sir Tristram and Gouvernail with him, and Sir Tristram took his harp with him, and so he was put to sea, for to sail into Ireland, and so by good fortune he arrived up into Ireland even fast by a castle where the king and the queen were, and at his arriving he sat and harped in his bed a merry lay, such one had they never heard in Ireland afore that time. And when it was told the king and the queen of such a knight that was such a harper, anon the king sent for him, and let search his wound, and then he asked him what was his name. He answered and said,

"I am of the country of Lyonesse, and my name is Tramtrist, [and I have] been wounded in a battle as I fought for a lady's right."

"Truly," said King Anguish, "ye shall have all the help in this land that ye may have here. But I let you wit in Cornwall I had a great loss as ever had king, for there I lost the best knight of the world, his name was Marhaus, a full noble knight, and knight of the Table Round;" and there he told Sir Tristram wherefore Sir Marhaus was slain. Sir Tristram made semblant [*like*] as he had been sorry, and better knew he how it was than the king.

Then the king for great favour made Tramtrist to be put in his daughter's ward and keeping, because she was a noble surgeon. And when she had searched his wound, she found in the bottom of his wound that there was poison, and within a little while she healed him, and therefore Tramtrist cast great love to la Belle Isolde, for she was at that time the fairest lady of the world, and then Sir Tramtrist [taught] her to harp, and she began to have a great fantasy unto Sir Tramtrist. And at that time Sir Palamides, that was a Saracen, was in that country, and was well cherished both of the king and the queen, and he proffered her many great gifts, for he loved her passing well. And all that espied right well Sir Tramtrist, and full well he knew Sir Palamides for a noble knight and a mighty man.

Thus was there great envy between Sir Tramtrist and

Sir Palamides. Then it befell that King Anguish let cry a great joust and a great tournament for a lady which was called the lady of the lawns, and she was nigh cousin unto the king, and what man that should win her should wed her three days after, and have all her lands. This cry was made in England, Wales, and Scotland, and also in France and in Britain. It befell upon a day la Belle Isolde came to Sir Tramtrist and told him of this tournament.

"Ah! Tramtrist," said la Belle Isolde, "why will ye not have to do at that tournament? well I wot Sir Palamides will be there and do what he may, and therefore, Sir Tramtrist, I pray you to be there, for else Sir Palamides is like to win the degree."

"Madam," said Sir Tramtrist, "as for that he may do so, for he is a proved knight, and I am but a young knight and late made, and the first battle that I did it mishapped me to be sore wounded as ye see. But and I wist [*if I knew*] that ye would be my better lady, at that tournament I will be, so that ye will keep my counsel, and let no creature have knowledge that I shall joust but yourself, and such as ye will to keep your counsel; my poor person shall I jeopard there for your sake, that peradventure Sir Palamides shall know when that I come."

"Thereto," said la Belle Isolde, "do your best, and as I can," said la Belle Isolde, "I shall purvey horse and armor for you at my devise."

"As ye will so be it," said Sir Tramtrist, "I will be at your commandment."

So at the day of jousts there came Sir Palamides with a

black shield, and he overthrew many knights, that all the people had marvel of him. For he put to the worse Sir Gawaine, Gaheris, Agravaine, Bagdemagus, Kay, Dodinas le Savage, Sagramor le Desirous, Gumret le Petit, and Griflet le Fise de Dieu. All these the first day Sir Palamides strake down to the earth. And then all manner of knights were adread of Sir Palamides, and many called him the knight with the black shield. So that day Sir Palamides had great worship. Then came King Anguish unto Tramtrist and asked him why he would not joust.

"Sir," said he, "I was but late hurt, and as yet I dare not adventure me."

And so on the morn Sir Palamides made him ready to come into the field as he did the first day. And there he smote down the king with the hundred knights, and the King of Scotland. Then had la Belle Isolde ordained and well arrayed Sir Tramtrist in white horse and harness. And right so she let put him out at a privy postern, and so he came into the field as it had been a bright angel. And anon Sir Palamides espied him, and therewith he feutered [*laid in rest*] a spear unto Sir Tramtrist, and he again unto him. And there Sir Tristram smote down Sir Palamides unto the earth. And then there was a great noise of people: some said Sir Palamides had a fall, some said the knight with the black shield had a fall. And wit you well la Belle Isolde was passing glad. And then Sir Gawaine and his fellows nine had marvel what knight it might be that had smitten down Sir Palamides. Then would there none joust with Tramtrist, but all that were there forsook him, most and least. And when Sir Palamides had received this fall, wit ye well he was sore ashamed; and as privily as he might he withdrew him out of the field. All that espied Sir Tristram, and lightly he rode after Sir Palamides, and overtook him, and bade him turn, for better he would assay him or ever he departed. Then Sir Palamides turned him, and either lashed at other with their swords. But at the first stroke Sir Tristram smote down Palamides, and gave him such a stroke upon the head that he fell to the earth. So then Tristram bade yield him and do his commandment, or else he would slay him. And when Sir Palamides beheld his countenance, he dread sore his buffets, so that he granted him all his asking.

"Well," said Sir Tristram unto him, "this shall be your charge. First, upon pain of your life, that ye forsake my lady la Belle Isolde, and in no manner of wise that ye draw unto her, and also these twelve months and a day that ye bear none armor nor in like wise no harness of war. Now promise me this, or here shalt thou die."

"Alas!" said Sir Palamides, "now am I for ever shamed."

And then he swore as Sir Tristram had commanded him. Then for great despite and anger, Sir Palamides cut off his harness and threw it away.

And then Sir Tristram rode privily unto the postern where la Belle Isolde kept him, and then she made him good cheer, and thanked God of his good speed.

Thus was Sir Tramtrist long there well cherished with the king and queen and namely [*likewise*] with la Belle Isolde.

So upon a day the queen and la Belle Isolde made a bayne [*bath*] for Sir Tramtrist, and when he was in his bayne, the queen and her daughter la Belle Isolde roamed up and down in the chamber, and there whiles Gouvernail and Hebes attended upon Tramtrist, and the queen beheld his sword whereas it lay upon his bed. And then by unhap the queen drew out his sword and beheld it a long while, and both they thought it a passing fair sword, but within a foot and an half of the point there was a great piece broken out of the edge. And when the queen espied that gap in the sword, she remembered of a piece of a sword that was found in the brain-pan of the good knight Sir Marhaus that was her brother.

"Alas!" said she then to her daughter la Belle Isolde. "This is the same traitorous knight that slew my brother thine uncle."

When la Belle Isolde heard her say so, she was then passing sore abashed, for she loved Sir Tramtrist passingly well, and right well she knew the cruelness of her mother the queen. And so anon therewith the queen went in all the haste that she might unto her own chamber, and then she sought in a coffer that she had, and there she found and took out the piece of the sword that was taken out of her brother's head Sir Marhaus, after that he was dead. And then anon she ran with the same piece of iron unto Sir Tramtrist's sword which lay upon the bed, and so when she put the same piece of steel and iron unto the same sword, it was then as fit as ever it might be when it was first new broken. And so forthwith the queen caught that sword fiercely in her hand, and with all her might she ran straight unto Tramtrist where he sat in a bayne, and there she had run him through had not Sir Hebes gotten her in his arms and pulled the sword from her, and else she had thrust him through. When she was thus letted of her evil will, she ran to King Anguish her husband, and fell on her knees before him, saying, "Oh, my lord and husband, here have ye in your house that traitor knight that slew my brother and your servant, that noble knight Sir Marhaus."

"Who is that," said King Anguish, "and where is he?"

"Sir," said she, "it is Sir Tramtrist, the same knight that my daughter hath healed."

"Alas!" said King Anguish, "therefore am I right neavy, for he is a full noble knight as ever I saw in field, but I charge you," said the king to the queen, "that ye have not to do with this knight, but let me deal with him."

Then the king went into the chamber to Sir Tramtrist, that then was gone unto his chamber, and then the king found him all armed, ready to mount upon his horse. And when the king saw him all ready armed to mount on horseback, the king said, "Nay, Tramtrist, it will not avail thee to compare against me. But thus much will I do for my worship, and for thy love: in so much as thou art within this court, it were no worship for me to slay thee, therefore upon this condition I will give thee leave to depart from this court in safety, so that thou wilt tell me who is thy father, and what is thy name, and if thou slew my brother Sir Marhaus."

"Sir," said Sir Tristram, "now shall I tell you all the truth; my father's name is Meliodas, King of Lyonesse, and my mother hight Elizabeth, that was sister unto King Mark of Cornwall, and my mother died of me in the forest, and because thereof she commanded or she died that when I were christened that they should name me Tristram, and because I would not be known in this country, I turned my name, and let call me Tramtrist; and for the truage of Cornwall, I fought for mine uncle's sake, and for the right of Cornwall that ye had possessed many years. And wit ye well," said Tristram unto the king, "I did the battle for the love of mine uncle King Mark, and for the love of the country of Cornwall, and for to increase mine honor. For that same day that I fought with Sir Marhaus I was made knight, and never or then did I know battle with no knight, and from me he went alive, and left his shield and his sword behind."

"Truly," said the king, "I may not say but ye did as a knight should, and it was your part to do for your quarrel, and to increase your worship as a knight should; howbeit I may not maintain you in this country with my worship, unless that I should displease my barons, and my wife, and her kin."

"Sir," said Tristram, "I thank you of your good lordship that I have had with you here, and the great goodness my lady your daughter hath showed me, and therefore," said Sir Tristram, "it may so happen that ye shall win more by my life than by my death, for in the parts of England it may happen I may do you service at some season that ye shall be glad that ever ye showed me your good lordship. With more I promise you as I am true knight, that in all places I shall be my lady your daughter's servant and knight in right and in wrong, and I shall never fail her to do as much as a knight may do. Also I beseech your good grace that I may take my leave at my lady your daughter, and at all the barons and knights."

"I will well," said the king.

Then Sir Tristram went unto la Belle Isolde, and took his leave of her. And then he told her all, what he was, and how he had changed his name because he would not be known, and how a lady told him that he should never be whole till he came into this country where the poison was made: "Wherethrough I was near my death, had not your ladyship been."

"Oh, gentle knight," said la Belle Isolde, "full woe am I of thy departing, for I saw never man that I owed so good will to." And therewithal she wept heartily.

"Madam," said Sir Tristram, "ye shall understand that my name is Sir Tristram de Lyonesse, and I promise you faithfully that I shall be all the days of my life your knight."

"Sir, gramercy," said la Belle Isolde, "and there again I promise you that I shall not be married of this seven year but if it be by your assent, and to whom ye will I shall be married, him shall I have, if he will have me, if ye will consent."

And then Sir Tristram gave her a ring, and she gave him another, and therewith he departed from her, leaving her making full great moan and lamentation, and he went straight unto the court among all the barons, and there he took his leave of most and least, and openly among them all he said: "Fair lords, now it is so that I must depart from hence, if there be any man here that I have offended unto, or that any man be with me grieved, let him complain here before me or I depart from hence, and I shall amend it unto my power. And if there be any that will proffer me wrong, or to say of me wrong or shame behind my back, say it now or never, and here is my body to make it good, body against body."

And all they stood still, there was not one that would say one word, yet were there some knights which were of the queen's blood and of Sir Marhaus' blood, but they would not meddle with him.

So Sir Tristram departed and took the sea, and with good wind he arrived up at Tintagil in Cornwall. And when King Mark was whole and in his prosperity, there came tidings that Sir Tristram was arrived and whole of his wound, whereof King Mark was passing glad, and so were all the barons. And when he saw his time, he rode unto his father King Meliodas, and there he had all the cheer that the king and the queen could make him. And then largely King Meliodas and his queen parted of their lands and goods unto Sir Tristram. So then by the license [*leave*] of King Meliodas his father, he returned again unto the court of King Mark, and there he lived in great joy long time, until at the last there befell a jealousy and an unkindness between King Mark and Sir Tristram.

Then King Mark cast always in his heart how he might destroy Sir Tristram. And then he imagined in himself to send Sir Tristram into Ireland for la Belle Isolde. For Sir

Tristram had so praised her beauty and her goodness that King Mark said he would wed her, whereupon he prayed Sir Tristram to take his way into Ireland for him on message. And all this was done to the intent to slay Sir Tristram. Notwithstanding, Sir Tristram would not refuse the message for no danger nor peril that might fall for the pleasure of his uncle, but to go he made him ready in the most goodliest wise that might be devised. So Sir Tristram departed and took the sea with all his fellowship. And anon as he was in the broad sea, a tempest took him and his fellowship and drove them back into the coast of England, and there they arrived fast by Camelot, and full fain they were to take the land. And when they were landed Sir Tristram set up his pavilion upon the land of Camelot, and there he let hang his shield upon the pavilion.

Then when Sir Tristram was in his rich pavilion, Gouvernail his man came and told him how King Anguish of Ireland was come there, and how he was put in great distress; and there Gouvernail told to Sir Tristram how King Anguish of Ireland was summoned and accused of murder.

"So God me help," said Sir Tristram, "these be the best tidings that ever came to me this seven year, for now shall the King of Ireland have need of my help, for I dare say there is no knight in this country that is not of King Arthur's court dare do no battle with Sir Blamor de Ganis; and for to win the love of the King of Ireland, I shall take the battle upon me; and therefore, Gouvernail, I charge thee to bring me to the king."

And so Gouvernail went unto King Anguish of Ireland, and saluted him fair. The king welcomed him, and asked him what he would.

"Sir," said Gouvernail, "here is a knight near hand which desireth to speak with you; and he bade me say that he would do you service."

"What knight is he?" said the king.

"Sir," said he, "it is Sir Tristram de Lyonesse, that for the good grace that ye showed unto him in your land, he will reward you in this country."

"Come on, good fellow," said the king, "with me, and show me Sir Tristram."

So the king took a little hackney and a little company with him, until he came unto Sir Tristram's pavilicn. And when Sir Tristram saw King Anguish, he ran unto him, and would have holden his stirrup. But anon the king leapt lightly from his horse, and either halsed [*embraced*] other in their arms.

"My gracious lord," said Sir Tristram, "gramercy of your great goodness that ye showed to me in your marches and lands. And at that time I promised you to do you service and ever it lay in my power."

"Ah, worshipful knight," said the king unto Sir Tristram, "now have I great need of you; for never had I so great need of no knight's help."

"How so, my good lord?" said Sir Tristram.

"I shall tell you," said King Anguish; "I am summoned and appealed from my country for the death of a knight that was kin unto the good knight Sir Launcelot, wherefore

Sir Blamor de Ganis, brother to Sir Bleoberis, hath appealed me to fight with him, other [*or else*] to find a knight in my stead. And well I wot," said the king, "these that are come of King Ban's blood, as Sir Launcelot and these other, are passing good knights, and hard men for to win in battle as any that I know now living."

"Sir," said Sir Tristram, "for the good lordship ye showed me in Ireland, and for my lady your daughter's sake, la Belle Isolde, I will take the battle for you upon this condition that ye shall grant me two things: that one is, that ye shall swear to me that ye are in the right, that ye were never consenting to the knight's death; sir, then," said Sir Tristram, "when that I have done this battle, if God give me grace that I speed, that ye shall give me a reward, what thing reasonable that I will ask of you."

"Truly," said the king, "ye shall have whatsoever ye will ask."

"It is well said," said Sir Tristram.

Then were the lists made ready, and Sir Tristram and Sir Blamor de Ganis, in the presence of the kings, judges, and knights, feutered [*laid in rest*] their spears and came together as it had been thunder, and there Sir Tristram through great might smote down Sir Blamor and his horse to the earth. Then anon Sir Blamor avoided his horse, and pulled out his sword and threw his shield afore him, and bade Sir Tristram alight; "for though an horse hath failed me, I trust the earth will not fail me."

And then Sir Tristram alighted and dressed him unto

battle, and there they lashed together strongly as racing and tracing, foining and dashing many sad strokes, that the kings and knights had great wonder that they might stand, for ever they fought like two wild men, so that there were never knights seen fight more fiercely than they did; for Sir Blamor was so hasty that he would have no rest, that all men wondered that they had breath to stand on their feet; all the place was bloody that they fought in. And at the last Sir Tristram smote Sir Blamor such a buffet upon the helm that he fell down upon his side, and Sir Tristram stood and beheld him.

Then when Sir Blamor might speak, he said thus:—

"Sir Tristram de Lyonesse, I require thee, as thou art a noble knight, and the best knight that ever I found, that thou wilt slay me out of hand [*straightway*], for I had liever die with worship than live with shame, and needs, Sir Tristram, thou must slay me, or else thou shalt never win the field, for I will never say the loth word [*of surrender*]; and therefore, if thou dare slay me, slay me, I require thee."

And when Sir Tristram heard him say so knightly, he wist not what to do with him. And then Sir Tristram started aback and went to the kings which were judges; and there he kneeled down before them, and besought them for their worship, and for King Arthur and Sir Launcelot's sake, that they would take this matter in their hands:

"For, fair lords," said Sir Tristram, "it were shame and pity that this noble knight that yonder lieth should be slain, for ye may well hear that shamed he will not be, and I pray to God that he never be slain nor shamed for me. And as for the king for whom I do this battle, I shall require him, as I am his true champion and true knight in this field, that he will have mercy upon this good knight."

"So God me help," said King Anguish to Sir Tristram, "I will be ruled for your sake as ye will have me. For I know you for my true knight, and therefore I will heartily pray the kings that be here as judges for to take it into their hands."

And then the kings which were judges called Sir Bleoberis unto them and demanded his advice.

"My lord," said Sir Bleoberis, "though that my brother be beaten and both the worse through might of arms, I dare well say though Sir Tristram hath beaten his body he hath not beaten his heart; I thank God he is not shamed this day. And rather than he should be shamed, I require you," said Sir Bleoberis, "let Sir Tristram slay him out of hand [*immediately*]."

"It shall not be so," said the kings, "for his adverse party, both the king and the champion, hath pity of Sir Blamor's knighthood."

"My lords," said Sir Bleoberis, "I will right well as ye will."

Then the kings called to them the King of Ireland, and found him good and treatable [*willing to agree*]. And then by all their advices Sir Tristram and Sir Bleoberis took up Sir Blamor. And the two brethren were accorded with King Anguish; and kissed each other and were made friends for ever. And then Sir Blamor and Sir Tristram kissed each other, and then the two brethren made their oaths that they would never fight with Sir Tristram. And Sir Tristram made the same oath. And for that gentle battle all the blood of Sir Launcelot loved Sir Tristram for ever more. Then King Anguish and Sir Tristram took their leave and sailed into Ireland with great joy and nobleness. So when they were in Ireland, the king let make it be known throughout all the land how and in what manner Sir Tristram had done for him. And then the queen and all the estates that were there made as much of him as ever they might make; but the joy that la Belle Isolde made of Sir Tristram, that might no tongue tell, for of men living she loved him most.

Then upon a day King Anguish asked Sir Tristram why he asked not his boon, for whatsoever he had promised him he should have it without fail.

"Sir," said Sir Tristram, "now is it time, this is all that I will desire, that ye will give me la Belle Isolde, your daughter, not for myself, but for mine uncle King Mark, that shall have her to wife, for so have I promised him."

"Alas," said the king, "I had liever than all the land that I have ye would wed her yourself."

"Sir, and I did, then were I shamed for ever in this world, and false of my promise. Therefore," said Sir Tristram, "I pray you hold your promise that ye promised me, for this is my desire, that ye will give me la Belle Isolde to go with me into Cornwall, for to be wedded to King Mark mine uncle."

"As for that," said King Anguish, "ye shall have her with you, to do with her what it please you, that is for to say if that ye list to wed her yourself, that is to me lievest;

and if ye will give her unto King Mark your uncle, that is in your choice."

So to make a short conclusion, la Belle Isolde was made ready to go with Sir Tristram, and dame Bragwaine went with her for her chief gentlewoman, with many other.

And anon they were richly wedded with great nobleness. But ever Sir Tristram and la Belle Isolde loved ever together.

Then was there great jousts and great tourneying, and many lords and ladies were at that feast, and Sir Tristram was most praised of all other.

[Then, as time passed by, Sir Tristram grieved sorely in his heart that la Belle Isolde was wedded to King Mark, till that he became as a wood man, and mounted his horse and rode forth into the forest away from Tintagil. So Sir Palamides sent a damsel to inquire after Sir Tristram.]

And she went to the lady of [a certain] castle, and told her of the misadventure of Sir Tristram.

"Alas," said the lady of that castle, "where is my lord Sir Tristram?"

"Right here by your castle," said the damsel.

"In good time," said the lady, "is he so nigh me: he shall have meat and drink of the best, and a harp I have of his whereupon he taught me, — for of goodly harping he beareth the prize in the world."

So this lady and the damsel brought him meat and drink, but he eat little thereof. Then upon a night he put his horse from him, and then he unlaced his armor, and then Sir Tristram would go into the wilderness, and burst down the trees and boughs; and otherwhile, when he found the harp that the lady sent him, then would he harp and play thereupon and weep together. And sometime when Sir Tristram was in the wood, that the lady wist not where he was, then would she sit her down and play upon that harp; then would Sir Tristram come to that harp and hearken thereto, and sometime he would harp himself. Thus he there endured a quarter of a year. Then at the last he ran his way, and she wist not where he was become. And then was he naked, and waxed lean and poor of flesh, and so he fell into the fellowship of herdmen and shepherds, and daily they would give him of their meat and drink. And when he did any shrewd deed they would beat him with rods, and so they clipped him with shears and made him like a fool.

And upon a day Sir Dagonet, King Arthur's fool, came into Cornwall, with two squires with him, and as they rode through the forest they came by a fair well where Sir Tristram was wont to be, and the weather was hot, and they alighted to drink of that well, and in the meanwhile their horses brake loose. Right so Sir Tristram came unto them, and first he soused Sir Dagonet in that well, and after his squires, and thereat laughed the shepherds, and forthwithal he ran after their horses, and brought them again one by one, and right so, wet as they were, he made them leap up and ride their ways. Thus Sir Tristram endured here an half year naked, and would never come in town nor village.

And there was a giant in that country that hight Tauleas,

and for fear of Sir Tristram more than seven years he durst not much go out at large, but for the most part he kept him in a sure castle of his own. And so this Sir Tauleas heard tell that Sir Tristram was dead by the noise of the court of King Mark, and then Sir Tauleas went daily at large. And so it happened upon a day he came to the herdmen wandering and lingering, and there he set him down to rest among them. The meanwhile there came a knight of Cornwall that led a lady with him, and his name was Sir Dinant. And when the giant saw him, he went from the herdmen and hid him under a tree. And so the knight came to the well, and there he alighted to rest him. And as soon as he was from his horse, the giant Sir Tauleas came between the knight and his horse, and leaped upon him. So forthwith he rode unto Sir Dinant, and took him by the collar, and drew him before him on his horse, and there would have stricken off his head. Then the herdmen said unto Sir Tristram, "Help yonder knight."

"Help ye him," said Sir Tristram.

"We dare not," said the herdmen.

Then Sir Tristram was ware of the sword of the knight where it lay, and thither he ran and took up the sword, and smote off Sir Tauleas' head, and so went his way to the herdmen again.

Then the knight took up the giant's head, and bare it with him unto King Mark, and told him what adventure betid him in the forest, and how a naked man rescued him from the grimly giant Tauleas.

"Where had ye this adventure?" said King Mark.

"Forsooth," said Sir Dinant, "at the fair fountain in your forest, where many adventurous knights meet, and there is the mad man."

"Well," said King Mark, "I will see that mad man."

So within a day or two King Mark commanded his knights and his hunters that they should be ready on the morrow for to hunt. And on the morrow he went unto the forest. And when the king came to the well, he found there lying by that well a fair naked man, and a sword by him. Then the king blew and screked [*called shrilly*] and therewith his knights came to him. And then the king commanded his knights to take that naked man with fairness, "and bring him to my castle." So they did softly and fair, and cast mantles upon Sir Tristram, and so led him unto Tintagil; and there they bathed him and washed him, and gave him hot suppings, till they had brought him well to his remembrance. But all this while there was no creature that knew Sir Tristram, nor what man he was. So it fell upon a day that the queen la Belle Isolde heard of such a man that ran naked in the forest, and how the king had brought him home to the court. Then la Belle Isolde called unto her dame Bragwaine, and said, "Come on with me, for we will go see this man that my lord brought from the forest the last day."

So they passed forth, and asked where was the sick man. And then a squire told the queen that he was in the garden taking his rest, and reposing him against the sun. So when the queen looked upon Sir Tristram she was not remembered of [*did not remember*] him. But ever she said unto dame Bragwaine, "Me seemeth I should have seen him heretofore in many places."

But as soon as Sir Tristram saw her he knew her well enough, and then he turned away his visage and wept. Then the queen had always a little brachet with her, that Sir Tristram gave her the first time that ever she came into Cornwall, and never would that brachet depart from her, but if Sir Tristram was nigh there as was la Belle Isolde; and this brachet was sent from the king's daughter of France unto Sir Tristram for great love. And anon as this little brachet felt a savor of Sir Tristram, she leaped upon him, and licked his learis [*cheeks*] and his ears, and then she whined and quested, and she smelled at his feet and at his hands, and on all parts of his body that she might come to.

"Ah, my lady," said dame Bragwaine unto la Belle Isolde, "alas, alas!" said she, "I see it is mine own lord Sir Tristram."

And thereupon Isolde fell down in a sowne [*swoon*], and so lay a great while; and when she might speak, she said: "My lord Sir Tristram, blessed be God ye have your life, and now I am sure ye shall be discovered by this little brachet, for she will never leave you; and also I am sure that as soon as my lord King Mark shall know you, he will banish you out of the country of Cornwall, or else he will destroy you. For God's sake, mine own lord, grant King Mark his will, and then draw you unto the court of King Arthur, for there are ye beloved."

Then la Belle Isolde departed, but the brachet would

not from him. And therewith came King Mark, and the brachet set upon him, and bayed at them all. And therewith Sir Andret spake and said: "Sir, this is Sir Tristram, I see by the brachet."

"Nay," said the king, "I cannot suppose that it is he."

So the king asked him upon his faith what he was, and what was his name.

"So God help," said he, "my name is Sir Tristram de Lyonesse, and now ye may do with me what ye list."

And so, by the advice of them all, Sir Tristram was banished out of the country of Cornwall for ten year, and thereupon he took his oath.

And then were many barons brought him into his ship. And when Sir Tristram was in the ship, he said thus: "Greet well King Mark and all mine enemies, and tell them I will come again when I may. And well I am rewarded for the fighting with Sir Marhaus, and delivering all the country from servage [*subjection*]. And well I am rewarded for the fetching and costs of la Belle Isolde out of Ireland, and the danger that I was in first and last, and by the way coming home what danger I had to bring again Queen Isolde from the castle. And well I am rewarded when I fought with Sir Bleoberis for Sir Segwarides' wife. And well am I rewarded when I fought with Sir Blamor de Ganis for King Anguish, father unto la Belle Isolde. And well am I rewarded when I smote down the good knight Sir Lamorake de Galis at King Mark's request. And well am I rewarded when I fought with the king with the hundred knights, and the King of Northgalis, and both these would have put his land in servage, and by me they were put to a rebuke. And well am I rewarded for the slaying of Tauleas the mighty giant, and many moe deeds have I done for him, and now have I my guerdon. And tell the King Mark that many noble knights of the Round Table have spared the barons of this country for my sake. Also I am not well rewarded when I fought with the good knight Sir Palamides, and rescued Queen Isolde from him. And at that time King Mark said before all his barons I should have been better rewarded." And therewith he took the sea.

[In those days was holden a great tournament at the Castle of Maidens, and thereto came Sir Tristram, for King Arthur was there, with his knights, and a goodly press of other kings, lords and ladies. And Sir Tristram let make him a black shield, and therewith was he ever to be known in the midst of the knights. And Sir Tristram overthrew eleven knights of Sir Launcelot's kin in one day, and jousted with King Arthur and with Sir Launcelot in such wise that all men wondered. And at the last Sir Tristram was sore wounded, and rode away into a forest. But Sir Launcelot held away the stour [*fight*] like as a man enraged that took no heed to himself.] And because Sir Launcelot was the last in the field the prize was given him. But Sir Launcelot would neither for king, queen, nor knight have the prize; but when the cry was cried through the field, "Sir Launcelot, Sir Launcelot, hath won the field this day!" Sir Launcelot let make another cry contrary to that cry: "Sir Tristram hath won the field, for he began first, and last he hath endured, and so hath he done the first day, the second, and the third day."

[And so King Arthur and Sir Launcelot and more knights rode forth for to find Sir Tristram. And after many adventures it happened that Sir Launcelot passed by the tomb of Sir Lanceor (him that was slain by Balin) and his lady Colombe. And by that same tomb came Sir Tristram: and neither knew the other, but Sir Tristram weened it to have been Sir Palamides. Then they two fought, and each wounded other wonderly sore, that the blood ran out upon the grass. And thus they fought the space of four hours. And at the last either knew other. Then cried Sir Launcelot,] "Oh, what adventure is befallen me!"

And therewith Sir Launcelot kneeled down and yielded him up his sword. And therewithal Sir Tristram kneeled adown, and yielded him up his sword. And so either gave other the degree. And then they both forthwithal went to the stone, and set them down upon it, and took off their helms to cool them, and either kissed other an hundred times. And then anon after they took their helms and rode to Camelot. And there they met with Sir Gawaine and with Sir Gaheris that had made promise to Arthur never to come again to the court till they had brought Sir Tristram with them.

Then King Arthur took Sir Tristram by the hand, and led him unto the Round Table. Then came Queen Guenever, and many ladies with her, and all these ladies said, all with one voice, "Welcome, Sir Tristram;" "welcome," said the damsels; "welcome," said the knights; "welcome," said King Arthur, "for one of the best knights and gentlest of the world, and knight of the most worship; for of all manner of hunting thou bearest the prize, and of all measures of blowing thou art the beginner, and of all the terms of hunting and hawking ye are the beginner; of all instruments of music ye are the best. Therefore, gentle knight," said King Arthur, "ye are right heartily welcome unto this court. And also I pray you," said King Arthur, "grant me a boon."

"It shall be at your commandment," said Sir Tristram.

"Well," said King Arthur, "I will desire of you that ye will abide in my court."

"Sir," said Sir Tristram, "thereto am I loth, for I have to do in many countries."

"Not so," said King Arthur, "ye have promised it me, ye may not say nay."

"Sir," said Sir Tristram, "I will as ye will."

Then went King Arthur unto the sieges about the Round Table, and looked in every siege which were void that lacked knights. And the king then saw in the siege of Marhaus letters that said:—

"This is the siege of the noblest knight Sir Tristram."

And then King Arthur made Sir Tristram knight of the Round Table, with great nobleness and great feast as might be thought.

Then King Mark had great despite of the renown of Sir Tristram. So he sent on his part men to espy what deeds he did. And when the messengers were come home, they told the truth as they heard, that he passed all other knights but if it were the noble knight Sir Launcelot. Then in great despite he took with him two good knights and two squires, and disguised himself, and took his way into England, to the intent to slay him.

[And it happened that Sir Dinadan met King Mark, and began to mock him for a Cornish knight of no worship. And] right as they stood thus talking together, they saw come riding to them over a plain six knights of the court of King Arthur, well armed at all points. And there by their shields Sir Dinadan knew them well. The first was the good knight Sir Uwaine, the son of King Uriens; the second was the noble knight Sir Brandiles; the third was Ozana le Cure Hardy; the fourth was Uwaine les Adventurous; the fifth was Sir Agravaine; the sixth Sir Mordred, brother to Sir Gawaine. When Sir Dinadan had seen these six knights, he thought in himself he would bring King Mark by some wile to joust with one of them.

"Lo," said Sir Dinadan, "yonder are knights errant that will joust with us."

"God forbid," said King Mark, "for they be six, and we but two."

"As for that," said Sir Dinadan, "let us not spare, for I will assay the foremost."

And therewith he made him ready. When King Mark saw him do so, as fast as Sir Dinadan rode toward them King Mark rode from them with all his menial company. So when Sir Dinadan saw King Mark was gone, he set the spear out of the rest, and threw his shield upon his back, and came riding to the fellowship of the Table Round. And anon Sir Uwaine knew Sir Dinadan, and welcomed him, and so did all his fellowship.

"What knight is that," said Sir Brandiles, "that so suddenly departed from you, and rode over yonder field?"

"Sir," said he, "it was a knight of Cornwall, and the most horrible coward that ever bestrode horse."

"What is his name?" said all the knights.

"I wot not," said Sir Dinadan.

Said Sir Griflet, "Here have I brought Sir Dagonet, King Arthur's fool, that is the best fellow and the merriest in the world."

[Then said Sir Mordred,] "Put my shield and my harness upon Sir Dagonet, and let him set upon the Cornish knight."

"That shall be done," said Sir Dagonet, "by my faith."

Then anon was Dagonet armed in Mordred's harness and his shield, and he was set on a great horse and a spear in his hand.

"Now," said Dagonet, "show me the knight, and I trow I shall bear him down."

So all these knights rode to a woodside, and abode till King Mark came by the way. Then they put forth Sir Dagonet, and he came on all the while his horse might run, straight upon King Mark. And when he came nigh King Mark, he cried as he were wood, and said, "Keep thee, knight of Cornwall, for I will slay thee."

Anon as King Mark beheld his shield he said to himself, "Yonder is Sir Launcelot: alas, now am I destroyed."

And therewithal he made his horse to run as fast as it might through thick and thin. And ever Sir Dagonet followed King Mark crying and rating him as a wood man through a great forest. When Sir Uwaine and Sir Brandiles saw Dagonet so chase King Mark, they laughed all as they were wood. And then they took their horses and rode after to see how Sir Dagonet sped. For they would not for no good that Sir Dagonet were hurt, for King Arthur loved him passing well, and made him knight with his own hands.

When Sir Uwaine and Sir Brandiles with his fellows came to the court of King Arthur, they told the king, Sir Launcelot, and Sir Tristram how Sir Dagonet the fool chased King Mark through the forest. There was great laughing and jesting at King Mark and at Sir Dagonet.

King Arthur on a day said unto King Mark, —

"Sir, I pray you to give me a gift that I shall ask you."

"Sir," said King Mark, "I will give you whatsoever ye desire, and it be in my power."

"Sir, gramercy," said King Arthur, "this I will ask you, that ye be a good lord unto Sir Tristram, for he is a man of great honor; and that ye will take him with you into Cornwall, and let him see his friends, and there cherish him for my sake."

"Sir," said King Mark, "I promise you by the faith of my body, and by the faith I owe to God and to you, I shall worship him for your sake in all that I can or may."

"Sir," said Arthur, "and I will forgive you all the evil

will that ever I owed you, and so be that ye swear that upon a book afore me."

"With a good will," said King Mark.

And so he there sware upon a book afore him and all his knights, and therewith King Mark and Sir Tristram took either other by the hands hard knit together. But for all this King Mark thought falsely, as it proved after, for he put Sir Tristram in prison, and cowardly would have slain him. Then soon after King Mark took his leave to ride into Cornwall, and Sir Tristram made him ready to ride with him, wherefore the most part of the Round Table were wroth and heavy; and in especial Sir Launcelot, and Sir Lamorak, and Sir Dinadan were wroth out of measure. For well they wist King Mark would slay or destroy Sir Tristram.

Now turn we unto Sir Tristram, that, as he rode on hunting, he met with Sir Dinadan, that was come into that country for to seek Sir Tristram. Then Sir Dinadan told Sir Tristram his name, but Sir Tristram would not tell his name; wherefor Sir Dinadan was wroth.

"For such a foolish knight as ye are," said Sir Dinadan, "I saw but late to-day lying by a well, and he fared as he had slept, and there he lay like a fool grinning and would not speak, and his shield lay by him, and his horse stood by him, and well I wot he was a lover."

"Ah, fair sir," said Sir Tristram, "are ye not a lover?"

"Marry, fie upon that craft," said Sir Dinadan.

"That is evil said," quoth Sir Tristram, "for a knight may never be of prowess, but if he be a lover."

"It is well said," quoth Sir Dinadan; "now tell me your name, sith ye be a lover, or else I shall do battle with you."

"As for that," said Sir Tristram, "it is no reason to fight with me but I tell you my name; as for that, my name shall ye not know as at this time."

"Fie for shame," said Sir Dinadan, "art thou a knight and darest not tell me thy name? therefore I will fight with thee."

"As for that," said Sir Tristram, "I will be advised, for I will not fight but if me list; and if I do battle," said Sir Tristram, "ye are not able for to withstand me."

"Fie on thee, coward," said Sir Dinadan.

And thus as they still hoved, they saw a knight come riding against them.

"Lo," said Sir Tristram, "see where cometh a knight riding that will joust with you."

Anon, as Sir Dinadan beheld him, he said, "It is the same doting knight that I saw lie by the well neither sleeping nor waking."

"Well," said Sir Tristram, "I know that knight full well with the covered shield of azure; he is the king's son of Northumberland, his name is Epinegris, and he is as great a lover as I know, and he loveth the king's daughter of Wales, a full fair lady. And now I suppose," said Sir Tristram, "and ye require him he will joust with you; and then shall ye prove whether a lover be a better knight or ye that will not love no lady."

"Well," said Sir Dinadan, "now shalt thou see what I shall do."

Therewithal Sir Dinadan spake on high and said, "Sir knight, make thee ready to joust with me, for it is the custom of errant knights one to joust with the other."

"Sir," said Epinegris, "is it the rule of you errant knights for to make a knight to joust will he or nill?"

"As for that," said Dinadan, "make thee ready, for here is for me."

And therewithal they spurred their horses, and met together so hard that Epinegris smote down Sir Dinadan. Then Sir Tristram rode to Sir Dinadan, and said, "How now? me seemeth the lover hath right well sped."

"Fie upon thee, coward," said Sir Dinadan, "and if thou be any good knight, now revenge my shame."

"Nay," said Sir Tristram, "I will not joust as at this time, but take your horse and let us go from hence."

"God defend me," said Sir Dinadan, "from thy fellowship, for I never sped well sith I met with thee."

And so they departed.

"Well," said Sir Tristram, "peradventure I could tell you tidings of Sir Tristram."

"God defend me," said Sir Dinadan, "from thy fellowship, for Sir Tristram were much the worse and he were in thy company."

And then they departed.

"Sir," said Sir Tristram, "yet it may happen that I shall meet with you in other places."

And so Sir Tristram rode unto Joyous Gard, and there heard in that town great noise and cry.

"What meaneth this noise?" said Sir Tristram.

"Sir," said they, "here is a knight of this castle which hath been long among us, and right now he is slain with two knights, and for none other cause but that our knight said that Sir Launcelot was a better knight than was Sir Gawaine."

"That was but a simple cause," said Sir Tristram, "to slay a good knight because he said well by his master."

"That is but a little remedy unto us," said the men of the town; "for if Sir Launcelot had been here, soon we should have been revenged upon those false knights."

When Sir Tristram heard them say so, incontinent he sent for his shield and for his spear, and lightly within a little while he had overtaken them, and bade them turn and amend that they had misdone.

"What amends wouldst thou have?" said that one knight.

And therewith they took their course, and either met other so hard, that Sir Tristram smote down that knight over his horse's crupper. Then the other knight dressed him unto Sir Tristram, and in the same wise as he served the first knight, so he served him. And then they gat them upon their feet as well as they might, and dressed their shields and their swords to do their battle unto the uttermost.

"Knights," said Sir Tristram, "ye shall tell me of whence ye are and what be your names."

"Wit thou well, sir knight," said they, "we fear us not to tell thee our names, for my name is Sir Agravaine, and my name is Gaheris, brethren unto the good knight Sir Gawaine, and we be nephews unto King Arthur."

"Well," said Sir Tristram, "for King Arthur's sake I shall let you pass as at this time. But it is shame," said Sir Tristram, "that Sir Gawaine and ye that be come of so great a blood, that ye four brethren are so named as ye be. For ye be called the greatest destroyers and murderers of good knights that be now in this realm; for it is but as I heard say, that Sir Gawaine and ye slew among you a better knight than ever ye were, that was the noble knight Sir Lamorak de Galis; and it had pleased God," said Sir Tristram, "I would I had been by Sir Lamorak at his death."

"Then shouldest thou have gone the same way," said Sir Gaheris.

"Fair knight," said Sir Tristram, "there must have been many more knights than ye are."

And therewithal Sir Tristram departed from them towards Joyous Gard. And when he was departed they took their horses, and the one said to the other, "We will overtake him and be revenged upon him in the despite of Sir Lamorak."

So when they had overtaken Sir Tristram, Sir Agravaine bade him, "Turn, traitor knight."

"That is evil said," said Sir Tristram; and therewith he pulled out his sword, and smote Sir Agravaine such a buffet upon the helm that he tumbled down off his horse in a swoon, and he had a grievous wound. And then he turned to Gaheris, and Sir Tristram smote his sword and his helm together with such a might that Gaheris fell out of his saddle; and so Sir Tristram rode unto Joyous Gard, and there he alighted and unarmed him. So Sir Tristram told la Belle Isolde of all his adventure as ye have heard tofore. And when she heard him tell of Sir Dinadan, "Sir," she said, "is not that he that made the song by King Mark?"

"That same is he," said Sir Tristram, "for he is the best joker and jester, and a noble knight of his hands, and the best fellow that I know, and all good knights love his fellowship."

"Alas, sir," said she, "why brought ye not him with you?"

"Have ye no care," said Sir Tristram, "for he rideth to seek me in this country, and therefore he will not away till he have met with me."

And there Sir Tristram told la Belle Isolde how Sir Dinadan held against all lovers. Right so there came in a varlet and told Sir Tristram how there was come an errant knight into the town with such colors upon his shield.

"That is Sir Dinadan," said Sir Tristram. "Wit ye what ye shall do?" said Sir Tristram; "send ye for him, my lady Isolde, and I will not be seen, and ye shall hear the merriest knight that ever ye spake withal, and the maddest talker, and I pray you heartily that ye make him good cheer."

Then anon la Belle Isolde sent into the town, and prayed Sir Dinadan that he would come into the castle and rest him there with a lady.

"With a good will," said Sir Dinadan; and so he mounted upon his horse, and rode into the castle; and there he alighted, and was unarmed and brought into the castle. Anon la Belle Isolde came unto him, and either saluted other. Then she asked him of whence he was.

"Madam," said Sir Dinadan, "I am of King Arthur's court, and knight of the Round Table, and my name is Sir Dinadan."

"What do ye in this country?" said la Belle Isolde.

"Madam," said he, "I seek the noble knight Sir Tristram, for it was told me that he was in this country."

"It may well be," said la Belle Isolde, "but I am not ware of him."

"Madam," said Sir Dinadan, "I marvel of Sir Tristram and moe other lovers, what aileth them to be so mad and so assotted upon women."

"Why," said la Belle Isolde, "are ye a knight and be ye no lover? it is a shame unto you; wherefore ye may not be called a good knight, but if that ye make a quarrel for a lady."

"God defend me," said Sir Dinadan, "for the joy of love is too short, and the sorrow and what cometh thereof endureth over long."

"Ah!" said la Belle Isolde, "say ye not so, for here fast by was the good knight Sir Bleoberis, which fought with three knights at once for a damsel's sake, and he won her before the King of Northumberland."

"It was so," said Sir Dinadan, "for I know him well for a good knight and a noble, and come of noble blood; for all be noble knights of whom he is come of, that is Sir Launcelot du Lake."

"Now I pray you," said la Belle Isolde, "tell me will ye fight for my love with three knights that did me great wrong? and insomuch as ye be a knight of King Arthur's court, I require you to do battle for me."

Then Sir Dinadan said, "I shall say unto you, ye are as fair a lady as ever I saw any, and much fairer than is my lady Queen Guenever; but wit ye well at one word that I will not fight for you with three knights, Jesu defend me."

Then Isolde laughed, and had good game at him. So he had all the cheer that she might make him; and there he lay all that night. And on the morn early Sir Tristram armed him, and la Belle Isolde gave him a good helm; and then he promised her that he would meet with Sir Dinadan, and they two would ride together unto Lonazep, where the tournament should be, "and there shall I make ready for you, where ye shall see the tournament." Then departed Sir Tristram with two squires that bare his shield and his spears that were great and long.

Then after that, Sir Dinadan departed and rode his way a great pace until he had overtaken Sir Tristram. And when Sir Dinadan had overtaken him, he knew him anon, and he hated the fellowship of him above all other knights.

"Ah," said Sir Dinadan, "art thou that coward knight that I met with yesterday, keep thee, for thou shalt joust with me, maugre thy head."

"Well," said Sir Tristram, "and I am loth to joust."

And so they let their horses run, and Sir Tristram missed

of him a purpose, and Sir Dinadan brake a spear upon Sir Tristram; and therewith Sir Dinadan dressed himself to draw out his sword.

"Not so," said Sir Tristram, "why are ye so wroth? I will not fight."

"Fie on thee, coward," said Sir Dinadan, "thou shamest all knights."

"As for that," said Sir Tristram, "I care not, for I will wait upon you and be under your protection, for because ye are so good a knight ye may save me."

"The devil deliver me of thee," said Sir Dinadan, "for thou art as goodly a man of arms and of thy person as ever I saw, and the most coward that ever I saw. What wilt thou do with those great spears that thou carriest with thee?"

"I shall give them," said Sir Tristram, "to some good knight when I come to the tournament; and if I see you do best I shall give them to you."

So thus as they rode talking they saw where came an errant knight afore them dressing him for to joust.

"Lo," said Sir Tristram, "yonder is one will joust; now dress thee to him."

"Ah! shame betide thee!" said Sir Dinadan.

"Nay, not so," said Sir Tristram, "for that knight seemeth a shrew."

"Then shall I," said Sir Dinadan.

And so they dressed their shields and their spears, and they met together so hard that the other knight smote down Sir Dinadan from his horse.

"Lo," said Sir Tristram, "it had been better that ye had left."

"Fie on thee, coward!" said Sir Dinadan.

Then Sir Dinadan started up, and gat his sword in his hand, and proffered to do battle on foot.

"Whether in love or in wrath?" said the other knight.

"Let us do battle in love," said Sir Dinadan.

"What is your name?" said that knight, "I pray you tell me."

"Wit ye well my name is Sir Dinadan."

"Ah, Sir Dinadan," said that knight, "and my name is Sir Gareth, the youngest brother unto Sir Gawaine."

Then either made of other great joy, for this Sir Gareth was the best knight of all those brethren, and he proved a full good knight. Then they took their horses, and there they spake of Sir Tristram, how he was such a coward. And every word Sir Tristram heard, and laughed them to scorn. Then were they ware where there came a knight before them well horsed and well armed.

"Fair knights," said Sir Tristram, "look between you who shall joust with yonder knight, for I warn you I will not have to do with him."

"Then shall I," said Sir Gareth.

And so they encountered together, and there that knight smote down Sir Gareth over his horse's crupper.

"How now?" said Sir Tristram unto Sir Dinadan, "dress thee now, and revenge the good knight Sir Gareth."

"That shall I not," said Sir Dinadan, "for he hath stricken down a much bigger knight than I am."

"Ah!" said Sir Tristram, "now Sir Dinadan, I see and perceive full well that your heart faileth you, therefore now shall ye see what I shall do."

And then Sir Tristram hurled unto that knight, and smote him quite from his horse. And when Sir Dinadan saw that, he marvelled greatly, and then he deemed in himself that it was Sir Tristram. Then this knight that was on foot pulled out his sword to do battle.

"What is your name?" said Sir Tristram.

"Wit ye well," said the knight, "my name is Sir Palamides."

"What knight hate ye most?" said Sir Tristram.

"Sir knight," said he, "I hate Sir Tristram to the death, for and I may meet with him the one of us shall die."

"Ye say well," said Sir Tristram, "and wit ye well that I am Sir Tristram de Lyonesse, and now do your worst."

When Sir Palamides heard him say so he was astonished, and then he said thus, "I pray you, Sir Tristram, forgive me all mine evil will, and if I live I shall do you service above all other knights that be living, and there as I have owed you evil will me sore repenteth. I wot not what aileth me, for me seemeth that ye are a good knight, and none other knight that named himself a good knight should not hate you; therefore I require you, Sir Tristram, take no displeasure at mine unkind words."

"Sir Palamides," said Sir Tristram, "ye say well, and well I wot ye are a good knight, for I have seen you proved, and many great enterprises have ye taken upon you, and well achieved them; therefore," said Sir Tristram, "and ye have any evil will to me, now may ye right it, for I am ready at your hand."

"Not so, my lord Sir Tristram; I will do you knightly service in all things as ye will command."

"And right so I will take you," said Sir Tristram.

And so they rode forth on their ways, talking of many things.

"Oh my lord Sir Tristram," said Dinadan, "foul have ye mocked me, for truly I came into this country for your sake, and by the advice of my lord Sir Launcelot, and yet would not Sir Launcelot tell me the certainty of you, where I should find you."

"Truly," said Sir Tristram, "Sir Launcelot wist well where I was, for I abode within his own castle."

Thus they rode until they were ware of the Castle of Lonazep, and then were they ware of four hundred tents and pavilions, and marvellous great ordinance. "So God me help," said Sir Tristram, "yonder I see the greatest ordinance that ever I saw."

"Sir," said Sir Palamides, "me seemeth there was as great an ordinance at the Castle of Maidens upon the rock, where ye won the prize, for I saw myself where ye forjousted thirty knights."

"Sir," said Sir Dinadan, "and in Surluse, at that tournament that Sir Galahalt of the long isles made, the which lasted seven days, was as great a gathering as is here, for there were many nations."

"Who was the best?" said Sir Tristram.

"Sir, it was Sir Launcelot du Lake, and the noble knight Sir Lamorak de Galis; Sir Launcelot won the degree."

"I doubt not," said Sir Tristram, "but he won the degree, so that he had not been overmatched with many knights. And of the death of Sir Lamorak," said Sir Tristram, "it was over great pity, for I dare say that he was the cleanest mighted man, and the best winded of his age that was on live, for I knew him that he was the biggest knight that ever I met withal, but if it were Sir Launcelot. Alas!" said Sir Tristram, "full woe is me of his death, and, if they were all the cousins of my lord King Arthur that slew him, they should die for it, and all those that were consenting to his death. And for such things," said Sir Tristram, "I fear to draw unto the court of my lord King Arthur. I will that ye wit it," said Sir Tristram to Sir Gareth.

"Sir, I blame you not," said Sir Gareth, "for well I understand the vengeance of my brethren Sir Gawaine, Sir Agravaine, Sir Gaheris, and Sir Mordred; but for me," said Gareth, "I meddle not of their matters, therefore there is none of them that loveth me, and, for I understand they be murderers of good knights, I left their company, and would God I had been by," said Sir Gareth, "when the noble knight Sir Lamorak was slain."

"Now as Jesu be my help," said Sir Tristram, "it is well said of you, for I had liever than all the gold between this and Rome I had been there."

"Truly," said Sir Palamides, "I would I had been there, and yet I had never the degree at no jousts there as he was, but he put me to the worse on foot or on horseback, and that day that he was slain he did the most deeds of arms that ever I saw knight do all the days of my life. And when the degree was given him by my lord King Arthur, Sir Gawaine and his three brethren, Sir Agravaine, Sir Gaheris, and Sir Mordred, set upon Sir Lamorak in a privy place, and there they slew his horse, and so they fought with him on foot more than three hours, both before him and behind him. And Sir Mordred gave him his death wound behind him at his back, and all to-hewed him; for one of his squires told me that saw it."

"Fie upon treason," said Sir Tristram, "for it killeth my heart to hear this tale."

"So doth it mine," said Sir Gareth; "brethren as they be mine, I shall never love them nor draw me to their fellowship for that deed."

"Now speak we of other deeds," said Sir Palamides, "and let him be, for his life ye may not get again."

"That is the more pity," said Sir Dinadan, "for Sir Gawaine and his brethren (except you, Sir Gareth) hate all the good knights of the Round Table for the most part; for well I wot, and they might privily, they hate my lord Sir Launcelot and all his kin, and great privy despite they have at him, and that is my lord Sir Launcelot well ware of, and that causeth him to have the good knights of his kindred about him."

"Sir," said Palamides, "let us leave off this matter, and let us see how we shall do at this tournament. By mine advice," said Palamides, "let us four hold together against all that will come."

"Not by my counsel," said Sir Tristram, "for I see by their pavilions there will be four hundred knights, and doubt ye not," said Sir Tristram, "but there will be many good knights, and be a man never so valiant nor so big yet he may be over-matched. And so I have seen knights done many times: and when they wend best to have won worship they lost it. For manhood is not worth but if it be meddled [*mingled*] with wisdom: and as for me," said Sir Tristram, "it may happen I shall keep mine own head as well as another."

So thus they rode until that they came to Humber bank, where they heard a cry and a doleful noise. Then were they ware in the wind where came a rich vessel covered over with red silk, and the vessel landed fast by them. Therewith Sir Tristram alighted and his knights. And so Sir Tristram went afore and entered into that vessel. And when he came within, he saw a fair bed richly covered, and thereupon lay a dead seemly knight, all armed, save the head was all be-bled, with deadly wounds upon him: the which seemed to be a passing good knight.

"How may this be," said Sir Tristram, "that this knight is thus slain?" Then Sir Tristram was ware of a letter in the dead knight's hand. "Master mariners," said Sir Tristram, "what meaneth that letter?"

"Sir," said they, "in that letter ye shall hear and know how he was slain, and for what cause, and what was his name; but, sir," said the mariners, "wit ye well that no man shall take that letter and read it but if he be a good knight, and that he will faithfully promise to revenge his death, else shall there no knight see that letter open."

"Wit ye well," said Sir Tristram, "that some of us may revenge his death as well as others; and if it be as ye say it shall be revenged." And therewith Sir Tristram took the letter out of the knight's hand, and it said thus: "Hermance, king and lord of the Red City, I send to all knights errant recommendation, and unto you, noble knights of King Arthur's court, I beseech them all among them to find one knight that will fight for my sake with two brethren, that I brought up of nought, and feloniously and traitorously they have slain me, wherefore I beseech one good knight to revenge my death; and he that revengeth my death I will that he have my Red City and all my castles."

"Sir," said the mariners, "wit ye well this king and knight that here lieth was a full worshipful man, and of full great prowess, and full well he loved all manner of knights errant."

"Truly," said Sir Tristram, "here is a piteous case, and full fain I would take this enterprise upon me, but I have made such a promise that needs I must be at this great tournament or else I am shamed. For well I wot for my sake in especial my lord Arthur let make this jousts and tournament in this country; and well I wot that many worshipful people will be there at that tournament for to see me. Therefore I fear me to take this enterprise upon me, that I shall not come again betimes to this jousts."

"Sir," said Palamides, "I pray you give me this enterprise, and ye shall see me achieve it worshipfully, or else I shall die in this quarrel."

"Well," said Sir Tristram, "and this enterprise I give you, with this that ye be with me at this tournament, that shall be as at this day seven night."

"Sir," said Palamides, "I promise you that I shall be with you by that day if I be unslain or unmaimed."

Then departed Sir Tristram, Gareth, and Sir Dinadan, and left Sir Palamides in the vessel; and so Sir Tristram beheld the mariners how they sailed along Humber. And when Sir Palamides was out of their sight, they took their horses, and beheld about them. And then were they ware of a knight that came riding against them unarmed, and nothing about him but a sword. And when this knight came nigh them he saluted them, and they him again.

"Fair knights," said that knight, "I pray you insomuch as ye be knights errant, that ye will come and see my castle, and take such as ye find there; I pray you heartily."

And so they rode with him into his castle; and there they were brought to the hall, that was well apparelled, and so they were unarmed and set at a board. And when this knight saw Sir Tristram, anon he knew him; and then this knight waxed pale and wroth at Sir Tristram. When Sir Tristram saw his host make such cheer, he marvelled greatly, and said, "Sir mine host, what cheer make ye?"

"Wit thou well," said he, "I fare much the worse for thee; for I know thee well, Sir Tristram de Lyonesse, thou slewest my brother, and therefore I give thee summons that I will slay thee and I may get thee at large."

"Sir knight," said Sir Tristram, "I am not advised that

ever I slew any brother of yours; and if ye say that I did it, I will make you amends unto my power."

"I will none of your amends," said the knight, "but keep thee from me."

So when he had dined, Sir Tristram asked his arms and departed; and so they rode forth on their way. And within a little while Sir Dinadan saw where came a knight riding all armed and well horsed without shield.

"Sir Tristram," said Sir Dinadan, "take heed to yourself, for I undertake that yonder cometh your host that will have to do with you."

"Let him come," said Sir Tristram, "I shall abide him as well as I may."

Anon that knight when he came nigh Sir Tristram he cried to him, and bade him abide and keep him well. So they hurled together, but Sir Tristram smote the other knight so sore that he bare him to the ground. And that knight arose lightly, and took his horse again, and so rode fiercely to Sir Tristram, and smote him twice full hard upon the helm. "Sir knight," said Sir Tristram, "I pray you to leave off and smite me no more, for I would be loth to deal with you and I might choose, for I have your meat and your drink within my body." For all that he would not leave; and then Sir Tristram gave him such a buffet upon the helm that he tumbled upside down from his horse, that the blood brast out at the ventails of his helm; and there he lay still likely to have died. Then Sir Tristram said, "Me repenteth sore of this buffet that I smote so sore, for, as I suppose, he is dead."

And so they departed and rode forth on their way. So they had not ridden but a while but they saw coming against them two full likely knights, well armed and horsed, and goodly servants about them. The one was called the king with the hundred knights, and that other was Sir Segwarides, which were renowned two noble knights. So as they came either by other, the king looked upon Sir Dinadan, which at that time had Sir Tristram's helm upon his shoulder, which helm the king had seen before with the Queen of Northwales, and that helm the Queen of Northwales had given unto la Belle Isolde, and the Queen la Belle Isolde gave it unto Sir Tristram.

"Sir knight," said [the king], "where had ye that helm?"

"What would ye?" said Sir Dinadan.

"For I will have ado with thee," said the king, "for the love of her that owned that helm, and therefore keep you."

So they departed and came together with all the mights of their horses; and there the king with the hundred knights smote Sir Dinadan, horse and all, to the earth; and then he commanded his servant, "Go and take thou his helm off, and keep it."

So the varlet went to unbuckle his helm.

"What helm? What wilt thou do?" said Sir Tristram; "leave that helm."

"To what intent," said the king, "will ye, sir knight, meddle with that helm?"

"Wit you well," said Sir Tristram, "that helm shall not depart from me, or it be dearer bought."

"Then make you ready," said [the king] unto Sir Tristram.

So they hurtled together, and there Sir Tristram smote him down over his horse's tail. And then the king arose lightly, and gat his horse lightly again, and then he struck fiercely at Sir Tristram many great strokes. And then Sir Tristram gave [the king] such a buffet upon the helm that he fell down over his horse, sore stunned.

"Lo," said Sir Dinadan, "that helm is unhappy to us twain, for I had a fall for it, and now, sir king, have ye another fall."

Then Segwarides asked, "Who shall joust with me?"

"I pray thee," said Sir Gareth unto Dinadan, "let me have this jousts."

"Sir," said Dinadan, "I pray you take it as for me."

"That is no reason," said Tristram, "for this jousts should be yours."

"At a word," said Sir Dinadan, "I will not thereof."

Then Gareth dressed him to Sir Segwarides, and there Sir Segwarides smote Sir Gareth and his horse to the earth.

"Now," said Sir Tristram to Dinadan, "joust with yonder knight."

"I will not thereof," said Dinadan.

"Then will I," said Sir Tristram.

And then Sir Tristram ran to him and gave him a fall, and so they left them on foot. And Sir Tristram rode unto Joyous Gard, and there Sir Gareth would not of his courtesy have gone into the castle, but Sir Tristram would not suffer him to depart; and so they alighted, and unarmed them, and had there great cheer. But when Sir Dinadan came afore la Belle Isolde, he cursed the time that ever he bare the helm of Sir Tristram, and there he told her how Sir Tristram had mocked him. Then was there good laughing and sport at Sir Dinadan, that they wist not what to do to keep them from laughing.

Now will we leave them merry within Joyous Gard, and speak we of Sir Palamides. Then Sir Palamides sailed even along Humber unto the coast of the sea, where was a fair castle, and at that time it was early in the morning afore day. Then the mariners went unto Sir Palamides, that was fast on sleep: "Sir knight," said the mariners, "ye must arise, for here is a castle into the which ye must go."

"I assent me thereto," said Sir Palamides.

And therewithal he arrived; and then he blew his horn, the which the mariners had given him. And when they that were within the castle heard that horn, they put forth many knights, and there they stood upon the walls and said with one voice, "Welcome be ye to this castle." And then it waxed clear day, and Sir Palamides entered into the castle. And within a while he was served with many divers meats. Then Sir Palamides heard about him much weeping and great dole. "What may this mean?" said Sir Palamides: "I love not to hear such a sorrow, and fain I would know what it meaneth."

Then there came afore him one whose name was Sir Ebel, that said thus, "Wit ye well, sir knight, this dole and sorrow is here made every day, and for this cause: we had a king that hight Hermance, and he was King of the Red City, and this king that was lord was a noble knight, large and liberal of his expense. And in the world he loved nothing so much as he did errant knights of King Arthur's court, and all jousting, hunting, and all manner of knightly games; for so kind a king and knight had never the rule of poor people as he was; and because of his goodness and gentleness we bemoan him and ever shall. And all kings and estates may beware by our lord, for he was destroyed in his own default, for had he cherished them of his blood he had yet lived with great riches and rest; but all estates may beware of our king. But alas," said Ebel, "that we shall give all other warning by his death."

"Tell me," said Palamides, "in what manner was your lord slain, and by whom?"

"Sir," said Sir Ebel, "our king brought up of children two men that now are perilous knights, and these two knights our king had so in charity, that he loved no man nor trusted no man of his blood, nor none other that was about him. And by these two knights our king was governed, and so they ruled him peaceably, and his lands, and never would they suffer none of his blood to have no rule with our king. And also he was so free and so gentle, and they so false and deceivable, that they ruled him peaceably; and that espied the lords of our king's blood, and departed from him unto their own livelihood. Then when these two traitors understood that they had driven all the lords of his blood from him, they were not pleased with that rule, but then they thought to have more, as ever it is an old saw, Give a churl rule, and thereby he will not be sufficed; for whatsoever he be that is ruled by a villain born, and the lord of the soil to be a gentleman born, the same villain shall destroy all the gentlemen about him; therefore all estates and lords beware whom ye take about you. And if ye be a knight of King Arthur's court, remember this tale, for this is the end and conclusion. My lord and king rode unto the forest by the advice of these false traitors, and there he chased at the red deer, all armed of all pieces, full like a good knight; and so for labor he waxed dry, and then he alighted and drank at a well. And when he was alighted, by the assent of these two false traitors, the one that hight Helius suddenly smote our king through the body with a spear, and so they left him there; and when they were departed, then by fortune I came unto the well and found my lord and king wounded unto the death; and when I heard his complaint, I let bring him to the water side, and in that same ship I put him alive. And when my lord King Hermance was in that vessel, he required me for the true faith that I owed unto him for to write a letter in this manner: —

" 'Recommending unto King Arthur and unto all the knights errant, beseeching them all in so much as I, King Hermance, King of the Red City, thus am slain by felony and treason, through two knights of mine own, and of mine own bringing up and of mine own making, that some worshipful knight will revenge my death, in so much as I have been ever to my power well willing unto King Arthur's court; and who that will adventure his life with these two traitors for my sake in one battle, I, King Hermance, King of the Red City, freely give all my lands and tenements that ever I possessed in all my life.' This letter," said Sir Ebel, "I wrote by my lord's commandment, and then he received his Maker [*took the Holy Communion*]. And when he was dead, he commanded me, or ever he were cold, to put this letter fast in his hand; and then he commanded me to put forth that same vessel down Humber, and I should give these mariners in commandment never to stint until that they came unto Logris, where all the noble knights shall assemble at this time, 'and there shall some good knight have pity on me to revenge my death, for there was never king nor lord falselier ne traitorlier slain than I am here to my death.'"

Thus was the complaint of our king Hermance.

"Now," said Sir Ebel, "ye know all how our lord was betrayed, we require you for God's sake have pity upon his death, and worshipfully revenge his death, and then may ye hold all these lands. For we all wit well that, and ye may slay these two traitors, the Red City and all those that be therein will take you for their lord."

"Truly," said Sir Palamides, "it grieveth my heart for to hear you tell this doleful tale. And to say the truth, I saw the same letter that ye speak of; and one of the best knights on the earth read that letter to me, and by his commandment I came hither to revenge your king's death; and therefore have done, and let me wit where I shall find those traitors, for I shall never be at ease in my heart till that I be in hands with them."

"Sir," said Sir Ebel, "then take your ship again, and

that ship must bring you unto the Delectable Isle, fast by the Red City, and we in this castle shall pray for you and abide your again-coming; for this same castle, and ye speed well, must needs be yours; for our king Hermance let make this castle for the love of the two traitors, and so we kept it with strong hand, and therefore full sore are we threated."

"Wot ye what ye shall do," said Sir Palamides; "whatsoever come of me, look ye keep well this castle. For, and it misfortune me so to be slain in this quest, I am sure there will come one of the best knights of the world for to revenge my death, and that is Sir Tristram de Lyonesse, or else Sir Launcelot du Lake."

Then Sir Palamides departed from that castle. And as he came nigh unto the city, there came out of a ship a goodly knight all armed against him, with his shield upon his shoulder, and his hand upon his sword; and anon as he came nigh Sir Palamides, he said, "Sir knight, what seek ye here in this country? leave this quest, for it is mine, and mine it was or it was yours, and therefore I will have it."

"Sir knight," said Sir Palamides, "it may well be that this quest was yours or it was mine, but when the letter was taken out of the dead king's hand, at that time by likelihood there was no knight had undertaken to revenge the death of King Hermance; and so at that time I promised to revenge his death, and so I shall, or else I am shamed."

"Ye say well," said the knight, "but wit ye well then will I fight with you, and he that is the better knight of us both let him take the battle in hand."

"I assent me," said Sir Palamides.

And then they dressed their shields, and drew out their swords, and lashed together many a sad stroke, as men of might, and thus they fought more than an hour. And at the last Sir Palamides waxed big and better winded, so that then he smote that knight such a stroke that he made him to kneel upon both his knees. Then that knight spoke on high and said, "Gentle knight, hold thy hand."

Sir Palamides was courteous and withdrew his hand.

Then this knight said, "Wit ye well, sir knight, that ye be better worthy to have this battle than I, and I require thee of thy knighthood to tell me thy name."

"Sir, my name is Sir Palamides, a knight of King Arthur's court and of the Round Table, that hither am come to revenge the death of this dead king."

"Ah, well be ye found," said the knight unto Sir Palamides, "for of all knights that be now living (except three) I had lievest have you. The first is Sir Launcelot du Lake, the second is Sir Tristram de Lyonesse, and the third Sir Lamorak de Galis; and I am brother unto King Hermance that is dead, and my name is Sir Hermind."

"It is well said," quoth Sir Palamides, "and ye shall see how I shall speed; and if I be there slain, go ye unto my lord Sir Launcelot or unto my lord Sir Tristram, and pray them to revenge my death, for as for Sir Lamorak, him shall ye never see in this world."

"Alas," said Sir Hermind, "how may that be?"

"He is slain," said Sir Palamides, "by Sir Gawaine and his brethren."

"Truly," said Hermind, "there was not one for one that slew him."

"That is truth," said Sir Palamides, "for they were four dangerous knights that slew him, as Sir Gawaine, Sir Agravaine, Sir Gaheris, and Sir Mordred; but Sir Gareth, the fifth brother, was away, the best knight of them all."

And so Sir Palamides told Hermind all the manner, and how they slew Sir Lamorak all only by treason. So Sir Palamides took his ship, and arrived up at the Delectable Isle. And in the meanwhile Sir Hermind, that was the king's brother, he arrived up at the Red City, and there he told them how there was come a knight of King Arthur's to avenge King Hermance's death; and his name is Sir Palamides the good knight. Then all the city made great joy. For mickle had they heard of Sir Palamides, and of his noble prowess. So let they ordain a messenger and sent unto the two brethren, and bade them to make them ready, for there was a knight come that would fight with them both. So the messenger went unto them where they were at a castle there beside. And there he told them how there was a knight come of King Arthur's court to fight with them both at once.

"He is welcome," said they. "But tell us, we pray you, if it be Sir Launcelot, or any of his blood."

"He is none of that blood," said the messenger.

"Then we care the less," said the two brethren, "for with none of the blood of Sir Launcelot we keep not to have to do withal."

"Wit ye well," said the messenger, "that his name is

Sir Palamides, the which is not yet christened, a noble knight."

"Well," said they, "and if he be now unchristened, he shall never be christened."

So they appointed for to be at the city within two days. And when Sir Palamides was come unto the city, they made passing great joy of him. And when they beheld him, [they] saw that he was well made, cleanly and bigly, and unmaimed of his limbs, and neither too young nor too old, and so all the people praised him; and though he was not christened, yet he believed in the best manner, and was faithful and true of his promise, and also well conditioned; and because he made his avow never to take full christendom unto the time that he had done seven battles within the lists.

So within the third day there came to this city these two brethren, the one hight Sir Helius, and that other hight Sir Helake, the which were men of great prowess, howbeit they were false and full of treason, and but poor men born, yet were they noble knights of their hands.

And with them they brought forty knights, to the intent they should be big enough for the Red City. Thus came the two brethren with great bobance [*boasting*] and pride, for they had put the Red City in fear and damage. Then they were brought into the lists; and Sir Palamides came into the place, and thus he said, "Be ye the two brethren, Sir Helius and Sir Helake, that slew your king and lord Sir Hermance by felony and treason, for whom I am come hither for to revenge his death?"

'Wit thou well," said Sir Helius and Sir Helake, "that we are the same knights that slew King Hermance. And wit thou well, Sir Palamides, Saracen, that we shall handle thee so or thou depart that thou shalt wish that thou werest christened."

"It may well be," said Sir Palamides, "for yet I would not die or I were christened, and yet so am I not afeared of you both, but I trust to God that I shall die a better Christian man than any of you both; and doubt ye not," said Sir Palamides, "either ye or I shall be left dead in this place."

Then they departed, and the two brethren came against Sir Palamides, and he against them, as fast as their horses might run. And by fortune Sir Palamides smote Helake through his shield, and through the breast more than a fathom. All this while Sir Helius held up his spear, and for pride and presumption he would not smite Sir Palamides with his spear. But when he saw his brother lie on the earth, and saw he might not help himself, then he said unto Sir Palamides, "Help thyself": and therewith he came hurtling unto Sir Palamides with his spear, and smote him quite from his saddle. Then Sir Helius rode over Sir Palamides twice or thrice. And therewith Sir Palamides was ashamed, and gat the horse of Sir Helius by the bridle, and therewithal the horse areared, and Sir Palamides helped after, and so they fell both to the earth, but anon Sir Helius started up lightly, and there he smote Sir Palamides a mighty stroke upon the helm, so that he kneeled upon his own knee. Then they lashed together many sad strokes, and traced and traversed, now backward, now sideling, hurtling together like two boars, and that same time they fell both grovelling to the earth. Thus they fought still without any reposing two hours, and never breathed, and then Sir Palamides waxed faint and weary, and Sir Helius waxed passing strong, and doubled his strokes, and drove Sir Palamides overthwart and endlong all the field, that they of the city, when they saw Sir Palamides in this case, they wept and cried, and made a sorrowful dole; and that other party made great joy. "Alas," said the men of the city, "that this noble knight should thus be slain for our king's sake!"

And as they were thus weeping and crying [for] Sir Palamides that had endured well an hundred strokes, that it was wonder that he stood upon his feet, at the last Sir Palamides beheld as well as he might the common people how they wept for him. And then he said unto himself, "Ah, fie for shame, Sir Palamides, wherefore hangest thou thy head so low?" And therewith he bare up his shield, and looked Sir Helius in the visage, and smote him a great stroke upon the helm, and after that another, and another. And then he smote Sir Helius with such a might, that he fell upon the ground grovelling; and then he started lightly to him, and rashed off his helm from his head, and there he smote him such a buffet that he departed his head from the body. And then were the people of the city the joyfullest people that might be. So they brought him unto his lodging with great solemnity, and there all the people became his men; and then Sir Palamides prayed them all for to take heed unto the lordship of King Hermance. "For, fair sirs, wit ye well, I may not at this time abide with you, for I must in all the haste be with my lord King Arthur at the Castle of Lonazep, which I have promised."

So then were the people full heavy of his departing; for all that city proffered Sir Palamides the third part of their goods so that he would abide with them; but in no wise at that time he would abide; and so Sir Palamides departed. And then he came unto the castle whereas Sir Ebel was lieutenant; and when they that were in the castle knew how Sir Palamides had sped, there was a joyful meyny [*household*]. And Sir Palamides departed, and came to the Castle of Lonazep. And when he wist that Sir Tristram was not there, he took his way unto Humber, and came unto Joyous Gard, whereas Sir Tristram was and la Belle Isolde. So it had been commanded that what knight errant came within the Joyous Gard, as in the town, that they should warn Sir Tristram. So there came a man of the town, and told Sir Tristram how there was a knight in the town, a passing goodly man.

"What manner of man is he?" said Sir Tristram, "and what sign beareth he?"

So the man told Sir Tristram all the tokens of him.

"That is Palamides," said Dinadan.

"It may well be," said Sir Tristram: "go ye to him," said Sir Tristram unto Dinadan.

So Dinadan went unto Sir Palamides, and there either made of other great joy, and so they lay together that night, and on the morn early came Sir Tristram and Sir Gareth, and took them in their beds, and so they arose and brake their fast.

[And so, having done many great deeds of arms, after many days it happened that Sir Tristram rode forth for to rescue Sir Palamides, but Sir Launcelot, in disguise, had already rescued him or [*before*] that Sir Tristram could come. And then Sir Tristram and Sir Palamides went with the unknown knight to his castle, which was Sir Launcelot's castle of Joyous Gard.]

And when they were come within Joyous Gard, they alighted, and their horses were led into a stable, and then they unarmed them. And when Sir Launcelot had put off his helm, Sir Tristram and Sir Palamides knew him. Then Sir Tristram took Sir Launcelot in his arms; and Sir Palamides kneeled down upon his knees and thanked Sir Launcelot. When Sir Launcelot saw Sir Palamides kneel, he lightly took him up, and said, —

"Wit thou well, Sir Palamides, I and any knight in this land of worship ought of very right succor and rescue so noble a knight as ye are proved and renowned throughout all this realm, endlong and overthwart."

Then Sir Launcelot within three or four days departed; and with him rode Sir Ector de Maris; and Dinadan and Sir Palamides were there left with Sir Tristram a two months and more. But ever Sir Palamides faded and mourned, that all men had marvel wherefore he faded so away. So upon a day, in the dawning Sir Palamides went into the forest by himself alone, and there he found a well. And therewithal he laid him down by the well. And then he began to make a rhyme of la Belle Isolde and him. And in the meanwhile Sir Tristram was that same day ridden into the forest to chase the hart of greese [*the fat hart*]. And so as Sir Tristram rode into that forest up and down, he heard one sing marvellously loud; and that was Sir Palamides, that lay by the well. And then Sir Tristram rode softly thither, for he deemed there was some knight errant that was at the well.

And when Sir Tristram came nigh him, he descended down from his horse, and tied his horse fast to a tree, and then he came near him on foot. And anon he was ware where lay Sir Palamides by the well. And ever the complaints were of that noble queen la Belle Isolde, the which was marvellously and wonderfully well made and full dolefully and piteously. And all the whole song the noble knight Sir Tristram heard from the beginning to the ending, the which grieved and troubled him sore. But then at last, when Sir Tristram had heard all Sir Palamides' complaints, he was wroth out of measure, and thought for to slay him there as he lay. Then Sir Tristram remembered himself that Sir Palamides was unarmed, and of the noble name that Sir Palamides had, and the noble name that himself had, and then he made a restraint of his anger, and so he went unto Sir Palamides a soft pace, and said, —

"Sir Palamides, I have heard your complaint, and of thy treason that thou hast owed me so long. And wit thou well therefore thou shalt die. And if it were not for shame of knighthood thou shouldest not escape my hands, for now I know well thou hast awaited me with treason. Tell me," said Sir Tristram, "how thou wilt acquit thee."

"Sir," said Palamides, "thus I will acquit me: as for queen la Belle Isolde, ye shall wit well that I love her above all other ladies of the world; and well I wot it shall befall me as for her love as befell to the noble knight Sir Kehidius, that died for the love of la Belle Isolde; and now, Sir Tristram, I will that ye wit that I have loved la Belle Isolde many a day, and she hath been the causer of my worship. And else I had been the most simplest knight in the world. For by her, and because of her, I have won the worship that I have: for when I remembered me of la Belle Isolde, I won the worship wheresoever I came, for the most part; and yet had I never reward nor bounty of her the days of my life, and yet have I been her knight guerdonless; and therefore, Sir Tristram, as for any death I dread not, for I had as lief die as to live. And if I were armed as thou art, I should lightly do battle with thee."

"Well have ye uttered your treason," said Sir Tristram.

"I have done to you no treason," said Sir Palamides, "for love is free for all men, and though I have loved your lady she is my lady as well as yours; and yet shall I love her to the uttermost days of my life as well as ye."

"Then," said Sir Tristram, "I will fight with you unto the uttermost."

"I grant," said Sir Palamides, "for in a better quarrel keep I never to fight, for and I die of your hands, of a better knight's hands may I not be slain. And sithen [*since*] I understand that I shall never rejoice the queen la Belle Isolde, I have as good a will to die as to live."

"Then set ye a day of battle," said Sir Tristram.

THE
BOY'S
KING
ARTHUR

So the child was delivered unto Merlin, and so he bare it forth

And when they came to the sword that the hand held, King Arthur took it up

"I am Sir Launcelot du Lake, King Ban's son of Benwick, and knight of the Round Table"

And lived by fruit and such as he might get

It hung upon a thorn, and there he blew three deadly notes

The lady Lyoness . . . had the dwarf in examination

"Oh, gentle knight," said la Belle Isolde, "full woe am I of thy departing"

"They fought with him on foot more than three hours, both before him and behind him"

King Mark slew the noble knight Sir Tristram as he sat harping before his lady la Belle Isolde

When Sir Percival came nigh the brim, and saw the water so boisterous, he doubted to overpass it

Sir Mador's spear brake all to pieces, but the other's spear held

He rode his way with the queen unto Joyous Gard

Then the king . . . ran towards Sir Mordred, crying, " Traitor, now is thy death day come"

Then Sir Launcelot saw her visage, but he wept not greatly, but sighed

"This day fifteen days," said Sir Palamides, "will I meet with you hereby in the meadow under Joyous Gard."

"Fie for shame!" said Sir Tristram, "will ye set so long a day? let us fight to-morrow."

"Not so," said Sir Palamides, "for I am feeble and lean, and have been long sick for the love of la Belle Isolde, and therefore I will rest me till that I have my strength again."

So then Sir Tristram and Sir Palamides promised faithfully to meet at the well as that day fifteen days.

Right so departed Sir Tristram and Sir Palamides; and so Sir Palamides took his horse and his harness, and rode unto King Arthur's court, and there Sir Palamides gat him four knights and three sergeants of arms; and so he returned again towards Joyous Gard. And in the meanwhile Sir Tristram chased and hunted at all manner of venery [*game*]; and about a three days afore that the battle should be, as Sir Tristram chased an hart, there was an archer shot at the hart, and by misfortune he smote Sir Tristram in the thickest of the thigh and wounded him right sore, and the arrow slew Sir Tristram's horse; and when Sir Tristram was so sore hurt, he was passing heavy, and wit ye well he bled sore. And then he took another horse, and rode unto Joyous Gard with full great heaviness.

Then when the fifteenth day was come, Sir Palamides came to the well with four knights with him of King Arthur's court, and three sergeants of arms. And the one sergeant brought his helm, the other his spear, and the third his sword. So Sir Palamides came into the field, and there he abode nigh two hours, and then he sent a squire unto Sir Tristram, and desired him to come into the field for to hold his promise. When the squire was come to Joyous Gard, and that Sir Tristram heard of his coming, he commanded that the squire should come to his presence there as he lay in his bed.

"My lord Sir Tristram," said Palamides' squire, "wit you well, my lord Palamides abideth you in the field, and he would wit whether ye would do battle or not."

"Ah, my fair brother," said Sir Tristram, "wit thou well that I am right heavy for these tidings, therefore tell Sir Palamides and I were well at ease I would not lie here, nor he should have no need to send for me, and I might either ride or go: and for thou shalt say that I am no liar," Sir Tristram showed him his thigh, that the wound was six inches deep: — "and now thou hast seen my hurt, tell thy lord that this is no feigned matter; and tell him that I had liever than all the gold of King Arthur that I were whole; and tell Sir Palamides, as soon as I am whole I shall seek him endlong and overthwart, and that I promise you as I am true knight; and if ever I may meet with him he shall have battle of me his fill."

And with this the squire departed. And then departed Sir Palamides where as fortune led him. And within a month Sir Tristram was whole of his hurt. And then he took his horse, and rode from country to country, and all strange adventures he achieved wheresoever he rode, and always he inquired for Sir Palamides.

[When Sir Tristram was returned, he heard how there should be a great feast at King Arthur's court on the Pentecost next following. And so when that day was nigh Sir Tristram set forth unarmed towards Camelot.]

And within a mile after, Sir Tristram saw before him where Sir Palamides had stricken down a knight, and had almost wounded him to death. Then Sir Tristram repented him that he was not armed, and then he hoved still. With that Sir Palamides knew Sir Tristram, and cried on high: "Sir Tristram, now be we met, for or we depart we will redress our old sores."

"As for that," said Sir Tristram, "there was never yet Christian man that might make his boast that ever I fled from him, and wit thou well, Sir Palamides, thou that art a Saracen shall never make thy boast that Sir Tristram de Lyonesse shall flee from thee."

And therewithal Sir Tristram made his horse to run with all his might, came he straight upon Sir Palamides, and brake his spear upon him in an hundred pieces, and forthwith Sir Tristram drew his sword, and then he turned his horse and struck at Sir Palamides six great strokes upon his helm. And then Sir Palamides stood still, and beheld Sir Tristram, and marvelled of his woodness and of his great folly; and then Sir Palamides said to himself, "And Sir Tristram were armed it were hard to cease him of this battle, and if I turn again and slay him I am shamed wheresoever that I go."

Then Sir Tristram spake and said, "Thou coward knight, what castest thou to do? why wilt thou not do battle with me, for have thou no doubt I shall endure all thy malice."

"Ah, Sir Tristram," said Sir Palamides, "full well thou wottest I may not fight with thee for shame, for thou art here naked, and I am armed, and if I slay thee dishonor shall be mine. And well thou wottest I know thy strength and thy hardiness to endure against a good knight."

"That is truth," said Sir Tristram, "I understand thy valiantness well."

"Ye say well," said Sir Palamides, "now I require you tell me a question that I shall say to you."

"Tell me what it is," said Sir Tristram, "and I shall answer you the truth."

"I put the case," said Sir Palamides, "that ye were armed at all rights as well as I am, and I naked as ye be, what would ye do to me now by your true knighthood?"

"Ah," said Sir Tristram, "now I understand thee well, Sir Palamides, for now must I say my own judgment, and, as God me bless, that I shall say shall not be said for no fear that I have of thee. But this is all; wit, Sir Palamides, as at this time thou shouldest depart from me, for I would not have ado with thee."

"No more will I," said Sir Palamides, "and therefore ride forth on thy way."

"As for that I may choose," said Sir Tristram, "either to ride or to abide. But Sir Palamides," said Sir Tristram, "I marvel of one thing, that thou that art so good a knight, that thou will not be christened, and thy brother Sir Safere hath been christened many a day."

"As for that," said Sir Palamides, "I may not yet be christened for one avow that I have made many years agone; howbeit in my heart I believe in Jesus Christ and his mild mother Mary; but I have but one battle to do, and when that is done I will be baptized with a good will."

"By my head," said Sir Tristram, "as for one battle thou shalt not seek it no longer. For God defend," said Sir Tristram, "that through my default thou shouldest longer live thus a Saracen. For yonder is a knight that ye, Sir Palamides, have hurt and smitten down; now help me that I were armed in his armor, and I shall soon fulfil thine avows."

"As ye will," said Sir Palamides, "so it shall be."

So they rode unto that knight that sat upon a bank, and then Sir Tristram saluted him, and he weakly saluted him again.

"Sir knight," said Sir Tristram, "I require you tell me your right name."

"Sir," he said, "my name is Sir Galleron of Galway, and knight of the Table Round."

"Truly," said Sir Tristram, "I am right heavy of your hurts: but this is all, I must pray you to lend me all your whole armor, for ye see I am unarmed, and I must do battle with this knight."

"Sir," said the hurt knight, "ye shall have it with a good will; but ye must beware, for I warn you that knight is wight [*strong*]. Sir," said Galleron, "I pray you tell me your name, and what is that knight's name that hath beaten me."

"Sir, as for my name, it is Sir Tristram de Lyonesse, and as for the knight's name that hath hurt you, it is Sir Palamides, brother unto the good knight Sir Safere, and yet is Sir Palamides unchristened."

"Alas," said Sir Galleron, "that is pity that so good a knight and so noble a man of arms should be unchristened."

"Truly," said Sir Tristram, "either he shall slay me, or I him, but that he shall be christened or ever we depart in sunder."

"My lord Sir Tristram," said Sir Galleron, "your renown and worship is well known through many realms and God save you this day from shame."

Then Sir Tristram unarmed Galleron, the which was a noble knight and had done many deeds of arms, and he was a large knight of flesh and bone. And when he was unarmed he stood upon his feet, for he was bruised in the back with a spear; yet, so as Sir Galleron might, he armed Sir Tristram. And then Sir Tristram mounted upon his own horse, and in his hand he gat Sir Galleron's spear. And therewithal Sir Palamides was ready, and so they came hurtling together, and either smote other in the midst of their shields, and therewithal Sir Palamides' spear brake, and Sir Tristram smote down the horse; and then Sir Palamides, as soon as he might, avoided his horse, and dressed his shield, and pulled out his sword. That saw Sir Tristram, and therewith he alighted, and tied his horse to a tree.

And then they came together as two wild boars, lashing together, tracing and traversing as noble men that oft had been well proved in battle; but ever Sir Palamides dreaded the might of Sir Tristram, and therefore he suffered him to breathe him. Thus they fought more than two hours; and often Sir Tristram smote such strokes at Sir Palamides that he made him to kneel; and Sir Palamides brake and cut away many pieces of Sir Tristram's shield, and then Sir Palamides wounded Sir Tristram, for he was a well fighting man. Then Sir Tristram was wood wrath out of measure, and rashed upon Sir Palamides with such a might that Sir Palamides fell grovelling to the earth, and therewithal he leapt up lightly upon his feet, and then Sir Tristram wounded Sir Palamides sore through the shoulder. And ever Sir Tristram fought still in like hard, and Sir Palamides failed not, but gave him many sad strokes. And at the last Sir Tristram doubled his strokes, and by fortune Sir Tristram smote Sir Palamides' sword out of his hand, and if Sir Palamides had stooped for his sword, he had been slain. Then Sir Palamides stood still and beheld his sword with a sorrowful heart.

"How now," said Sir Tristram unto Sir Palamides, "now have I thee at advantage as thou hadst me this day, but it shall never be said in no court, nor among good knights, that Sir Tristram shall slay any knight that is weaponless, and therefore take thou thy sword, and let us make an end of this battle."

"As for to do this battle," said Sir Palamides, "I dare right well end it; but I have no great lust to fight no more, and for this cause, mine offence to you is not so great but that we may be friends. All that I have offended is and was for the love of la Belle Isolde. And as for her, I dare say she is peerless above all other ladies, and also I proffered her never no dishonor; and by her I have gotten the most part of my worship, and sithen I offended never as to her own person. And as for the offence that I have done, it was against your own person, and for that offence ye have given me this day many sad strokes, and some I have given you again; and now I dare say I felt never man of your might, nor so well breathed, but if it were Sir Launcelot du Lake. Wherefore I require you, my lord, forgive me all that I have offended unto you. And this same day have me to the next church, and first let me be clean confessed, and after see you now that I be truly baptized. And then will we all ride together unto the court of Arthur, that we be there at the high feast."

"Now take your horse," said Sir Tristram, "and as ye say, so it shall be; and all your evil will God forgive it you, and I do. And here, within this mile, is the suffragan of Carlisle, that shall give you the sacrament of baptism."

Then they took their horses, and Sir Galleron rode with them. And when they came to the suffragan Sir Tristram told him their desire. Then the suffragan let fill a great vessel with water. And when he had hallowed it, he then confessed clean Sir Palamides, and Sir Tristram and Sir Galleron were his god-fathers. And then soon after they departed, riding towards Camelot, where King Arthur and Queen Guenever was, and for the most part all the knights of the Round Table. And so the king and all the court were glad that Sir Palamides was christened. And Sir Tristram returned again towards Joyous Gard.

[And so, after years, and many mighty deeds of arms, the] traitor King Mark slew the noble knight Sir Tristram as he sat harping before his lady la Belle Isolde, with a trenchant glaive; for whose death was much bewailing of every knight in Arthur's days. And la Belle Isolde died swooning upon the corpse of Sir Tristram, whereof was great pity. And all that were with King Mark consenting to the death of Sir Tristram were slain.

BOOK V

OF SIR GALAHAD AND SIR PERCIVAL

AND THE QUEST OF THE HOLY GRAIL

BOOK V

OF SIR GALAHAD AND SIR PERCIVAL

AND THE QUEST OF THE HOLY GRAIL

AT the vigil of Pentecost, when all the fellowship of the Round Table were come unto Camelot, and there they all heard their service, and all the tables were covered, ready to set thereon the meat, right so entered into the hall a full fair gentlewoman on horseback, that had ridden full fast, for her horse was all to-besweat; [and she besought Sir Launcelot that he would come forth with her into the forest for to dub a knight.] Right so departed Sir Launcelot with the gentlewoman, and rode till they came into a forest, and into a great valley, where he saw an abbey of nuns; and there was a squire ready to open the gates. And so there came in twelve nuns, which brought with them Galahad, the which was passing fair and well made, that unneth [*hardly*] men in the world might not find his match; and all those ladies wept.

"Sir," said the ladies, "we bring here this child, the which we have nourished, and we pray you for to make him a knight; for of a more worthier man's hand may he not receive the order of knighthood."

Sir Launcelot beheld that young squire, and saw he was seemly and demure as a dove, with all manner of good features, that he wend of his age never to have seen so fair a man of form.

Then said Sir Launcelot, "Cometh this desire of himself?"

He and all they said, "Yea."

"Then shall he," said Sir Launcelot, "receive the high order of knighthood as to-morrow at the reverence of the high feast."

That night Sir Launcelot had passing good cheer, and on the morrow at the hour of prime, at Galahad's desire, he made him knight; and said, "God make him a good man, for beauty faileth him not as any that liveth."

So when the king and all the knights were come from service, the barons espied in the sieges of the Round Table, all about written with gold letters: "Here ought to sit" he, and he "ought to sit here." And thus they went so long until that they came to the Siege Perilous, where they found letters newly written of gold, that said: "Four hundred winters and fifty-four accomplished after the passion of our Lord Jesu Christ ought this siege to be fulfilled."

Then all they said, "This is a marvellous thing, and an adventurous."

"In the name of God," said Sir Launcelot; and then he accounted the term of the writing, from the birth of our Lord unto that day.

"It seemeth me," said Sir Launcelot, "this siege ought to be fulfilled this same day, for this is the feast of Pentecost after the four hundred and four and fifty year; and if it would please all parties, I would none of these letters were seen this day, till he be come that ought to achieve this adventure."

Then made they to ordain a cloth of silk for to cover these letters in the Siege Perilous. Then the king bade haste unto dinner.

"Sir," said Sir Kay the steward, "if ye go now unto your meat, ye shall break your old custom of your court. For ye have not used on this day to sit at your meat or that ye have seen some adventure."

"Ye say sooth," said the king, "but I had so great joy of Sir Launcelot and of his cousins, which be come to the court whole and sound, that I bethought me not of my old custom."

So as they stood speaking, in came a squire, and said unto the king, "Sir, I bring unto you marvellous tidings."

"What be they?" said the king.

"Sir, there is here beneath at the river a great stone, which I saw fleet [*float*] above the water, and therein saw I sticking a sword."

The king said, "I will see that marvel."

So all the knights went with him, and when they came unto the river, they found there a stone fleeting, as it were of red marble, and therein stuck a fair and a rich sword, and in the pommel thereof were precious stones, wrought with subtle letters of gold. Then the barons read the letters, which said in this wise: "Never shall man take me hence, but only he by whom I ought to hang, and he shall be the best knight of the world."

When the king had seen these letters, he said unto Sir

Launcelot, "Fair sir, this sword ought to be yours, for I am sure that ye be the best knight of the world."

Then Sir Launcelot answered soberly, "Certainly, sir, it is not my sword. Also, sir, wit ye well I have no hardiness to set my hand to it, for it belongeth not to hang by my side. Also, who assayeth for to take that sword, and faileth of it, he shall receive a wound by that sword that he shall not be whole long after. And I will that ye wit that this same day will the adventures of the Sancgreal (that is called the holy vessel) begin."

So when they were served, and all the sieges fulfilled save only the Siege Perilous, anon there befell a marvellous adventure, that all the doors and the windows of the palace shut by themselves, but for all that the hall was not greatly darked, and therewith they were all abashed both one and other. Then King Arthur spake first, and said, "Fair fellows and lords, we have seen this day marvels, but or night I suppose we shall see greater marvels."

In the meanwhile came in a good old man and an ancient, clothed all in white; and there was no knight that knew from whence he came. And with him he brought a young knight, both on foot, in red arms, without sword or shield, save a scabbard hanging by his side; and these words he said, "Peace be with you, fair lords." Then the old man said unto King Arthur, "Sir, I bring you here a young knight that is of king's lineage, and of the kindred of Joseph of Arimathea, whereby the marvels of this court and of strange realms shall be fully accomplished."

The king was right glad of his words, and said unto the good man, "Sir, ye be right heartily welcome, and the young knight with you."

Then the old man made the young knight to unarm him; and he was in a coat of red sendall, and bare a mantle upon his shoulder that was furred with fine ermines, and put that upon him. And the old man said unto the young knight, "Sir, follow after."

And anon he led him unto the Siege Perilous, where beside sat Sir Launcelot; and the good man lifted up the cloth, and found there letters that said thus: "This is the siege of Galahad the haut [*high*] prince."

Then all the knights of the Table Round marvelled them greatly of Sir Galahad, that he durst sit there in that Siege Perilous, and was so tender of age, and wist not from whence he came, but all only by God, and said, This is he by whom the Sancgreal shall be achieved, for there sat never none but he, but he were mischieved. Then Sir Launcelot beheld his son, and had great joy of him.

Then came King Arthur unto Sir Galahad, and said, "Sir, ye be welcome, for ye shall move many good knights unto the quest of the Sancgreal, and ye shall achieve that never knight might bring to an end."

Then the king took him by the hand, and went down from the palace to show Sir Galahad the adventure of the stone.

The queen heard thereof, and came after with many ladies, and showed them the stone where it hoved on the water. "Sir," said the king unto Sir Galahad, "here is a great marvel as ever I saw, and right good knights have assayed and failed."

"Sir," said Galahad, "that is no marvel, for this adventure is not theirs, but mine, and for the surety of this sword I brought none with me; for here by my side hangeth the scabbard."

And anon he laid his hand on the sword, and lightly drew it out of the stone, and put it in the sheath, and said unto the king, "Now it goeth better than it did aforehand."

"Sir," said the king, "a shield God shall send you."

"Now have I," said Sir Galahad, "that sword that sometime was the good knight's Balin le Savage, and he was a passing good man of his hands. And with this sword he slew his brother Balan, and that was great pity, for he was a good knight, and either slew other through a dolorous stroke that Balan gave unto my grandfather King Pelles, the which is not yet whole, nor not shall be till I heal him."

Therewith the king and all espied where came riding down the river a lady on a white palfrey towards them. Then she saluted the king and the queen, and asked if that Sir Launcelot was there? And then he answered himself, "I am here, fair lady."

Then she said, all with weeping, "How your great doing is changed sith this day in the morn."

"Damsel, why say ye so?" said Launcelot.

"I say you sooth," said the damsel, "for ye were this day the best knight of the world, but who should say so now should be a liar, for there is now one better than ye. And well it is proved by the adventures of the sword whereto ye durst not set your hand, and that is in remembrance, that ye shall not ween from henceforth that ye be the best knight of the world."

"As touching that," said Sir Launcelot, "I know well I was never the best."

"Yes," said the damsel, "that were ye, and yet are of any sinful man of the world; and, sir king, Nacien the hermit sendeth thee word that to thee shall befall the greatest worship that ever befell king in Britain, and I shall tell you wherefore, for this day the Sancgreal appeared in this thy house, and fed thee and all thy fellowship of the Round Table."

And so the damsel took her leave, and departed the same way that she came.

Then the king [caused that Queen Guenever should see Sir Galahad] in the visage; and when she beheld him she said, "Soothly I dare well say that he is Sir Launcelot's son, for never two men resembled more in likeness, therefore it is no marvel though he be of great prowess."

So a lady that stood by the queen said: "Madam, for God's sake, ought he of right to be so good a knight?"

"Yea, forsooth," said the queen, "for he is of all parties come of the best knights of the world, and of the highest lineage, for Sir Launcelot is come but of the eighth degree from our Lord Jesu Christ, and Sir Galahad is of the ninth degree from our Lord Jesu Christ, therefore I dare well say that they be the greatest gentlemen of all the world."

And then the king and all the estates went home unto

Camelot, and so went to even-song to the great minster; and so after that they went to supper, and every knight sat in their place as they were beforehand. Then anon they heard cracking and crying of thunder, that them thought the place should all to-rive [*burst*]; in the midst of the blast entered a sunbeam more clear by seven times than ever they saw day, and all they were alighted of the grace of the Holy Ghost. Then began every knight to behold other, and either saw other by their seeming fairer than ever they saw afore, [and] there was no knight that might speak one word a great while, and so they looked every man on other, as they had been dumb. Then there entered into the hall the Holy Grail covered with white samite, but there was none might see it, nor who bare it. And there was all the hall full filled with good odors, and every knight had such meats and drinks as he best loved in this world; and when the Holy Grail had been borne through the hall, then the holy vessel departed suddenly, that they wist not where it became. Then had they all breath to speak. And then the king yielded thankings unto God of His good grace that He had sent them.

"Now," said Sir Gawaine, "we have been served this day of what meats and drinks we thought on, but one thing beguiled us, we might not see the Holy Grail, it was so preciously covered: wherefore I will make here avow, that to-morn, without longer abiding, I shall labor in the quest of the Sancgreal, that I shall hold me out a twelvemonth and a day, or more if need be, and never shall I return again unto the court till I have seen it more openly than it hath been seen here: and if I may not speed, I shall return again as he that may not be against the will of our Lord Jesu Christ."

When they of the Table Round heard Sir Gawaine say so, they arose up the most part, and made such avows as Sir Gawaine had made.

Anon as King Arthur heard this he was greatly displeased, for he wist well that they might not gainsay their avows.

"Alas!" said King Arthur unto Sir Gawaine, "ye have nigh slain me with the avow and promise that ye have made. For through you ye have bereft me of the fairest fellowship and the truest of knighthood that ever were seen together in any realm of the world. For when they depart from hence, I am sure they all shall never meet more in this world, for they shall die many in the quest. And so it forethinketh [*repenteth*] me a little, for I have loved them as well as my life, wherefore it shall grieve me right sore the departing of this fellowship. For I have had an old custom to have them in my fellowship."

And therewith the tears fell into his eyes, and he said: "Sir Gawaine, Sir Gawaine, ye have set me in great sorrow, for I have great doubt that my true fellowship shall never meet more here again."

When the queen, ladies, and gentlewomen wist these tidings, they had such sorrow and heaviness that no tongue might tell it, for those knights had holden them in honor and charity, but among all other, Queen Guenever made great sorrow. "I marvel," said she, "my lord will suffer them to depart from him." Thus was all the court troubled, because those knights should depart.

After this the queen came unto Sir Galahad, and asked him of whence he was, and of what country; he told her of whence he was, and son unto Sir Launcelot she said he was.

And then they went to rest them; and in the honor of the highness of Sir Galahad he was led into King Arthur's chamber, and there he rested him in his own bed; and as soon as it was daylight the king arose, for he had taken no rest of all that night for sorrow.

So anon Sir Launcelot and Sir Gawaine commanded their men to bring their arms; and when they [were all armed, then the king would know how many they were, and they found by tale [*count*] that they were an hundred and fifty, and all knights of the Round Table.]

And so they mounted their horses, and rode through the streets of Camelot, and there was weeping of the rich and poor, and the king turned away and might not speak for weeping.

So within a while they came to a city and a castle that hight [*was named*] Vagon; there they entered into the castle, and the lord of that castle was an old man that hight Vagon, and he was a good man of his living, and set open the gates, and made them all the good cheer that he might.

And then they departed on the morrow with weeping and mourning cheer, and every knight took the way that him best liked.

Now rideth Sir Galahad yet without shield; and so he rode four days without any adventure, and at the fourth day after even-song he came to a white abbey, and there he was received with great reverence, and led to a chamber; and there he was unarmed, and then was he ware of two knights of the Round Table, one was King Bagdemagus, and that other was Sir Uwaine. And when they saw him, they went unto him and made of him great solace, and so they went to supper.

"Sirs," said Sir Galahad, "what adventure brought you hither?"

"Sir," said they, "it is told us that within this place is a shield that no man may bear about his neck but if that he be mischieved or dead within three days, or else maimed forever."

"Ah, sir," said King Bagdemagus, "I shall bear it to-morrow for to assay this strange adventure."

"In the name of God," said Sir Galahad.

"Sir," said King Bagdemagus, "and I may not achieve the adventure of this shield, ye shall take it upon you, for I am sure ye shall not fail."

"Sir," said Sir Galahad, "I agree right well thereto, for I have no shield."

So on the morrow they arose and heard mass. Then King Bagdemagus asked where the adventurous shield was; anon a monk led him behind an altar, where the shield hung as white as any snow, but in the midst was a red cross.

"Sir," said the monk, "this shield ought not to be hanged about no knight's neck, but he be the worthiest knight of the world, and therefore I counsel you knights to be well advised."

"Well," said King Bagdemagus, "I wot well that I am not the best knight of the world, but yet shall I assay to bear it."

And so he bare it out of the monastery; and then he said unto Sir Galahad, "If it will please you, I pray you abide here still, till ye know how I shall speed."

"I shall abide you here," said Galahad.

Then King Bagdemagus took with him a squire, the which should bring tidings unto Sir Galahad how he sped. Then when they had ridden a two mile, and came in a fair valley afore an hermitage, then they saw a goodly knight come from that part in white armor, horse and all, and he came as fast as his horse might run with his spear in the rest, and King Bagdemagus dressed his spear against him, and brake it upon the white knight; but the other struck him so hard that he brake the mails, and thrust him through the right shoulder, for the shield covered him not as at that time, and so he bare him from his horse, and therewith he alighted and took the white shield from him, saying, "Knight, thou hast done thyself great folly, for this shield ought not to be borne but by him that shall have no peer that liveth."

And then he came to King Bagdemagus' squire and said, "Bear this shield unto the good knight Sir Galahad, that thou left in the abbey, and greet him well from me."

And the squire went unto Bagdemagus and asked him whether he were sore wounded or not?

"Yea, forsooth," said he, "I shall escape hard from the death."

Then he fetched his horse, and brought him with great pain unto an abbey. Then was he taken down softly, and unarmed, and laid in a bed, and there was looked to his wounds. And he lay there long, and escaped hard with the life.

"Sir Galahad," said the squire, "that knight that wounded Bagdemagus sendeth you greeting, and bade that ye should bear this shield, wherethrough great adventures should befall."

"Now blessed be God and fortune," said Sir Galahad.

And then he asked his arms, and mounted upon his horse, and hung the white shield about his neck, and commended them unto God. And Sir Uwaine said he would bear him fellowship, if it pleased him.

"Sir," said Sir Galahad, "that may ye not, for I must go alone, save this squire that shall bear me fellowship." And so departed Sir Uwaine.

Then within a while came Sir Galahad there as the white knight abode him by the hermitage, and every each saluted other courteously.

"Sir," said Sir Galahad, "by this shield been fall many marvels."

"Sir," said the knight, "it befell, after the passion of our Lord Jesu Christ thirty year, that Joseph of Arimathea, the gentle knight that took down our Lord from the cross, at that time he departed from Jerusalem with a great part of his kindred with him, and so they labored till they came to a city that hight Sarras. And at that same hour that Joseph came unto Sarras, there was a king that hight Evelake, that had great war against the Saracens, and in especial against one Saracen, the which was King Evelake's cousin, a rich king and a mighty, the which marched nigh this land, and his name was called Tollome le Feintes. So upon a day these two met to do battle. Then Joseph, the son of Joseph of Arimathea, went unto King Evelake, and told him that he would be discomfited and slain but if he left his believe of the old law and believe upon the new law. And then he showed him the right believe of the Holy Trinity, the which he agreed with all his heart, and there this shield was made for King Evelake, in the name of Him that died upon the cross; and then through his good believe he had the better of King Tollome. For when King Evelake was in the battle, there was a cloth set afore the shield, and when he was in the greatest peril he let put away the cloth, and then anon his enemies saw a figure of a man upon the cross, wherethrough they were discomfited. And so it befell that a man of King Evelake's had his hand smitten off, and bare his hand in his other hand, and Joseph called that man unto him, and bade him go with good devotion and touch the cross; and as soon as that man had touched the cross with his hand it was as whole as ever it was before. Not long after that, Joseph was laid in his death bed, and when King Evelake saw that, he made great sorrow, and said: 'For thy love I have left my country, and sith [*since*] thou shalt out of this world, leave me some token that I may think on thee.' 'That will I do right gladly,' said Joseph. 'Now bring me the shield that I took you when ye went into the battle against King Tollome.' Then Joseph bled sore that he might not by no means be stanched, and there upon that same shield he made a cross of his own blood. 'Now ye shall never see this shield but that ye shall think on me, and it shall be always as fresh as it is now, and never shall no man bear this shield about his neck but he shall repent it, unto the time that Galahad the good knight bear it, and the last of my lineage shall have it about his neck, that shall do many marvellous deeds.' 'Now,' said King Evelake, 'where shall I put this shield, that this worthy knight may have it?' 'Ye shall leave it there as Nacien the hermit shall be put after his death. For thither shall that good knight come the fifteenth day after that he shall receive the order of knighthood. And so that day that they set is this time that ye have his shield. And in the same abbey lieth Nacien the hermit.'"

And then the white knight vanished away. Anon, as the squire had heard these words, he alighted off his hackney, and kneeled down at Galahad's feet, and prayed him that he might go with him till he had made him knight. So Sir Galahad granted him, and turned again unto the abbey there they came from. And there men made great joy of Sir Galahad.

Then as Sir Galahad heard this, he thanked God, and took his horse, and he had not ridden but half a mile, he saw in a valley before him a strong castle with deep ditches, and there ran beside a fair river, the which hight Sevarne; and there he met with a man of great age, and either saluted other, and Sir Galahad asked him what was the castle's name.

"Fair sir," said he, "it is the Castle of Maidens."

"That is a cursed castle," said Sir Galahad, "and all they that been conversant therein, for all pity is out thereof, and all hardiness and mischief is therein."

"Therefore I counsel you, sir knight," said the old man, "to return again."

"Sir," said Sir Galahad, "wit ye well I shall not return again."

Then looked Sir Galahad on his armor that nothing failed him, and then he put his shield afore him; and anon there met him seven maidens, that said unto him, "Sir knight, ye ride here in a great folly, for ye have the waters for to pass over."

"Why should I not pass the water?" said Sir Galahad.

So rode he away from them, and met with a squire that said, "Knight, those knights in the castle defy you, and forbid you ye go no further till that they wit what ye would."

"Fair sir," said Galahad, "I come for to destroy the wicked custom of this castle."

"Sir, and ye will abide by that, ye shall have enough to do."

"Go you now," said Galahad, "and haste my needs."

Then the squire entered into the castle. And anon after there came out of the castle seven knights, and all were brethren. And when they saw Galahad, they cried, "Knight, keep thee, for we assure thee nothing but death."

"Why," said Galahad, "will ye all have ado with me at once?"

"Yea," said they, "thereto mayest thou trust."

Then Galahad put forth his spear, and smote the foremost to the earth, that near he brake his neck. And therewith all the other smote him on his shield great strokes, so that their spears brake. Then Sir Galahad drew out his sword, and set upon them so hard that it was marvel to see it, and so, through great force, he made them to forsake the field; and Galahad chased them till they entered into the castle, and so passed through the castle at another gate. And there met Sir Galahad an old man clothed in religious clothing, and said, "Sir, have here the keys of this castle."

Then Sir Galahad opened the gates, and saw so much people in the streets that he might not number them, and all said, "Sir, ye be welcome, for long have we abiden here our deliverance."

Then came to him a gentlewoman, and said, "These knights be fled, but they will come again this night, and here to begin again their evil custom."

"What will ye that I shall do?" said Galahad.

"Sir," said the gentlewoman, "that ye send after all the knights hither that hold their lands of this castle, and make them to swear for to use the customs that were used heretofore of old time."

"I will well," said Galahad.

And there she brought him an horn of ivory, bounden with gold, and said, "Sir, blow ye this horn, which will be heard two mile about this castle."

And when Sir Galahad had blown the horn, he set him down upon a bed. Then came there a priest unto Sir Galahad, and said, "Sir, it is past a seven year that these seven brethren came into this castle, and herborowed [*harbored*] with the lord of this castle, which hight the duke Lianour; and he was lord of all this country. And so when they espied the duke's daughter that was a fair woman, then by their false covin [*conspiracy*] they slew him and his eldest son, and then they took the maiden and the treasure of the castle. And then by great force they held all the knights of this castle against their will under their obeisance, and in great servage and truage, robbing and pilling [*pillaging*] the poor common people of all that they had. So it happened upon a day that the duke's daughter said, 'Ye have done to me great wrong to slay mine own father and my brother, and thus to hold our lands; not for then,' said she, 'ye shall not hold this castle for many years; for by one knight ye shall be overcome.' Thus she prophesied seven year before. 'Well,' said the seven knights, 'sithence [*since*] ye say so, there shall never lady nor knight pass this castle, but they shall abide mauger [*spite of*] their heads, or die therefore, till that knight be come by whom we shall leese [*lose*] this castle.' And therefore it is called the maidens' castle, for they have devoured many maidens."

"Now," said Sir Galahad, "is she here for whom this castle was lost?"

"Nay," said the priest, "she died within three nights after, and sithence have they kept her young sister, which endureth great pain, with moe other ladies."

By this were the knights of the country come. And then he made them do homage and fealty to the duke's daughter, and set them in great ease of heart. And in the morn there came one to Galahad, and told him how that Gawaine, Gareth, and Uwaine had slain the seven brethren.

"I suppose well," said Sir Galahad: and took his armor and his horse, and commended them unto God.

So when Sir Galahad was departed from the Castle of Maidens, he rode till he came to a waste forest, and there he met with Sir Launcelot and Sir Percival, but they knew him not, for he was new disguised. Right so, Sir Launcelot his father dressed his spear, and brake it upon Sir Galahad, and Sir Galahad smote him so again, that he smote down horse and man. And then he drew his sword, and dressed him unto Sir Percival, and smote him so on the helm that it rove to the coif of steel, and had not the sword swerved Sir Percival had been slain, and with the stroke he fell out of his saddle. This joust was done before the hermitage where a recluse dwelled. And when she saw Sir Galahad ride, she said, "God be with thee, best knight of the world. Ah, certes," said she all aloud, that Launcelot and Percival might hear it, "and yonder two knights had known thee as well as I do, they would not have encountered with thee."

When Sir Galahad heard her say so he was sore adread to be known: therewith he smote his horse with his spurs, and then rode a great pace froward them. Then perceived they both that he was Galahad, and up they gat on their horses, and rode fast after him, but in a while he was out of their sight.

[Then it fell that Sir Percival's horse was slain; and he gat him a hackney from a yeoman that he met, and the hackney was slain. Then Sir Percival] cast away his helm and sword, and said, "Now am I a very wretch, cursed, and most unhappy above all other knights."

So in this sorrow he abode all that day, till it was night, and then he was faint, and laid him down and slept till it was midnight. And then he awaked, and saw afore him a woman which said unto him, "Abide me here, and I shall go fetch you an horse."

And so she came soon again, and brought an horse with her that was black. When Sir Percival beheld that horse, he marvelled that it was so great and so well apparelled; and for then he was so hardy, he leaped upon him, and took none heed of himself. And so anon as he was upon him he thrust to him with his spurs, and so rode by a forest, and the moon shone clear. And within an hour and less, he bare him four days' journey thence, till he came to a rough water the which roared, and his horse would have borne him into it.

And when Sir Percival came nigh the brim, and saw the water so boisterous, he doubted to overpass it. And then he made the sign of the cross in his forehead. When the fiend felt him so charged, he shook off Sir Percival, and he went into the water, crying and roaring, making great sorrow; and it seemed unto him that the water burnt. Then Sir Percival perceived it was a fiend, the which would have brought him unto his perdition.

And so he prayed all that night, till on the morn that it was day. Then he saw that he was in a wild mountain the which was closed with the sea nigh all about, that he might see no land about him which might relieve him, but wild beasts. And then he went into a valley, and there he saw a young serpent bring a young lion by the neck, and so he came by Sir Percival. With that came a great lion crying and roaring after the serpent. And as fast as Sir Percival saw this, he marvelled, and hied him thither, but anon the lion had overtaken the serpent, and began battle with him. And then Sir Percival thought to help the lion, for he was the more natural beast of the two; and therewith he drew his sword, and set his shield afore him, and there gave the serpent such a buffet that he had a deadly wound. When the lion saw that, he made no semblant to fight with him, but made him all the cheer that a beast might make a man. Then Sir Percival perceived that, and cast down his shield, which was broken, and then he did off his helm for to gather wind, for he was greatly enchafed with the serpent. And the lion went alway about him fawning as a spaniel. And then he stroked him on the neck and on the shoulders. And then he thanked God of the fellowship of that beast. And about noon, the lion took his little whelp, and trussed him, and bare him there he came from. Then was Sir Percival alone.

Thus when Sir Percival had prayed, he saw the lion come towards him, and then he couched down at his feet. And so all that night the lion and he slept together; and when Sir Percival slept he dreamed a marvellous dream, that there two ladies met with him, and that one sat upon a lion, and that other sat upon a serpent, and that one of them was young, and the other was old, and the youngest him thought said, "Sir Percival, my lord saluteth thee, and sendeth thee word that thou array thee and make thee ready, for to-morrow thou must fight with the strongest champion of the world."

[Then, after many great deeds, it befell on a certain day that as the good knight Galahad rode, he was met by a damsel on a palfrey, and she led him towards the sea. And so at the seaside they found a ship wherein they entered, and Sir Bors and Sir Percival being in that ship greeted them with joy.]

By then the ship went from the land of Logris, and by adventure it arrived up betwixt two rocks passing great and marvellous, but there they might not land, for there was a swallow of the sea, save there was another ship, and upon it they might go without danger.

"Go we thither," said the gentlewoman, "and there shall we see adventures, for so is our Lord's will."

And when they came thither, they found the ship rich enough, but they found neither man nor woman therein. But they found in the end of the ship two fair letters written, which said a dreadful word and a marvellous:—

"Thou man which shall enter into this ship, beware thou be in steadfast belief, for I am faith, and therefore beware how thou enterest, for and thou fail I shall not help thee."

Then said the gentlewoman, "Percival, wot ye what I am?"

"Certainly," said he, "not to my witting."

"Wit ye well," said she, "I am thy sister, that am daughter of King Pellinore, and therefore wit ye well that ye are the man in the world that I most love; and if ye be not in perfect belief, enter not in no manner of wise, for then should ye perish in the ship, for it is so perfect it will suffer no sin in it."

And when Sir Percival knew that she was his sister, he was inwardly glad, and said, "Fair sister, I shall enter therein, for if I be a miss-creature or an untrue knight, there shall I perish."

In the meanwhile Sir Galahad blessed him, and entered therein, and then next the gentlewoman, and then Sir Bors and Sir Percival. And when they were therein, they found it so marvellous fair and rich, that they had great marvel thereof. And in the midst of the ship was a fair bed, and Sir Galahad went thereto, and found there a crown of silk, and at the feet was a sword rich and fair, and it was drawn out of the sheath half a foot and more, and the sword was of divers fashions, and the pommel was of stone, and there was in him all manner of colors that any man might find, and every each of the colors had divers virtues, and the scales of the haft were of two ribs of divers beasts. The one beast was a serpent, which was conversant in Calidone, and is called the serpent of the fiend. And the bone of him is of such a virtue, that there is no hand that handleth him shall never be weary nor hurt. And the other beast is a fish which is not right great, and haunteth the flood of Eufrates; and that fish is called Ertanax, and his bones be of such a manner of kind, that who that handleth them shall have so much will that he shall never be weary, and he shall not think on joy nor sorrow that he hath had, but only that thing that he beholdeth before him. And as for this sword there shall never man begripe it at the handle but one, but he shall pass all other.

"In the name of God," said Sir Percival, "I shall essay to handle it."

So he set his hand to the sword, but he might not begripe it.

"By my faith," said he, "now have I failed."

Sir Bors set his hand thereto and failed. Then Sir Galahad beheld the sword, and saw the letters like blood, that said, "Let see who shall assay to draw me out of my sheath, but if he be more hardier than other, and who that draweth me, wit ye well that he shall never fail of shame of his body, or to be wounded to the death."

"By my faith," said Galahad, "I would draw this sword out of the sheath, but the offending is so great that I shall not set my hand thereto."

"Now sir," said the gentlewoman, "wit ye well that the drawing of this sword is forbidden to all men, save all only unto you. Also this ship arrived in the realm of Logris [*England*], and that time was deadly war between King Labor, which was father unto the maimed king, and King Hurlame, which was a Saracen. But then was he newly christened, so that men held him afterwards one of the wittiest men of the world. And so upon a day it befell that King Labor and King Hurlame had assembled their folk upon the sea, where this ship was arrived, and there King Hurlame was discomfit, and his men slain, and he was afeared to be dead, and fled to his ship, and there found this sword, and drew it, and came out and found King Labor, the man in the world of all Christendom in whom was then the greatest faith. And when King Hurlame saw King Labor, he dressed this sword, and smote him upon the helm so hard, that he clave him and his horse to the earth with the first stroke of his sword. And it was in the realm of Logris; and so befell great pestilence and great harm to both realms. For sith increased corn nor grass, nor well nigh no fruit, nor in the water was no fish, wherefore men call it the lands of the two marches, the waste land for the dolorous stroke. And when King Hurlame saw that this sword was so kerving [*sharp*], he returned again to fetch the scabbard, and so came into this ship, and entered and put the sword into the scabbard; and as soon as he had done so, he fell down dead before the bed. Thus was the sword proved, that none that drew it but he were dead or maimed."

"Sir," said she, "there was a king that hight Pelles the Maimed King. And while he might ride, he supported much Christendom, and holy Church. So upon a day he hunted in a wood of his which lasted unto the sea, and at the last he lost his hounds and his knights, save only one; and there he and his knight went till that they came toward Ireland, and there he found the ship. And when he saw the letters and understood them, yet he entered, for he was right perfect of his life; but his knight had none hardiness to enter, and there found he this sword, and drew it out as much as ye may see. So therewith entered a spear, wherewith he was smitten through both the thighs, and never sith might he be healed, nor nought shall, tofore we come to him. Thus, said she, was King Pelles, your grandsire, maimed for his hardiness."

"In the name of God, damsel," said Galahad.

So they went toward the bed to behold all about it, and above the head there hung two swords. Also there were two spindles which were as white as any snow, and other that were as red as blood, and other above green as any emerald: of these three colors were the spindles, and of natural color within, and without any painting.

"These spindles," said the damsel, "were when sinful Eve came to gather fruit, for which Adam and she were put out of paradise, she took with her the bough on which the apple hung. Then perceived she that the branch was fair and green, and she remembered her the loss which came from the tree, then she thought to keep the branch as long as she might; and because she had no coffer to keep it in, she put it into the ground. So by the will of our Lord the branch grew to a great tree within a little while, and was as white as any snow, branches, boughs, and leaves, that it was a token a maid planted it. And anon the tree, that was white, became as green as any grass, and all that came of it. And so it befell many days after, under the same tree, Cain slew his brother Abel, whereof befell full great marvel; for anon as Abel had received the death under the green tree, it lost the green color and became red, and that was in tokening of the blood; and anon all the plants died thereof, but the tree grew and waxed marvellous fair, and it was the fairest tree and the most delectable that any man might behold; and so died the plants that grew out of it before the time that Abel was slain under it. So long endured the tree till that Solomon, King David's son, reigned and held the land after his father. This Solomon was wise and knew the virtues of stones and of trees, and so he knew the course of the stars, and many other things. This King Solomon had an evil wife, wherethrough he wend that there had never been no good woman; and so he despised them in his books. So a voice answered him once, 'Solomon, if heaviness come unto a man by a woman, ne reck thou never; for yet shall there come a woman whereof there shall come greater joy unto man an hundred times more than this heaviness giveth sorrow, and that woman shall be born of thy lineage.' Then when Solomon heard these words, he held himself but a fool, and the truth he perceived by old books. Also the Holy Ghost showed him the coming of the glorious Virgin Mary. Then asked he of the voice if it should be in the end of his lineage. 'Nay,' said the voice, 'but there shall come a man which shall be a [pure man] of your blood, and he shall be as good a knight as Duke Josua thy brother-in-law.

'Now have I certified thee of that thou stoodst in doubt.' Then was Solomon glad that there should come any such of his lineage, but ever he marvelled and studied who that should be, and what his name might be. His wife perceived that he studied, and thought that she would know it at some season, and so she waited her time, and asked of him the cause of his studying, and there he told her altogether how the voice told him. 'Well,' said she, 'I shall let make a ship of the best wood and most durable that men may find.' So Solomon sent for all the carpenters of the land and the best. And when they had made the ship, the lady said to Solomon, 'Sir,' said she, 'since it is so that this knight ought to pass all other knights of chivalry which have been tofore him, and shall come after him, moreover I shall tell you,' said she, 'ye shall go into our Lord's temple, whereas is King David's sword, your father, the which is the marvellousest and sharpest that ever was taken in any knight's hand. Therefore take that, and take off the pommel, and thereto make ye a pommel of precious stones, that it be so subtilly made that no man perceive it but that they be all one. And after make there an hilt so marvellously and wonderly that no man may know it; and after make a marvellous sheath; and when you have made all this, I shall let make a girdle thereto, such as shall please you.' All this King Solomon let make as she devised, both the ship and all the remnant. And when the ship was ready in the sea for to sail, the lady let make a great bed and marvellous rich, and set her upon the bed's head covered with silk, and laid the sword at the bed's feet; and the girdles were of hemp. And therewith was the king angry. 'Sir, wit ye well,' said she, 'that I have none so high a thing that were worthy to sustain so big a sword, and a maid shall bring other knights thereto, but I wot not when it shall be, nor what time.' And there she let make a covering to the ship, of cloth of silk that shall never rot for no manner of weather. Yet went that lady and made a carpenter to come to that tree which Abel was slain under. 'Now,' said she, 'carve me out of this tree as much wood as will make me a spindle.' 'Ah!

madam,' said the carpenter, 'this is the tree the which our first mother planted.' 'Do it,' said she, 'or else I shall destroy thee.' Anon, as the carpenter began to work, there came out drops of blood, and then would he have left, but she would not suffer him. And so he took away as much wood as might well make a spindle; and so she made him to take as much of the green tree and of the white tree. And when these three spindles were shapen, she made them to be fastened on the bed. When Solomon saw this he said to his wife, 'Ye have done marvellously, for though all the world were here now, they could not tell wherefore all this was made, but our Lord himself, and thou that hast done it wottest not what it shall betoken.' 'Now let it be,' said she, 'for ye shall hear tidings sooner than ye ween.'

That night lay King Solomon before the ship with a small fellowship. And when King Solomon was on sleep, him thought there came from heaven a great company of angels, and alighted into the ship and took water which was brought by an angel in a vessel of silver, and besprent [*besprinkled*] all the ship; and after he came to the sword, and drew letters on the hilt. And after went to the ship's board, and wrote there other letters, which said: 'Thou man that wilt enter within me, beware that thou be full within the faith, for I ne [*not*] am but faith and belief.' When Solomon espied these letters he was abashed, so that he durst not enter, and so drew him aback, and the ship was anon shoven in the sea, and he went so fast that he lost sight of him within a little while. And then a little voice said, 'Solomon, the last knight of thy lineage shall rest in this bed.' Then went Solomon and awaked his wife and told her of the adventures of the ship."

Now a great while the three fellows [*Galahad, and his two friends*] beheld the bed and the three spindles. Then they were at certain that they were of natural colors, without painting. Then they lifted up a cloth which was above the ground, and there they found a rich purse by seeming. And Percival took it, and found therein a writ, and so he read it, and devised the manner of the spindles, and of the ship, whence it came, and by whom it was made.

"Now," said Galahad, "where shall we find the gentlewoman that shall make new girdles to the sword?"

"Fair sir," said Percival's sister, "dismay you not, for by the leave of God I shall let make a girdle to the sword, such one as shall belong thereto."

And then she opened a box, and took out girdles which were seemly wrought with golden threads, and thereupon were set full of precious stones, and a rich buckle of gold.

"Lo, lords," said the gentlewoman, "here is a girdle that ought to be set about the sword; and wit ye well that the greatest part of this girdle was made of my hair, the which I loved full well while I was a woman of the world; but as soon as I wist that this adventure was ordained me, I clipped off my hair, and made this girdle in the name of God."

"Ye are well found," said Sir Bors, "for truly ye have put us out of a great pain, wherein we should have entered ne had your teaching been."

Then went the gentlewoman and set it upon the girdle of the sword.

"Now," said the three fellows, "what is the right name of the sword, and what shall we call it?"

"Truly," said she, "the name of the sword is the Sword with the Strange Girdles, and the scabbard, Mover of Blood; for no man that hath blood in him shall never see the one part of the scabbard which was made of the tree of life."

Then they said unto Sir Galahad, "In the name of Jesu Christ, we pray you that ye gird you with this sword, which hath been so much desired in the realm of Logris."

"Now let me begin," said Sir Galahad, "to grip this sword for to give you courage; but wot ye well that it belongeth no more to me than it doth to you."

And then he gripped about it with his fingers a great deal, and then she girded him about the middle with the sword.

"Now reck I not though I die, for now I hold me one of the blessed maidens of the world, which hath made thee the worthiest knight of the world."

"Fair damsel," said Sir Galahad, "ye have done so much that I shall be your knight all the days of my life."

Then they went from that ship, and went into the other ship; and anon the wind drove them into the sea a great pace, but they had no victual. But it happened that they came on the morrow to a castle which men call Courteloise that was in the marches of Scotland. And when they had passed the port, the gentlewoman said, "Lords, here be men arriven that, and they wist that ye were of King Arthur's court, ye should be assailed anon."

"Damsel," said Galahad, "he that cast us out of the rock shall deliver us from them."

[And it happened after that Sir Percival's sister of her own wish died for the healing of a certain lady, and the lady was healed. Then, as she had desired beforehand, Sir Percival laid her in a barge and] covered it with silk; and the wind arose and drove the barge from land, and all knights beheld it till it was out of their sight.

When Sir Launcelot was come to the water of Mortaise, he was in great peril, and so he laid him down and slept, and took his adventure that God would send him. So when he was asleep, there came a vision unto him, and said, "Launcelot, arise up and take thine armor, and enter into the first ship that thou shalt find."

And when he had heard these words, he started up, and saw a great clearness about him; and then he lifted up his hand and blessed him, and so took his armor, and made him ready. And by adventure he came by a strand, and found a ship the which was without sail or oars; and as soon as he was within the ship, there he felt the most sweetest savor that ever he felt, and he was fulfilled with all things that he thought on or desired. And so in this joy he lay him down on the ship-board, and slept till daylight. And when he awoke, he found there a fair bed, and therein lying a gentlewoman dead, the which was Sir Percival's sister. And as Sir Launcelot beheld her, he espied in her right hand a writing, the which he read, wherein he found all the adventures as ye have heard before, and of what lineage she was come. So with this gentlewoman Sir Launcelot was a month and more.

So upon a night he went to play him by the water's side, for he was somewhat weary of the ship, and then he listened, and heard an horse come, and one riding upon him. And when he came nigh he seemed a knight. And so he let him pass, and went there as the ship was, and there he alighted, and took the saddle and the bridle and put the horse from him, and went into the ship. And then Launcelot dressed unto him and said, "Ye be welcome."

And he answered and saluted him again, and asked him, "What is your name? for much my heart giveth unto you."

"Truly," said he, "my name is Launcelot du Lake."

"Sir," said he, "then be ye welcome, for ye were the beginner of me in this world."

"Ah," said he, "are ye Galahad?"

"Yea forsooth," said he.

And so he kneeled down and asked him his blessing, and after took off his helm and kissed him. And there was great joy between them, for there is no tongue can tell the joy that they made either of other, and many a friendly word spoken between, as kind [*nature*] would, the which is no need here to be rehearsed. And there every each told other of their adventures and marvels that were befallen to them in many journeys, sith that they departed from the court. Anon as Galahad saw the gentlewoman dead in the bed, he knew her well enough, and told great worship of her, and that she was the best maid living, and it was great pity of her death. But when Launcelot heard how the marvellous sword was gotten, and who made it, and all the marvels rehearsed afore, then he prayed Galahad his son that he would show him the sword, and so he did. And anon he kissed the pommel, and the hilts, and the scabbard.

"Truly," said Launcelot, "never erst knew I of so high adventures done, and so marvellous and strange." So dwelled Launcelot and Galahad within that ship half a year, and served God daily and nightly with all their power. And often they arrived in isles far from folk, where there repaired none but wild beasts; and there they found many strange adventures and perilous, which they brought to an end.

[Then on a certain day, a knight in white called to Sir Galahad from the shore to leave that ship and fare on his quest, and Sir Galahad departed from his father Sir Launcelot, and rode off upon the shore. But Sir Launcelot drove a month through the sea, ever praying for news of the Sancgreal.]

So it befell on a night, at midnight he arrived afore a castle, on the back side, which was rich and fair. And there was a postern opened towards the sea, and was open without any keeping, save two lions kept the entry; and the moon shone clear. Anon Sir Launcelot heard a voice that said, "Launcelot, go out of this ship, and enter into the castle, where thou shalt see a great part of thy desire." Then he ran to his arms, and so armed him, and so he went to the gate, and saw the lions. Then set he hand to his sword, and drew it. Then there came a dwarf suddenly, and smote him on the arm so sore that the sword fell out of his hand.

Then took he again his sword, and put it up in his sheath, and make a cross in his forehead, and came to the lions, and they made semblant to do him harm. Notwithstanding he passed by them without hurt, and entered into the castle to the chief fortress, and there were they all at rest. Then Launcelot entered in so armed, for he found no gate nor door but it was open. And at the last he found a chamber whereof the door was shut, and he set his hand thereto to have opened it, but he might not.

Then he enforced him mickle [*much*] to undo the door. Then he listened, and heard a voice which sang so sweetly that it seemed none earthly thing. Then Sir Launcelot kneeled down before the chamber, for well wist he that there was the Sancgreal within that chamber. Then said he, "Fair sweet Father Jesu Christ, if ever I did thing that pleased the Lord, for thy pity have me not in despite for my sins done aforetime, and that thou show me something of that I seek!"

And with that he saw the chamber door open, and there came out a great clearness, that the house was as bright as all the torches of the world had been there. So came he to the chamber door, and would have entered. And anon a voice said to him, "Flee, Launcelot, and enter not, for thou oughtest not to do it: and if thou enter thou shalt forthink it." Then he withdrew him aback right heavy. Then looked he up in the midst of the chamber, and saw a table of silver, and the holy vessel covered with red samite, and many angels about it.

Right soon he entered into the chamber, and came towards

the table of silver; and, when he came nigh, he felt a breath, that him thought was entermedled [*mingled*] with fire, which smote him so sore in the visage, that him thought it all to-burnt his visage, and therewith he fell to the ground, and had no power to arise. Then felt he many hands about him, which took him up, and bare him out of the chamber without any amending of his sowne [*swoon*], and left him there seeming dead to all the people. So on the morrow, when it was fair daylight, they within were arisen, and found Sir Launcelot lying before the chamber door: all they marvelled how he came in. And so they took him by every part of the body, and bare him into a chamber, and laid him in a rich bed far from all folk.

[Thus lay Sir Launcelot twenty-four days and nights, like as it were a punishment for the twenty-four years that he had been a sinner. And at the last he recovered himself.]

So Sir Launcelot departed, and took his armor, and said that he would go see the realm of Logris, "which I have not seen in a twelvemonth." And therewith he [took his leave and] rode through many realms. And he turned unto Camelot, where he found King Arthur and the queen. But many of the knights of the Round Table were slain and destroyed, more than half. And so three were come home, Ector, Gawaine, and Lionel, and many other that need not to be rehearsed. And all the court was passing glad of Sir Launcelot; and the king asked him many tidings of his son Galahad. And there Launcelot told the king of his adventures that had befallen him since he departed. And also he told him of the adventures of Galahad, Percival, and Bors, which that he knew by the letter of the dead damsel, and as Galahad had told him.

"Now, God would," said the king, "that they were all three here."

"That shall never be," said Launcelot, "for two of them shall ye never see, but one of them shall come again."

[Now Sir Galahad rode many journeys in vain, and afterward, meeting with Sir Bors and Sir Percival, they knew many wonders and adventures; till on a certain day they came down into a ship, and in the midst thereof they found a table of silver and the Holy Grail all covered with white samite. And the Holy Grail wrought many miracles, comforting them in prison, feeding them, and healing the sick. And it befell that the Paynim king who had cast them in prison died, and the people by one accord chose Sir Galahad to be king, and he reigned there a year. And on a certain morning Sir Galahad, having risen early, and come unto the palace, saw before him the Holy Grail, and a man kneeling, and about him a great fellowship of angels. Then Sir Galahad knew that his hour was come. And he] went to Sir Percival, and kissed him and commended him to God; and he went to Sir Bors, and kissed him and commended him to God, and said, "Fair lord, salute me to my lord Sir Launcelot, my father."

And therewith he kneeled down before the table and made his prayers; and then suddenly his soul departed, and a great multitude of angels bare his soul up to heaven. Also the two fellows saw come from heaven an hand, but they saw not the body; and then it came to the [Holy Grail] and took it, and the spear, and so bare it to heaven.

Since was there never man so hardy to say that he had seen the Holy Grail.

[Then after a year and two months, Sir Percival, having lived a holy life in a hermitage, departed away from this world. And having buried him by his sister and Sir Galahad, Sir Bors entered into a ship and came at last to Logris, and rode fast to Camelot where King Arthur was. And there was great joy made of him, for they weened he had been dead.]

And anon Sir Bors said to Sir Launcelot, "Galahad, your own son saluted you by me, and after you King Arthur, and all the court, and so did Sir Percival: for I buried them with mine own hands in the city of Sarras. Also, Sir Launcelot, Galahad prayeth you to remember of this uncertain world, as ye behight him when ye were together more than half a year."

"This is true," said Launcelot; "now I trust to God his prayer shall avail me."

Then Launcelot took Sir Bors in his arms, and said, "Gentle cousin, ye are right welcome to me, and all that ever I may do for you and for yours, ye shall find my poor body ready at all times whiles the spirit is in it, and that I promise you faithfully, and never to fail. And wit ye well, gentle cousin Sir Bors, that ye and I will never depart in sunder whilst our lives may last."

"Sir," said he, "I will as ye will."

BOOK VI

OF THE FAIR MAID OF ASTOLAT

BOOK VI

OF THE FAIR MAID OF ASTOLAT

SO after the quest of the Sanc Greal was fulfilled, and all knights that were left on live were come again to the Table Round, then was there great joy, and in especial King Arthur and Queen Guenever made great joy of the remnant that were come home.

And then the queen let make a dinner in London unto the knights of the Round Table. All at that dinner she had Sir Gawaine and his brethren, that is to say, Sir Agravaine, Sir Gaheris, Sir Gareth, and Sir Mordred. Also there was Sir Bors de Ganis, Sir Blamor de Ganis, Sir Bleoberis de Ganis, Sir Galihud, Sir Galihodin, Sir Ector de Maris, Sir Lionel, Sir Palamides, Sir Safere his brother, Sir La Cote Mal Taile, Sir Persant, Sir Ironside, Sir Brandiles, Sir Kay le Seneschal, Sir Mador de la Porte, Sir Patrice, a knight of Ireland, [Sir] Aliduke, Sir Astomore, and Sir Pinel le Savage, the which was cousin to Sir Lamorak de Galis, the good knight that Sir Gawaine and his brethren slew by treason. And so these four and twenty knights should dine with the queen, and there was made a great feast of all manner of dainties. But Sir Gawaine had a custom that he used daily at dinner and at supper, that he loved well all manner of fruit, and in especial apples and pears. And therefore whosoever dined or feasted Sir Gawaine would commonly purvey for good fruit for him; and so did the queen for to please Sir Gawaine, she let purvey for him of all manner of fruit, for Sir Gawaine was a passing hot knight of nature. And this Pinel hated Sir Gawaine because of his kinsman Sir Lamorak de Galis, and therefore for pure envy and hate Sir Pinel enpoisoned certain apples, for to enpoison Sir Gawaine. And so this was well unto the end of the meat; and so it befell by misfortune a good knight named Patrice, cousin unto Sir Mador de la Porte, to take a poisoned apple. And when he had eaten it he swelled so till he burst, and there Sir Patrice fell down suddenly dead among them. Then every knight leaped from the board ashamed and enraged for wrath, nigh out of their wits. For they wist not what to say: considering Queen Guenever made the feast and dinner, they all had suspicion unto her.

"My lady, the queen," said Gawaine, "wit ye well, madam, that this dinner was made for me: for all folks that know my conditions understand that I love well fruit; and now I see well I had near been slain; therefore, madam, I dread lest ye will be shamed."

Then the queen stood still, and was sore abashed, that she wist not what to say.

"This shall not so be ended," said Sir Mador de la Porte, "for here have I lost a full noble knight of my blood, and therefore upon this shame and despite I will be revenged to the uttermost."

And thereupon Sir Mador appealed Queen Guenever of

the death of his cousin Sir Patrice.[1] Then stood they all still, that none of them would speak a word against him, for they had a great suspection [*suspicion*] unto Queen Guenever, because she let make the dinner. And the queen was so sore abashed that she could none otherwise do but wept so heartily that she fell in a swoon. With this noise and sudden cry came unto them King Arthur, and marvelled greatly what it might be; and when he wist of their trouble, and the sudden death of that good knight Sir Patrice, he was a passing heavy man.

And ever Sir Mador stood still before King Arthur, and ever he appealed Queen Guenever of treason; for the custom was such at that time that all manner of shameful death was called treason.

"Fair lords," said King Arthur, "me repenteth sore of this trouble, but the cause is so we may not have to do in this matter, for I must be a rightful judge, and that repenteth me that I may not do battle for my wife, for, as I deem, this deed came never of her; and therefore I suppose we shall not all be destitute, but that some good knight shall put his body in jeopardy for my queen rather than she should be brent [*burnt*] in a wrong quarrel; and therefore, Sir Mador, be not so hasty, for it may happen she shall not be all friendless, and therefore desire thou the day of battle, and she shall purvey her of some good knight which shall

[1] We have here the beginning of that series of quarrels which presently arrays Sir Gawaine and King Arthur (who with many protests allows himself to be guided by Sir Gawaine) on one side, against Queen Guenever and Sir Launcelot (who has taken the queen's part) on the other, and which ends with the great battle in which Arthur is slain and the Round Table broken up for ever.

answer you, or else it were to me great shame, and unto all my court."

"My gracious lord," said Sir Mador, "ye must hold me excused, for though ye be our king, in that degree ye are but a knight as we are, and ye are sworn unto knighthood as well as we, and therefore I pray you that ye will not be displeased; for there is none of the twenty knights that were bidden for to come unto this dinner, but all they have great suspection unto the queen. What say you all, my lords?" said Sir Mador.

Then they answered by and by, and said they could not excuse the queen, for why she made the dinner, and either it must come by her or by her servants.

"Alas," said the queen, "I made this dinner for a good intent, and never for none evil; so Almighty God help me in my right."

"My lord the king," said Sir Mador, "I require you, as ye be a righteous king, give me a day that I may have justice."

"Well," said the king, "I give the day this day fifteen days, that thou be ready armed on horseback in the meadow beside Westminster. And if it so fall that there be any knight to encounter with you, there mayest thou do the best, and God speed the right. And if it so fall that there be no knight at that day, then must my queen be burnt, and there shall she be ready to have her judgment."

"I am answered," said Sir Mador; and every knight went where it liked him.

So when the king and queen were together, the king asked the queen how this case befell?

The queen answered, "So God me help, I wot not how, nor in what manner."

"Where is Sir Launcelot?" said King Arthur, "and he were here, he would not grudge to do battle for you."

"Sir," said the queen, "I wot not where he is, but his brother and his kinsmen deem that he is not within this realm."

[For, within a little while before, it happened on a day that Queen Guenever was displeased with Sir Launcelot and forbade him the court, and that Sir Launcelot full sadly left the court and departed into his country and dwelt with the hermit Sir Brasias.]

"That me repenteth," said King Arthur, "for and he were here he would soon stint this strife. Then I will counsel you," said the king, "that ye go unto Sir Bors, and pray him to do that battle for you for Sir Launcelot's sake, and upon my life he will not refuse you; for right well I perceive that none of all these twenty knights that were with you in fellowship at your dinner will do battle for you: [which would be] great slander for you in this court."

"Alas!" said the queen, "I cannot do withal; but now I miss Sir Launcelot, for, and he were here, he would put me full soon unto my heart's ease."

"Now go your way," said the king unto the queen, "and require Sir Bors to do battle for you for Sir Launcelot's sake."

So the queen departed from the king, and sent for Sir Bors into her chamber; and when he was come, she besought him of succor.

"Madam," said he, "what would ye that I do? for I may not with my worship have to do in this matter, because I was at that same dinner, for dread that any of those knights would have me in suspection; also, madam," said Sir Bors, "now miss ye Sir Launcelot, for he would not have failed you, neither in right nor yet in wrong, as ye have well proved when ye have been in danger, and now have ye driven him out of this country, by whom ye and we all were daily worshipped.[1] Therefore, madam, I greatly marvel me how ye dare for shame require me to do any thing for you, in so much as ye have chased him out of your country by whom we were borne up and honored."

"Alas! fair knight," said the queen, "I put me wholly in your grace, and all that is done amiss I will amend as ye will counsel me."

And therewith she kneeled down upon both her knees, and besought Sir Bors to have mercy upon her, "or I shall have a shameful death, and thereto I never offended."

Right so came King Arthur, and found the queen kneeling afore Sir Bors. Then Sir Bors pulled her up, and said, "Madam, ye do to me great dishonor."

"Ah, gentle knight," said the king, "have mercy upon my queen, courteous knight, for I am now in certain she is untruly defamed. And therefore, courteous knight," said the king, "promise her to do battle for her: I require you, for the love of Sir Launcelot."

"My lord," said Sir Bors, "ye require me the greatest thing that any man may require me; and wit ye well, if I

[1] "Worshipped" *made of worth, honored.*

grant to do battle for the queen I shall wrath many of my fellowship of the Table Round; but as for that," said Bors, "I will grant my lord, for my lord Sir Launcelot's sake, and for your sake, I will at that day be the queen's champion, unless that there come by adventure a better knight than I am to do battle for her."

"Will ye promise me this," said the king, "by your faith?"

"Yea sir," said Sir Bors, "of that will I not fail you, nor her both, but if that there come a better knight than I am, and then shall he have the battle."

Then was the king and the queen passing glad, and so departed, and thanked him heartily. So then Sir Bors departed secretly upon a day, and rode unto Sir Launcelot, there as he was with the hermit Sir Brasias, and told him of all their adventure.

"Ah," said Sir Launcelot, "this is come happily as I would have it, and therefore I pray you make you ready to do battle, but look that ye tarry till ye see me come, as long as ye may. For I am sure Mador is an hot knight, when he is enchafed, for the more ye suffer him, the hastier will he be to battle."

"Sir," said Sir Bors, "let me deal with him; doubt ye not ye shall have all your will."

Then departed Sir Bors from him, and came to the court again. Then was it noised in all the court that Sir Bors should do battle for the queen: wherefore many knights were displeased with him, that he would take upon him to do battle in the queen's quarrel, for there were but few knights in the court but they deemed the queen was in the wrong, and that she had done that treason. So Sir Bors answered thus unto his fellows of the Table Round: "Wit ye well, my fair lords, it were shame to us all, and we suffered to see the most noble queen of the world to be shamed openly, considering her lord and our lord is the man of most worship in the world, and most christened, and he hath ever worshipped us all, in all places."

Many answered him again: "As for our most noble King Arthur, we love him and honor him as well as ye do; but as for Queen Guenever, we love her not, for because she is a destroyer of good knights."

"Fair lords," said Sir Bors, "me seemeth ye say not as ye should say, for never yet in all my days knew I nor heard say that ever she was a destroyer of any good knight; but at all times, as far as I ever could know, she was always a maintainer of good knights, and alway she hath been large and free of her goods to all good knights, and the most bounteous lady of her gifts and her good grace that ever I saw or heard speak of; and therefore it were great shame," said Sir Bors, "unto us all to our most noble king's wife, if we suffer her to be shamefully slain. And wit ye well," said Sir Bors, "I will not suffer it, for I dare say so much, the queen is not guilty of Sir Patrice's death, for she ought [*owed*] him never none evil will, nor none of the twenty-four knights that were at that dinner; for I dare well say that it was for good love she had us to dinner, and not for no mal engine [*bad design*], and that I doubt not shall be proved hereafter, for, howsoever the game goeth, there was treason among some of us."

Then some said to Sir Bors, "We may well believe your words."

And so some of them were well pleased, and some were not pleased.

The day came on fast until the even that the battle should be. Then the queen sent for Sir Bors, and asked him how he was disposed.

"Truly, madam," said he, "I am disposed in likewise as I promised you, [and I will not] fail you, unless by adventure there come a better knight than I to do battle for you; then, madam, I am discharged of my promise."

Then the queen went unto the king, and told him the answer of Sir Bors.

"Have ye no doubt," said the king, "of Sir Bors, for I call him now one of the best knights of the world, and the most profitable man."

And thus it passed on until the morn. And the king and the queen, and all manner of knights that were there at that time, drew them unto the meadow beside Westminster, where the battle should be. And so when the king was come with the queen, and many knights of the Round Table, then the queen was put there in the constable's ward, and a great fire made about an iron stake, that, and Sir Mador de la Porte had the better, she should be burnt. Such custom was used in those days, that neither for favor, neither for love, nor affinity, there should be none other but righteous judgment, as well upon a king as upon a knight, and as well upon a queen as upon another poor lady. So in this meanwhile came in Sir Mador de la Porte, and took his oath before the king, That the queen did this treason unto his cousin Sir Patrice, and unto his oath he would prove it with his body, hand for hand, who that would say the contrary. Right so came in Sir Bors, and said, that as for Queen Guenever, she is in the right, "and that will I make good with my hands, that she is not culpable of this treason that is put upon her."

"Then make thee ready," said Sir Mador, "and we shall prove whether thou be in the right or I."

"Sir Mador," said Sir Bors, "wit thou well I know you for a good knight: but I trust unto almighty God I shall be able to withstand your malice: but thus much have I promised my lord King Arthur, and my lady the queen, that I shall do battle for her in this case to the uttermost, unless that there come a better knight than I am, and discharge me."

"Is that all?" said Sir Mador; "either come thou off, and do battle with me, or else say nay."

"Take your horse," said Sir Bors, "and, as I suppose, ye shall not tarry long but that ye shall be answered."

Then either departed to their tents, and made them ready to mount upon horseback as they thought best. And anon Sir Mador de la Porte came into the field with his shield on his shoulder, and a spear in his hand; and so rode about the place, crying unto King Arthur, "Bid your champion come forth, and he dare."

Then was Sir Bors ashamed, and took his horse, and came to the lists' end. And then was he ware where as came out of a wood, there fast by, a knight all armed at all points upon a white horse, with a strange shield, and of strange arms; and he came riding all that he might run; and so he came to Sir Bors, and said, "Fair knight, I pray you be not displeased, for here must a better knight than ye are have this battle; therefore I pray you to withdraw you, for I would ye knew I have had this day a right great journey, and this battle ought to be mine, and so I promised you when I spake with you last, and with all my heart I thank you of your good will."

Then Sir Bors rode unto King Arthur, and told him how there was a knight come that would have the battle for to fight for the queen.

"What knight is he?" said the king.

"I wot not," said Sir Bors, "but such covenant he made with me to be here this day. Now my lord," said Sir Bors, "here am I discharged."

Then the king called to that knight, and asked him if he would fight for the queen. Then he answered to the king, "Therefore came I hither, and therefore, Sir king," he said, "tarry me no longer, for I may not tarry. For anon as I have finished this battle I must depart hence, for I have ado many matters elsewhere. For wit you well," said that knight, "this is dishonor to you all knights of the Round Table, to see and know so noble a lady and so courteous a queen as Queen Guenever is thus to be rebuked and shamed amongst you."

Then they all marvelled what knight that might be that so took the battle upon him, for there was not one that knew him, but if it were Sir Bors. Then said Sir Mador de la Porte unto the king, "Now let me wit with whom I shall have ado withal."

And then they rode to the lists' end, and there they couched their spears, and ran together with all their mights. And Sir Mador's spear brake all to pieces, but the other's spear held, and bare Sir Mador's horse and all backward to the earth a great fall. But mightily and suddenly he avoided his horse, and put his shield afore him, and then drew his sword, and bade the other knight alight and do battle with him on foot. Then that knight descended from his horse lightly like a valiant man, and put his shield afore him, and drew his sword, and so they came eagerly unto battle, and either gave other many great strokes, tracing and traversing, raising and foining, and hurtling together with their swords, as it were wild boars. Thus were they fighting nigh an hour, for this Sir Mador was a strong knight, and mightily proved in many strong battles. But at last this knight smote Sir Mador grovelling upon the earth, and the knight stepped near him to have pulled Sir Mador flatling upon the ground; and therewith suddenly Sir Mador arose, and in his rising he smote that knight through the thick of the thighs, that the blood ran out fiercely. And when he felt himself so wounded, and saw his blood, he let him arise upon his feet; and then he gave him such a buffet upon the helm that he fell to the earth flatling, and therewith he strode to him for to have pulled off his helm off his head. And then Sir Mador prayed that knight to save his life, and so he yielded him as overcome, and released the queen of his quarrel.

"I will not grant thee thy life," said that knight, "only that thou freely release the queen forever, and that no mention be made upon Sir Patrice's tomb that ever Queen Guenever consented to that treason."

"All this shall be done," said Sir Mador, "I clearly discharge my quarrel forever."

Then the knights parters of the lists [*knights who parted the combatants*] took up Sir Mador and led him to his tent, and the other knight went straight to the stair foot whereas King Arthur sat, and by that time was the queen come unto the king, and either kissed other lovingly. And when the king saw that knight, he stooped down unto him and thanked him, and in likewise did the queen. And then the king prayed him to put off his helm and to rest him, and to take a sop of wine; and then he put off his helm to drink, and then every knight knew that he was the noble knight Sir Launcelot. As soon as the king wist that, he took the queen by the hand, and went unto Sir Launcelot, and said, "Gramercy of your great travel that ye have had this day for me and for my queen."

"My lord," said Sir Launcelot, "wit ye well that I ought of right ever to be in your quarrel, and in my lady the queen's quarrel, to do battle, for ye are the man that gave me the high order of knighthood, and that day my lady your queen did me great worship, or else I had been shamed. For that same day ye made me knight, through my hastiness I lost my sword, and my lady your queen found it, and lapped it in her train, and gave me my sword when I had need thereof, or else had I been shamed among all knights. And therefore, my lord King Arthur, I promised her at that day ever to be her knight in right or in wrong."

"Gramercy," said King Arthur, "for this journey; and wit you well," said King Arthur, "I shall acquit you of [*repay you for*] your goodness."

And ever the queen beheld Sir Launcelot, and wept so tenderly that she sank almost down upon the ground for sorrow, that he had done to her so great goodness, whereas she had showed him great unkindness. Then the knights of his blood drew unto him, and there either of them made great joy of other; and so came all the knights of the Round Table that were there at that time, and he welcomed them. And then Sir Mador was had to leechcraft [*surgery*]; and Sir Launcelot was healed of his wound. And then was there made great joy and mirth in the court.

And so it befell that the damsel of the lake, which was called Nimue, the which wedded the good knight Sir Pelleas, and so she came to the court, for ever she did great goodness unto King Arthur and to all his knights, through her sorcery and enchantments. And so when she heard how the queen was [endangered] for the death of Sir Patrice, then she told it openly that she was never guilty; and there she disclosed by whom it was done, and named him Sir Pinel, and for what cause he did it; there it was openly disclosed, and so the queen was excused, and the knight Sir Pinel fled into his country. Then was it openly known that Sir Pinel empoisoned the apples of the feast, to the intent to have destroyed Sir Gawaine, because Sir Gawaine and his brethren destroyed Sir Lamorak de Galis, whom Sir Pinel was cousin unto.

And then Sir Mador sued daily and long to have the queen's good grace; and so, by the means of Sir Launcelot, he caused him to stand in the queen's grace, and all was forgiven. Thus it passed forth until our Lady Day the Assumption; within fifteen days of that feast King [Arthur let cry a great tournament] at Camelot, that is, Winchester, [where] he and the King of Scotland would joust against all that would come against them. And when this cry was made, thither came many knights. So there came thither the King of Northgalis, and King Anguish of Ireland, and the king with the hundred knights, and Sir Galahalt the haut prince, and the King of Northumberland, and many other noble dukes and earls of divers countries. So King Arthur made him ready to depart to these jousts, and would have had the queen with him; but at that time she would not, she said, for she was sick and might not ride at that time.

"That me repenteth," said the king, "for this seven year ye saw not such a fellowship together, except at Whitsuntide when Galahad departed from the court."

"Truly," said the queen to the king, "ye must hold me excused: I may not be there, and that me repenteth."

And so upon the morn early Sir Launcelot heard mass, and brake his fast, and so took his leave of the queen, and departed. And then he rode so much until he came to Astolat, that is Gilford; and there it happed him in the eventide he came to an old baron's place, that hight Sir Bernard of Astolat. And as Sir Launcelot entered into his lodging, King Arthur espied him as he did walk in a garden beside the castle, how he took his lodging, and knew him full well.

"It is well," said King Arthur unto the knights that were with him in that garden beside the castle, "I have now espied one knight that will play his play at the jousts to the which we be gone towards, I undertake he will do marvels."

"Who is that, we pray you tell us," said many knights that were there at that time.

"Ye shall not wit for me," said the king, "at this time."

And so the king smiled, and went to his lodging. So when Sir Launcelot was in his lodging, and unarmed him in his chamber, the old baron came unto him, making his reverence, and welcomed him in the best manner; but the old knight knew not Sir Launcelot.

"Fair sir," said Sir Launcelot to his host, "I would pray you to lend me a shield that were not openly known, for mine is well known."

"Sir," said his host, "ye shall have your desire, for me seemeth ye be one of the likeliest knights of the world, and therefore I shall show you friendship. Sir, wit ye well I have two sons which were but late made knights, and the eldest hight Sir Tirre, and he was hurt the same day that he was made knight, that he may not ride, and his shield ye shall have, for that is not known, I dare say, but here, and in no place else. And my youngest son hight Sir Lavaine, and if it please you he shall ride with you unto those jousts; and he is of his age strong and mighty, for much my heart giveth unto you that ye should be a noble knight, therefore I beseech you tell me your name," said Sir Bernard.

"As for that," said Sir Launcelot, "ye must hold me excused as at this time, and if God give me grace to speed well at the jousts, I shall come again and tell you; but I pray you heartily," said Sir Launcelot, "in any wise let me have your son Sir Lavaine with me, and that I may have his brother's shield."

"Also this shall be done," said Sir Bernard.

This old baron had a daughter that time that was called the fair maid of Astolat, and ever she beheld Sir Launcelot wonderfully; and she cast such a love unto Sir Launcelot that she could not withdraw her love, wherefore she died; and her name was Elaine la Blanche. So thus as she came to and fro, she besought Sir Launcelot to wear upon him at the jousts a token of hers.

"Fair damsel," said Sir Launcelot, "and if I grant you that, ye may say I do more for your love than ever I did for lady or damsel."

Then he remembered him that he would ride unto the jousts disguised, and for because he had never before that time borne no manner of token of no damsel, then he bethought him that he would bear one of hers, that none of his blood thereby might know him. And then he said, "Fair damsel, I will grant you to wear a token of yours upon my helmet, and therefore what it is show me."

"Sir," said she, "it is a red sleeve of mine, of scarlet well embroidered with great pearls."

And so she brought it him. So Sir Launcelot received it, and said, "Never or this time did I so much for no damsel."

And then Sir Launcelot betook [*gave*] the fair damsel his shield in keeping, and prayed her to keep it until he came again. And so that night he had merry rest and great cheer; for ever the fair damsel Elaine was about Sir Launcelot all the while that she might be suffered.

So upon a day in the morning, King Arthur and all his knights departed, for the king had tarried there three days to abide his knights. And so when the king was ridden, Sir Launcelot and Sir Lavaine made them ready for to ride, and either of them had white shields, and the red sleeve Sir Launcelot let carry with him. And so they took their leave of Sir Bernard the old baron, and of his daughter the fair maid of Astolat. And then they rode so long till that they came to Camelot, which now is called Winchester. And there was great press of knights, dukes, earls, and barons, and many noble knights; but there was Sir Launcelot privily lodged by the means of Sir Lavaine with a rich burgess, that no man in that town was ware what they were. And so they sojourned there till our Lady Day the Assumption, as the great feast should be. So then trumpets began to blow unto the field, and King Arthur was set on high upon a scaffold to behold who did best. But King Arthur would not suffer Sir Gawaine to go from him, for never had Sir Gawaine the better if Sir Launcelot were in the field. And many times was Sir Gawaine rebuked when Sir Launcelot came to any jousts disguised. Then some of the kings, as King Anguish of Ireland and the King of Scotland, were at that time turned upon King Arthur's side. And then upon the other side was the King of Northgalis, and the king with the hundred knights, and the King of Northumberland, and

Sir Galahalt the haut prince. But these three kings and this one duke were passing weak to hold against King Arthur's party; for with him were the noblest knights of the world. So then they withdrew them either party from other, and every man made him ready in his best manner to do what he might. Then Sir Launcelot made him ready, and put the red sleeve upon his head, and fastened it fast; and so Sir Launcelot and Sir Lavaine departed out of Winchester privily, and rode until [*unto*] a little leaved wood, behind the party that held against King Arthur's party, and there they held them still till the parties smote together. And then came in the King of Scots and the King of Ireland on Arthur's party; and against them came the King of Northumberland; and the king with the hundred knights smote down the King of Northumberland, and also the king with the hundred knights smote down King Anguish of Ireland. Then Sir Palamides, that was on Arthur's party, encountered with Sir Galahalt, and either of them smote down other, and either party holp their lords on horseback again. So there began a strong assail upon both parties. And then there came in Sir Brandiles, Sir Sagramor le Desirous, Sir Dodinas le Savage, Sir Kay le Seneschal, Sir Griflet le Fise de Dieu, Sir Mordred, Sir Meliot de Logris, Sir Ozanna le Cure Hardy, Sir Safere, Sir Epinogris, and Sir Galleron of Galway. All these fifteen knights were knights of the Table Round. So these with more others came in together, and beat back the King of Northumberland, and the King of North Wales. When Sir Launcelot saw this, as he hoved in a little leaved wood, then he said unto Sir Lavaine, "See yonder is a company of good knights, and they hold them together as boars that were chafed with dogs."

"That is truth," said Sir Lavaine.

"Now," said Sir Launcelot, "and ye will help me a little, ye shall see yonder fellowship which chaseth now these men in our side, that they shall go as fast backward as they went forward."

"Sir, spare not," said Sir Lavaine, "for I shall do what I may."

Then Sir Launcelot and Sir Lavaine came in at the thickest of the press, and there Sir Launcelot smote down Sir Brandiles, Sir Sagramor, Sir Dodinas, Sir Kay, Sir Griflet, and all this he did with one spear. And Sir Lavaine smote down Sir Lucan le Butler, and Sir Bedivere. And then Sir Launcelot gat another spear, and there he smote down Sir Agravaine, Sir Gaheris, and Sir Mordred, and Sir Meliot de Logris. And Sir Lavaine smote down Ozanna le Cure Hardy: and then Sir Launcelot drew his sword, and there he smote on the right hand and on the left hand, and by great force he unhorsed Sir Safere, Sir Epinogris, and Sir Galleron. And then the knights of the Table Round withdrew them aback, after they had gotten their horses as well as they might.

"Oh, mercy," said Sir Gawaine, "what knight is yonder, that doth so marvellous deeds of arms in that field?"

"I wot what he is," said King Arthur, "but as at this time I will not name him."

"Sir," said Sir Gawaine, "I would say it were Sir Launcelot, by his riding and his buffets that I see him deal: but ever me seemeth it should be not he, for that he beareth the red sleeve upon his head, for I wist him never bear token, at no jousts, of lady nor gentlewoman."

"Let him be," said King Arthur, "he will be better known and do more or ever he depart."

Then the party that were against King Arthur were well comforted, and then they held them together, that beforehand were sore rebuked. Then Sir Bors, Sir Ector de Maris, and Sir Lionel, called unto them the knights of their blood, as Sir Blamor de Ganis, Sir Bleoberis, Sir Aliduke, Sir Galihud, Sir Galihodin, Sir Bellangere le Beuse, so these nine knights of Sir Launcelot's kin thrust in mightily, for they were all noble knights. And they, of great hate and despite that they had unto him, thought to rebuke that noble knight Sir Launcelot, and Sir Lavaine, for they knew them not. And so they came hurtling together, and smote down many knights of Northgalis and of Northumberland. And when Sir Launcelot saw them fare so, he gat a spear in his hand, and there encountered with them all at once; Sir Bors, Sir Ector de Maris, and Sir Lionel smote him all at once with their spears.

And with force of themselves they smote Sir Launcelot's horse unto the ground; and by misfortune Sir Bors smote Sir Launcelot through the shield into the side, and the spear brake, and the head abode still in the side. When Sir Lavaine saw his master lie upon the ground, he ran to the King of Scotland and smote him to the ground, and by great force he took his horse and brought him to Sir Launcelot, and mauger [*in spite of*] them all he made him to mount upon that horse. And then Sir Launcelot gat him a great spear in his hand, and there he smote Sir Bors both horse and man to the ground; and in the same wise he served Sir Ector and Sir Lionel; and Sir Lavaine smote down Sir Blamor de Ganis. And then Sir Launcelot began to draw his sword, for he felt himself so sore hurt, that he wend there to have had his death; and then he smote Sir Bleoberis such a buffet upon the helm that he fell down to the ground in a swoon; and in the same wise he served Sir Aliduke and Sir Galihud. And Sir Lavaine smote down Sir Bellangere, that was the son of Sir Alisander Lorphelin. And by that time Sir Bors was horsed; and then he came with Sir Ector and Sir Lionel, and they three smote with their swords upon Sir Launcelot's helmet; and when he felt their buffets, and his wound that was so grievous, then he thought to do what he might whiles he might endure; and then he gave Sir Bors such a buffet that he made him to bow his head passing low; and therewithal he razed off his helm, and might have slain him, and so pulled him down. And in the same manner of wise he served Sir Ector and Sir Lionel, for he might have slain them. But when he saw their visages his heart might not serve him thereto, but left them there lying. And then after he hurled in among the thickest press of them all, and did there marvellous deeds of arms that ever any man saw or heard speak of. And alway the good knight Sir Lavaine was with him; and there Sir Launcelot with his sword smote and pulled down moe [*more*] than thirty knights, and the most part were of the Round Table. And Sir Lavaine did full well that day, for he smote down ten knights of the Round Table.

"Ah mercy, Jesu," said Sir Gawaine unto King Arthur, "I marvel what knight he is with the red sleeve."

"Sir," said King Arthur, "he will be known or he depart."

And then the king let blow unto lodging, and the prize was given by heralds to the knight with the white shield and that bare the red sleeve. Then came the king with the hundred knights, the King of Northgalis, and the King of Northumberland, and Sir Galahalt the haut prince, and said unto Sir Launcelot, "Fair knight, God thee bless, for much have ye done this day for us, therefore we pray you that ye will come with us that ye may receive the honor and the prize, as ye have worshipfully deserved it."

"My fair lords," said Sir Launcelot, "wit ye well, if I have deserved thanks, I have sore bought it, for I am like never to escape with my life; therefore I pray you that ye will suffer me to depart where me liketh, for I am sore hurt; I had liever [*rather*] to rest me than to be lord of all the world." And therewith he groaned piteously, and rode a great gallop away from them until he came to a wood side, and when he saw that he was from the field nigh a mile, that he was sure he might not be seen, then said he with a high voice, "O gentle knight Sir Lavaine, help me that this truncheon were out of my side, for it sticketh so sore that it nigh slayeth me."

"O mine own lord," said Sir Lavaine, "I would fain do

that might please you, but I dread me sore, and I draw out the truncheon, that ye shall be in peril of death."

"I charge you," said Sir Launcelot, "as ye love me draw it out."

And therewithal he descended from his horse, and right so did Sir Lavaine, and forthwith Sir Lavaine drew the truncheon out of his side. And he gave a great shriek, and a marvellous grisly groan, and his blood brast [*burst*] out nigh a pint at once, that at last he sank down, and so swooned pale and deadly.

"Alas," said Sir Lavaine, "what shall I do?"

And then he turned Sir Launcelot into the wind, but so he lay there nigh half an hour as he had been dead. And so at the last Sir Launcelot cast up his eyes, and said, "O Lavaine, help me that I were on my horse, for here is fast by within this two mile a gentle hermit, that sometime was a full noble knight and a great lord of possessions; and for great goodness he hath taken him to wilful poverty, and forsaken many lands, and his name is Sir Baldwin of Brittany, and he is a full noble surgeon, and a good leech. Now let see, help me up that I were there. For ever my heart giveth me that I shall never die of my cousin-german's hands."

And then with great pain Sir Lavaine holp him upon his horse; and then they rode a great gallop together, and ever Sir Launcelot bled that it ran down to the earth. And so by fortune they came to that hermitage, which was under a wood, and a great cliff on the other side, and a fair water running under it. And then Sir Lavaine beat on the gate with the butt of his spear, and cried fast, "Let in, for Jesu's sake."

And there came a fair child to them, and asked them what they would?

"Fair son," said Sir Lavaine, "go and pray thy lord the hermit for God's sake to let in here a knight that is full sore wounded, and this day tell thy lord that I saw him do more deeds of arms than ever I heard say that any man did."

So the child went in lightly, and then he brought the hermit, the which was a passing good man. So when Sir Lavaine saw him, he prayed him for God's sake of succor.

"What knight is he?" said the hermit, "is he of the house of King Arthur or not?"

"I wot not," said Sir Lavaine, "what is he, nor what is his name, but well I wot I saw him do marvellously this day, as of deeds of arms."

"On whose party was he?" said the hermit.

"Sir," said Sir Lavaine, "he was this day against King Arthur, and there he won the prize of all the knights of the Round Table."

"I have seen the day," said the hermit, "I would have loved him the worse because he was against my lord King Arthur, for sometime I was one of the fellowship of the Round Table, but I thank God now I am otherwise disposed. But where is he? let me see him."

Then Sir Lavaine brought the hermit to him.

And when the hermit beheld him as he sat leaning upon his saddle-bow, ever bleeding piteously, [then] alway the knight hermit thought that he should know him, but he could not bring him to knowledge, because he was so pale for bleeding.

"What knight are ye," said the hermit, "and where were ye born?"

"Fair lord," said Sir Launcelot, "I am a stranger and a knight adventurous, that laboreth throughout many realms for to win worship."

Then the hermit advised him better [*looked more closely*], and saw by a wound on the cheek that he was Sir Launcelot.

"Alas!" said the hermit, "mine own lord, why hide ye your name from me? forsooth I ought to know you of right, for ye are the most noble knight of the world, for well I know you for Sir Launcelot."

"Sir," said he, "sith ye know me, help me, and [*if*] ye may, for Christ's sake, for I would be out of this pain at once, either to death or to life."

"Have ye no doubt," said the hermit, "ye shall live and fare right well."

And so the hermit called to him two of his servants; and so he and his servants bare him into the hermitage, and lightly unarmed him, and laid him in his bed. And then anon the hermit stanched the blood; and then he made him to drink good wine; so by that Sir Launcelot was right well refreshed, and came to himself again. For in those days it was not the guise of hermits as it now is in these days, for there were no hermits in those days but that they had been men of worship and of prowess, and those hermits held great households, and refreshed people that were in distress.

Now turn we unto King Arthur, and leave we Sir Launcelot in the hermitage.

So when the kings were come together on both parties, and the great feast should be holden, King Arthur asked the King of Northgalis and their fellowship where was that knight that bare the red sleeve: "Bring him before me, that he may have his laud and honor and the prize, as it is right."

Then spake Sir Galahalt the haut prince and the king with the hundred knights: "We suppose that knight is mischieved, and that he is never like to see you, nor none of us all, and that is the greatest pity that ever we wist of any knight."

"Alas," said King Arthur, "how may this be? is he so hurt? What is his name?"

"Truly," said they all, "we know not his name, nor from whence he came, nor whither he would."

"Alas," said the king, "these be to me the worst tidings that came to me this seven year: for I would not for all the lands I hold, to know and wit it were so that that noble knight were slain."

"Know ye him?" said they all.

"As for that," said King Arthur, "whether I know him or know him not, ye shall not know for me what man he is, but Almighty Jesu send me good tidings of him."

And so said they all.

"By my head," said Sir Gawaine, "if it be so, that the good knight be so sore hurt, it is great damage and pity to all this land, for he is one of the noblest knights that ever I saw in a field handle a spear or a sword; and if he may be found, I shall find him, for I am sure that he is not far from this town."

"Bear you well," said King Arthur, "that ye may find him, without that he be in such a plight that he may not bestir himself."

"Jesu defend," said Sir Gawaine, "but I shall know what he is and if I may find him."

Right so Sir Gawaine took a squire with him, and rode upon two hackneys all about Camelot within six or seven mile; but as he went so he came again, and could hear no word of him. Then within two days King Arthur and all the fellowship returned to London again; and so as they rode by the way, it happened Sir Gawaine at Astolat to lodge with Sir Bernard, whereas Sir Launcelot was lodged. And so as Sir Gawaine was in his chamber for to take his rest, Sir Bernard the old baron came to him, and also his fair daughter Elaine, for to cheer him, and to ask him what tidings he knew, and who did best at the tournament at Winchester.

"So God help me," said Sir Gawaine, "there were two knights which bare two white shields, but the one of them bare a red sleeve upon his head, and certainly he was one of the best knights that ever I saw joust in field; for I dare make it good," said Sir Gawaine, "that one knight with the red sleeve smote down forty valiant knights of the Round Table, and his fellow did right well and right worshipfully."

"Now blessed be God," said the fair maid of Astolat,

"that the good knight sped so well, for he is the man in the world the which I first loved, and truly he shall be the last man that ever after I shall love."

"Now, fair maid," said Sir Gawaine, "is that good knight your love?"

"Certainly," said she; "wit ye well he is my love."

"Then know ye his name?" said Sir Gawaine.

"Nay, truly," said the maid, "I know not his name, nor from whence he came; but to say that I love him, I promise God and you that I love him."

"How had ye knowledge of him first?" said Sir Gawaine.

Then she told him as ye have heard before, and how her father betook [*intrusted*] him her brother to do him service, and how her father lent him her brother Sir Tirre's shield, "and here with me he left his own shield."

"For what cause did he so?" said Sir Gawaine.

"For this cause," said the damsel, "for his shield was too well known among many noble knights."

"Ah, fair damsel," said Sir Gawaine, "please it you let me have a sight of that shield."

"Sir," said she, "it is in my chamber covered with a case, and if it will please you to come in with me ye shall see it."

"Not so," said Sir Bernard unto his daughter; "let send for it."

So when the shield was come, Sir Gawaine took off the case, and when he beheld that shield he knew anon that it was Sir Launcelot's shield, and his own arms.

"Ah Jesu, mercy!" said Sir Gawaine, "now is my heart more heavier than ever it was before."

"Why?" said the damsel Elaine.

"For I have a great cause," said Sir Gawaine; "is that knight that oweth that shield your love?"

"Yea, truly," said she, "my love he is, God would that I were his love."

"So God me speed," said Sir Gawaine, "fair damsel, ye love the most honorable knight of the world, and the man of most worship."

"So me thought ever," said the damsel, "for never or that time for no knight that ever I saw loved I never none erst."

"God grant," said Sir Gawaine, "that either of you may rejoice other, but that is in a great adventure; but truly," said Sir Gawaine unto the damsel, "ye may say ye have a fair grace, for why I have known that noble knight this fourteen years, and never or that day I or none other knight, I dare make it good, saw nor heard that ever he bare token or sign of no lady, gentlewoman, nor maid, at no jousts nor tournament; and therefore, fair maid," said Sir Gawaine, "ye are much beholden to give him thanks; but I dread me," said Sir Gawaine, "ye shall never see him in this world, and that is great pity as ever was of earthly knight."

"Alas!" said she, "how may this be? is he slain?"

"I say not so," said Sir Gawaine, "but wit ye well that he is grievously wounded by all manner of signs, and by men's sight more likelier to be dead than to be alive, and wit ye well he is the noble knight Sir Launcelot, for by his shield I know him."

"Alas!" said the fair maid Elaine, "how may it be? what was his hurt?"

"Truly," said Sir Gawaine, "the man in the world that loveth him best hurt him so; and I dare say, and that knight that hurt him knew the very certainty that he had hurt Sir Launcelot, it would be the most sorrow that ever came to his heart."

"Now, fair father," said then Elaine, "I require you give me leave to ride and to seek him, or else I wot well I shall go out of my mind, for I shall never stint [*stop*] till that I find him and my brother Sir Lavaine."

"Do as it liketh you," said her father, "for me right sore repenteth of the hurt of that noble knight."

So the king and all came to London, and there Sir Gawaine openly disclosed to all the court that it was Sir Launcelot that jousted best.

So as the fair maid Elaine came to Winchester, she sought there all about, and by fortune Sir Lavaine was ridden to play him and to enchafe his horse. And anon, as fair Elaine saw him, she knew him, and then she cried aloud unto him; and when he heard her, anon he came unto her. And then she asked her brother, "How fareth my lord Sir Launcelot?"

"Who told you, sister, that my lord's name was Sir Launcelot?"

Then she told him how Sir Gawaine by his shield knew him. So they rode together till they came unto the hermitage, and anon she alighted; so Sir Lavaine brought her unto Sir Launcelot. And when she saw him lie so sick and pale in his bed, she might not speak, but suddenly she fell unto the ground in a swoon, and there she lay a great while. And when she was relieved, she sighed and said, "My lord Sir Launcelot, alas! why go ye in this plight?" and then she swooned again. And then Sir Launcelot prayed Sir Lavaine to take her up and to bring her to him. And when she came to herself, Sir Launcelot kissed her, and said, "Fair maiden, why fare ye thus? Ye put me to pain; wherefore make ye no more such cheer for, and ye be come to comfort me, ye be right welcome, and of this little hurt that I have, I shall be right hastily whole, by the grace of God. But I marvel," said Sir Launcelot, "who told you my name."

Then the fair maiden told him all how Sir Gawaine was lodged with her father. "And there by your shield he discovered your name."

"Alas," said Sir Launcelot, "that me repenteth, that my name is known, for I am sure it will turn unto anger."

So this maiden, Elaine, never went from Sir Launcelot, but watched him day and night and did such attendance to him that there was never woman did more kindlier for man than she did. Then Sir Launcelot prayed Sir Lavaine to make espies in Winchester for Sir Bors if he came there, and told him by what token he should know him by a wound in his forehead.

"For well I am sure," said Sir Launcelot, "that Sir Bors will seek me, for he is the good knight that hurt me."

Now turn we unto Sir Bors de Ganis, that came to Winchester to seek after his cousin Sir Launcelot. And so when he came to Winchester, anon there were men that Sir Lavaine had made to lie in watch for such a man, and anon Sir Lavaine had warning thereof. And then Sir Lavaine came to Winchester and found Sir Bors. And so they departed, and came unto the hermitage where Sir Launcelot was; and when Sir Bors saw Sir Launcelot lie in his bed all pale and discolored, anon Sir Bors lost his countenance, and for kindness and for pity he might not speak, but wept full tenderly a great while. And then when he might speak, he said unto him thus, "Alas! that ever such a caitiff knight as I am should have power by unhappiness to hurt the most noblest knight of the world. Where I so shamefully set upon you and overcharged you, and where ye might have slain me, ye saved me, and so did not I: for I, and your blood, did to you our uttermost I marvel that my heart or my blood would serve me, wherefore, my lord Sir Launcelot, I ask your mercy."

"Fair cousin," said Sir Launcelot, "I would with pride have overcome you all, and there in my pride I was near slain, and that was in mine own default, for I might have given you warning of my being there. Therefore, fair cousin," said Sir Launcelot, "let this speech overpass, and all shall be welcome that God sendeth; and let us leave off this matter, and let us speak of some rejoicing; for this that is done may not be undone, and let us find a remedy how soon that I may be whole."

And so upon a day they took their horses and took Elaine la Blanche with them; and when they came to Astolat, there they were well lodged and had great cheer of Sir Bernard the old baron and of Sir Tirre his son. And so on the morrow, when Sir Launcelot should depart, fair Elaine brought her father with her and her two brethren Sir Tirre and Sir Lavaine, and thus she said:

"My lord Sir Launcelot, now I see that ye will depart; fair and courteous knight, have mercy upon me, and suffer me not to die for your love."

"What would ye that I did?" said Sir Launcelot.

"I would have you unto my husband," said the maid Elaine.

"Fair damsel, I thank you," said Sir Launcelot; "but certainly," said he, "I cast me never to be married."

"Alas!" said she, "then must I needs die for your love."

"Ye shall not," said Sir Launcelot, "for wit ye well, fair damsel, that I might have been married and I had would, but I never applied me to be married; but because, fair damsel, that ye will love me as ye say ye do, I will, for your good love and kindness, show you some goodness, and that is this: that wheresoever ye will set your heart upon some good knight that will wed you, I shall give you together a thousand pound yearly to you and to your heirs; thus much will I give you, fair maid, for your kindness, and alway while I live to be your own knight."

"Of all this," said the damsel, "I will none, for, but if you will wed me, wit you well, Sir Launcelot, my good days are done."

"Fair damsel," said Sir Launcelot, "of [this] ye must pardon me."

Then she shrieked shrilly, and fell down in a swoon; and

then women bare her into her chamber, and there she made overmuch sorrow. And then Sir Launcelot would depart; and there he asked Sir Lavaine what he would do.

"What should I do," said Sir Lavaine, "but follow you, but if ye drive me from you, or command me to go from you?"

Then came Sir Bernard to Sir Launcelot, and said to him, "I cannot see but that my daughter Elaine will die for your sake."

"I may not do withal," said Sir Launcelot, "for that me sore repenteth; for I report me to yourself that my proffer is fair, and me repenteth," said Sir Launcelot, "that she loveth me as she doth: I was never the causer of it, for I report me to your son, I early nor late proffered her bounty nor fair behests; and I am right heavy of her distress, for she is a full fair maiden, good, and gentle, and well taught."

"Father," said Sir Lavaine, "she doth as I do, for since I first saw my lord Sir Launcelot I could never depart from him, nor nought I will and I may follow him."

Then Sir Launcelot took his leave, and so they departed, and came unto Winchester. And when King Arthur wist that Sir Launcelot was come, whole and sound, the king made great joy of him, and so did Sir Gawaine, and all the knights of the Round Table except Sir Agravaine and Sir Mordred.

Now speak we of the fair maiden of Astolat, that made such sorrow day and night, that she never slept, eat, nor drank; and ever she made her complaint unto Sir Launcelot. So when she had thus endured a ten days, that she feebled so that she must needs pass out of this world, then she shrived her clean, and received her Creator [*took the Holy Communion*]. Then her ghostly father bade her leave such thoughts. Then she said, "Why should I leave such thoughts? am I not an earthly woman? and all the while the breath is in my body I may complain me, for my belief is I do none offence though I love an earthly man, and I take God to my record I never loved none but Sir Launcelot du Lake, nor never shall. For our sweet Saviour Jesu Christ," said the maiden, "I take thee to record I was never greater offender against thy laws but that I loved this noble knight Sir Launcelot out of all measure, and of myself, good Lord, I might not withstand the fervent love wherefore I have my death."

And then she called her father Sir Bernard, and her brother Sir Tirre, and heartily she prayed her father that her brother might write a letter like as she would indite it. And so her father granted her. And when the letter was written word by word like as she had devised, then she prayed her father that she might be watched until she were dead, "And while my body is whole, let this letter be put into my right hand, and my hand bound fast with the letter until that I be cold, and let me be put in a fair bed with all the richest clothes that I have about me, and so let my bed and all my rich clothes be laid with me in a chariot to the next place whereas the Thames is, and there let me be put in a barge, and but one man with me, such as ye trust, to steer me thither, and that my barge be covered with black samite over and over. Thus, father, I beseech you let me be done."

So her father granted her faithfully that all this thing should be done like as she had devised. Then her father and her brother made great dole, for, when this was done, anon she died. And so when she was dead, the corpse and the bed and all was led the next day unto the Thames, and there a man and the corpse and all were put in a barge on the Thames, and so the man steered the barge to Westminster, and there he rowed a great while to and fro or any man espied it.

So by fortune King Arthur and Queen Guenever were speaking together at a window; and so as they looked into the Thames, they espied the black barge, and had marvel what it might mean.

Then the king called Sir Kay, and showed him it.

"Sir," said Sir Kay, "wit ye well that there is some new tidings."

"Go ye thither," said the king unto Sir Kay, "and take with you Sir Brandiles and Sir Agravaine, and bring me ready word what is there."

Then these three knights departed, and came to the barge, and went in; and there they found the fairest corpse lying in a rich bed that ever they saw, and a poor man sitting in the end of the barge, and no word would he speak. So these three knights returned unto the king again, and told him what they had found.

"That fair corpse will I see," said King Arthur.

And then the king took the queen by the hand and went thither. Then the king made the barge to be holden fast;

and then the king and the queen went in, with certain knights with them, and there they saw a fair gentlewoman lying in a rich bed, covered unto her middle with many rich clothes, and all was of cloth of gold; and she lay as though she had smiled. Then the queen espied the letter in the right hand, and told the king thereof. Then the king took it in his hand, and said, "Now I am sure this letter will tell what she was, and why she is come hither."

Then the king and the queen went out of the barge; and the king commanded certain men to wait upon the barge; and so when the king was come within his chamber, he called many knights about him, and said that he would wit openly what was written within that letter. Then the king brake it, and made a clerk to read it; and this was the intent of the letter: "Most noble knight, Sir Launcelot, now hath death made us two at debate for your love; I was your lover, that men called the fair maid of Astolat; therefore unto all ladies I make my moan; yet pray for my soul, and bury me at the least, and offer ye my mass-penny. This is my last request. Pray for my soul, Sir Launcelot, as thou art a knight peerless."

This was all the substance in the letter. And when it was read, the king, the queen, and all the knights wept for pity of the doleful complaints. Then was Sir Launcelot sent for. And when he was come, King Arthur made the letter to be read to him; and when Sir Launcelot heard it word by word, he said, "My lord Arthur, wit ye well I am right heavy of the death of this fair damsel. God knoweth I was never causer of her death by my willing, and that will I report me to her own brother; here he is, Sir Lavaine. I will not say nay, but that she was both fair and good, and much I was beholden unto her, but she loved me out of measure."

"Ye might have showed her," said the queen, "some bounty and gentleness, that might have preserved her life."

"Madam," said Sir Launcelot, "she would none other way be answered, but that she would be my wife, and of [this] I would not grant her; but I proffered her, for her good love that she showed me, a thousand pound yearly to her and to her heirs, and to wed any manner knight that she could find best to love in her heart. For, madam," said Sir Launcelot, "I love not to be constrained to love; for love must arise of the heart, and not by no constraint."

"That is truth," said the king, and many knights: "love is free in himself, and never will be bounden; for where he is bounden he looseth himself."

Then said the king unto Sir Launcelot, "It will be your worship that ye oversee that she be buried worshipfully."

"Sir," said Sir Launcelot, "that shall be done as I can best devise."

And so many knights went thither to behold the fair dead maid. And on the morrow she was richly buried; and Sir Launcelot offered her mass-penny, and all the knights of the Round Table that were there at that time offered with Sir Launcelot. And then when all was done, the poor man went again with the barge.

BOOK VII

OF THE DEATH OF ARTHUR

BOOK VII

OF THE DEATH OF ARTHUR[1]

BUT ever in these days the enemies of Sir Launcelot and of Queen Guenever lay in wait to do them harm, in especial Sir Mordred and Sir Agravaine. So it befell that the queen was again appealed of treason and was condemned to the fire, while Sir Launcelot was away. But when Sir Launcelot heard thereof, he came suddenly with his kindred and attacked them that guarded about the queen whereas she stood at the stake about to be burnt.]

Then was there spurring and plucking up of horses and right so they came to the fire, and who that stood against them there they were slain, there might none withstand Sir Launcelot. And in this rashing and hurling, as Sir Launcelot thrang [*rushed*] here and there, it mishappened him to slay Sir Gaheris and the noble knight Sir Gareth, for they were unarmed and unaware; for Sir Launcelot smote Sir Gareth and Sir Gaheris upon the brain-pans, wherethrough they were both slain in the field; howbeit in very truth Sir Launcelot saw them not, and so were they found dead among the thickest of the press. Then when Sir Launcelot had thus done, and had put them to

[1] This event — the death of King Arthur — gave name to the whole series of stories with some of the old editors: Caxton, for example, the first printer of Sir Thomas Malory's book, issued it under the title "La Mort Darthur," that is, *la mort* (French, *the death*) *d'Arthur* (*of Arthur*).

flight all they that would withstand him, then he rode straight unto Queen Guenever, and made a kirtle and a gown to be cast upon her, and then he made her to be set behind him, and prayed her to be of good cheer. Wit you well that the queen was glad when she escaped from death; and then she thanked God and Sir Launcelot. And so he rode his way with the queen unto Joyous Gard, and there he kept her as a noble knight should do, and many great lords and some kings sent Sir Launcelot many good knights; and many noble knights drew unto Sir Launcelot. When this was known openly, that King Arthur and Sir Launcelot were at debate, many knights were glad of their debate, and many knights were sorry of their debate.

[Then King Arthur made moan out of measure, for he knew that the Round Table was foredoomed and that great wars must come of these matters.]

"And now I dare say," said the king, "that there was never Christian king that held such a fellowship together. Alas! that ever Sir Launcelot and I should be at debate. Ah! Agravaine, Agravaine," said the king, "Jesu forgive it thy soul! for thine evil will that thou and thy brother Sir Mordred had unto Sir Launcelot hath caused all this sorrow."

And ever among these complaints King Arthur wept and swooned. Then there came one unto Sir Gawaine, and told him how the queen was led away with Sir Launcelot, and nigh twenty-four knights slain.

"Truly," said the man, "your two brethren, Sir Gareth and Sir Gaheris, be slain."

"Who slew [them]?" said Sir Gawaine.

"Sir," said the man, "Sir Launcelot slew them both."

"Alas!" said Sir Gawaine, "now is all my joy gone."

And then he fell down in a swoon, and long he lay there as he had been dead; and then when he arose out of his swoon, he cried out so ruefully, and said, "Alas!" And right so Sir Gawaine ran unto the king, crying and weeping: "Oh! King Arthur mine uncle, my good brother Sir Gaheris is slain, and my brother Sir Gareth also, the which were two noble knights."

"I know not how it was," said the king, "but so it is said, Sir Launcelot slew them both in the thickest of the press, and knew them not."

[Then fell Sir Gawaine into bitter hatred against Sir Launcelot and never stinted therein till the day of his death.]

"My most gracious lord and my uncle," said Sir Gawaine, "wit you well that now I shall make you a promise, the which I shall hold by my knighthood, that from this day I shall never fail Sir Launcelot, until the one of us hath slain the other; and therefore I require you, my lord and my king, dress you unto the war, for wit you well I shall be revenged upon Sir Launcelot. For I promise unto God," said Sir Gawaine, "for the death of my brother Sir Gareth I shall seek Sir Launcelot throughout seven kings' realms but I shall slay him, or else he shall slay me."

"Ye shall not need to seek him so far," said the king, "for, as I hear say, Sir Launcelot will abide me and you in the Joyous Gard, and much people draweth unto him as I hear say."

Then came King Arthur and Sir Gawaine with an huge

host, and laid a siege about Joyous Gard, both at the town and at the castle; and there they made full strong war on both parties. But in no wise Sir Launcelot would not ride out nor go out of the castle of a long time, neither he would suffer none of his good knights to issue out, neither none of the town nor of the castle, until fifteen weeks were past.

So it befell on a day in harvest that Sir Launcelot looked over the walls and spake on high to King Arthur and Sir Gawaine: "My lords both, wit ye well it is in vain that ye labor at this siege, for here win ye no worship but dishonor."

"Come forth," said King Arthur unto Sir Launcelot, "and thou darest, and I promise thee I shall meet thee in the midst of the field."

"God defend me," said Sir Launcelot, "that ever I should encounter with the most noble king that made me knight."

"Fie upon thy fair language," said the king, "for wit you well, and trust it, I am thy mortal foe, and ever will to my death day, for thou hast slain my good knights and full noble men of my blood, that I shall never recover again: also thou hast dishonored my queen, and holden her many winters, and like a traitor taken her from me by force."

"My most noble lord and king," said Sir Launcelot, "ye may say what ye will, for ye wot well with yourself I will not strive, but there as ye say I have slain your good knights, I wot well that I have done so, and that me sore repenteth, but I was enforced to do battle with them, in saving of my life, or else I must have suffered them to have slain me. And as for my lady Queen Guenever, oft-times, my lord, ye have consented that she should be burnt and destroyed in your heat, and then it fortuned me to do battle for her, and or I departed from her adversary they confessed their untruth, and she full worshipfully excused. And at such times, my lord Arthur," said Sir Launcelot, "ye loved me, and thanked me when I saved your queen from the fire, and then ye promised me for ever to be my good lord, and now me thinketh ye reward me full ill. For sithence I have done battles for your queen in other quarrels than in mine own, me seemeth now I had more right to do battle for her in a right quarrel. And therefore my good and gracious lord," said Sir Launcelot, "take your queen unto your good grace, for she is both fair, true, and good."

"Fie on thee, false recreant knight," said Sir Gawaine, "I let thee to wit that my lord mine uncle King Arthur shall have his queen and thee maugre [*in spite of*] thy visage, and slay you both whereas it shall please him."

"It may well be," said Sir Launcelot; "but wit ye well, my lord Sir Gawaine, and me list to come out of this castle, ye should win me and the queen more harder than ever ye won a strong battle."

"Fie upon thy proud words," said Sir Gawaine, "as for my lady the queen, I will never say of her shame. Ah! thou false recreant knight," said Sir Gawaine, "what cause hadst thou to slay my good brother Sir Gareth, that loved thee more than all thy kin? Alas! thou madest him knight with thine own hands, why slewest thou him that loved thee so well?"

"For to excuse me," said Sir Launcelot, "it helpeth me not. But, by Jesu," said Sir Launcelot, "and by the faith that I owe unto the high order of knighthood, I should with as good a will have slain my nephew Sir Bors de Ganis at that time. But alas! that ever I was so unhappy," said Sir Launcelot, "that I had not seen Sir Gareth and Sir Gaheris."

"Thou liest, false recreant knight," said Sir Gawaine, "thou slewest him in despite of me, and therefore wit thou well that I shall make war unto thee all the while that I may live."

"That me sore repenteth," said Sir Launcelot, "for well I understand that it helpeth me not to seek for none accordment whiles that ye, Sir Gawaine, are so mischievously set; and if ye were not, I would not doubt to have the good grace of my lord King Arthur."

[Then Sir Launcelot's kinsmen besought him that he would go out and do battle for the slanders that Sir Gawaine and his knights did put upon him.]

"Alas!" said Sir Launcelot, "for to ride out of this castle and do battle, I am full loth to do it."

Then Sir Launcelot spake on high unto King Arthur and Sir Gawaine: "My lords, I require you and beseech you, sith I am thus required and conjured to ride into the field, that neither you, my lord King Arthur, nor you, Sir Gawaine, come not into the field."

"What shall we do then?" said Sir Gawaine; "is not this the king's quarrel with thee to fight? and it is my quarrel to fight with thee, Sir Launcelot, because of the death of my brother Sir Gareth."

"Then must I needs unto battle," said Sir Launcelot.

And always Sir Launcelot charged all his knights in any wise to save King Arthur and Sir Gawaine.

And on the morrow at underne [*nine o'clock*] King Arthur was ready in the field with three great hosts. And then Sir Launcelot's fellowship came out at three gates in full good array, and Sir Lionel came in the foremost battle, and Sir Launcelot came in the middle battle, and Sir Bors came out at the third gate.

[Then was there spurring and thrusting and many strokes.]

And ever King Arthur was nigh about Sir Launcelot to have slain him, and Sir Launcelot suffered him, and would not strike again. So Sir Bors encountered with King Arthur, and there with a spear Sir Bors smote him down; and so he alighted and drew his sword, and said to Sir Launcelot, "Shall I make an end of this war?" and that he meant to have slain King Arthur.

"Not so hardy," said Sir Launcelot, "upon pain of thy head, that thou touch him no more: for I will never see that most noble king, that made me knight, neither slain ne shamed."

And therewithal Sir Launcelot alighted off his horse, and took up the king and horsed him again, and said thus, "My lord Arthur, for God's love stint this strife."

And when King Arthur was again on horseback, he looked upon Sir Launcelot, and then the tears burst out of his eyes thinking on the great courtesy that was in Sir Launcelot more than in any other man. And therewith the king rode forth his way, and might no longer behold him, and said to himself, "Alas! that ever this war began." And then either parties of the battles withdrew them for to rest them, and buried the dead bodies, and to the wounded men they laid soft salves; and thus they endured that night till on the morrow. And on the morrow, by underne, they made them ready to do battle, and then Sir Bors led them forward. So on the morrow came Sir Gawaine as grim as any bear, with a spear in his hand. And when Sir Bors saw him [they rode furiously together and either gave the other a great wound]. Then Sir Launcelot rescued Sir Bors, and sent him into the castle; but neither Sir Gawaine nor Sir Bors died not of their wounds, for they were both holpen.

"Alas!" said Sir Launcelot, "I have no heart to fight against my lord King Arthur; for always me seemeth I do not as I ought to do."

"My lord," said Sir Palamides, "though ye spare them all this day, they will never con you thank; and if they may get you at any vantage, ye are but dead."

So then Sir Launcelot understood well that they told him truth, and then he strained himself more. And then within a little while, by even-song time, Sir Launcelot and his party better stood, for their horses went in blood past the fetlocks, there was so much people slain. And then, for pity, Sir Launcelot withheld his knights, and suffered King Arthur's party for to withdraw them one side. And then Sir Launcelot's party withdrew them into his castle, and either party buried the dead bodies and put salve unto the wounded men. So when Sir Gawaine was hurt, they on King Arthur's party were not so orgulous [*arrogantly eager*] as they were beforehand to do battle. Of this war was noised through all christendom, and at the last it was noised afore the Pope; and he considering the great goodness of King Arthur [let send letters to Sir Launcelot how that he should bring the queen back to King Arthur. And so, when King Arthur had carried his host back to his own country, came Sir Launcelot to King Arthur's court and gave him again his queen].

[And then while Sir Launcelot was at court he strove hard to be accorded with Sir Gawaine, for he bore no malice neither to Sir Gawaine nor to King Arthur. But Sir Gawaine would not be accorded, and ever let King Arthur from being accorded, that would right gladly have received again his old faithful knight, Sir Launcelot. And ever more bitter grew Sir Gawaine: till at the last he said to Sir Launcelot:] "In this land thou shalt not abide past fifteen days, such warning I give thee. So the king and we were consented and accorded or thou camest hither; and else," said Sir Gawaine, "wit thou well that thou shouldst not have come hither, but if it were maugre thy head. And if that it were not for the Pope's commandment, I should do battle with my body against thy body, and prove it unto thee that thou hast been false unto mine uncle King Arthur and to me both, and that shall I prove upon thy body when thou art departed from hence, wheresoever I find thee."

Then Sir Launcelot sighed, and therewith the tears fell on his cheeks, and then he said these words: "Alas! most noble Christian realm, whom I have loved above all other realms, and in thee have I gotten a great part of my worship, and now I shall depart in this wise. Truly me repenteth that ever I came into this realm, that should be thus shamefully banished undeserved and causeless. But fortune is so variable and the wheel so mutable, there is no constant abiding, and that may be proved by many old chronicles of noble Hector, and Troilus, and Alisander the mighty conqueror, and many other moe [*more*]; when they were most in their royalty, they alighted lowest. And so fareth by me," said Sir Launcelot, "for in this realm I have had worship, and by me and mine all the whole Round Table hath been increased, more in worship by me and my blood than by any other. And therefore wit you well, Sir Gawaine, I may live as well upon my lands as any knight that is here. And if ye, my most renowned king, will come upon my lands with your nephew Sir Gawaine for to war upon me, I must endure you as well as I may; but as for you Sir Gawaine, if that ye come there, I pray you charge me not with treason nor felony, for, and ye do, I must answer you."

"Do thou thy best," said Sir Gawaine, "therefore hie thee fast that thou were gone, and wit thou well we shall soon come after, and break the strongest castle that thou hast upon thy head."

"That shall not need," said Sir Launcelot, "for and I were as orgulous set as ye are, wit ye well I should meet with you in midst of the field."

"Make thou no more language," said Sir Gawaine, "but deliver the queen from thee, and pike thee lightly out of this court."

And then Sir Launcelot said unto Queen Guenever, in hearing of the king and them all, "Madam, now I must depart from you and this noble fellowship for ever; and sithen it is so, I beseech you to pray for me, and say me well, and if ye be hard bestead by any false tongues, lightly, my lady, let send me word, and if any knight's hands may deliver you by battle, I shall deliver you."

And therewithal Sir Launcelot kissed the queen, and then he said all openly, "Now let see what he be in this place, that dare say the queen is not true unto my lord Arthur: let see who will speak, and he dare speak."

And therewith he brought the queen to the king, and then Sir Launcelot took his leave and departed; and there was neither king, duke ne earl, baron ne knight, lady nor gentlewoman, but all they wept as people out of their mind, except Sir Gawaine; and when the noble Sir Launcelot took his horse, to ride out of Carlisle, there was sobbing and weeping for pure dole of his departing; and so he took his way unto Joyous Gard. And afterwards he called it Dolorous Gard. And thus Sir Launcelot departed from the court for ever.

So leave we Sir Launcelot in his lands, and his noble knights with him, and return we again unto King Arthur and Sir Gawaine, that made a great host ready, to the number of threescore thousand, and all thing was ready for their shipping to pass over the sea. And so they shipped at Cardiff. And there King Arthur made Sir Mordred chief ruler of all England; and also he put Queen Guenever under his governance. And so King Arthur passed over the sea, and landed upon Sir Launcelot's land, and there he burnt and wasted, through the vengeance of Sir Gawaine, all that they might overrun.

Then spake King Bagdemagus unto Sir Launcelot, "Sir, your courtesy will shend [*ruin*] us all, and your courtesy hath caused all this sorrow; for and they thus override our lands, they shall by process of time bring us all to nought, whilst we thus hide us in holes."

Then said the good knight Sir Galihud to Sir Launcelot, "Sir, here be knights come of kings' blood, that will not long droop and they were without the walls; therefore give us leave, as we are knights, to meet them in the field, and we shall slay them, that they shall curse the time that ever they came into this country."

Then spake the seven brethren of North Wales, and they were seven noble knights as a man might seek in seven kings' lands, or he might find such seven knights, then they spake all with one voice, "Sir Launcelot, for Christ's sake let us ride out with Sir Galihud, for we been never wont to cower in castles nor in towns."

Then speake Sir Launcelot, which was master and governor of them all, "My fair lords, howbeit we will as at this time keep our strong walls, and I shall send a messenger unto my lord King Arthur, desiring him to take a treaty; for better is peace than always war."

So Sir Launcelot sent forth a damsel and a dwarf with her, requiring King Arthur to leave his war upon his lands. And so she started upon a palfrey, and the dwarf ran by her side.

[But Sir Gawaine would have no peace nor treaties, and sent vile messages back to Sir Launcelot, and presently led the host to Sir Launcelot's castle.]

So thus they endured well half a year, and much slaughter of people there was on both parties. Then it befell upon a day that Sir Gawaine came before the gates armed at all pieces upon a great courser, with a great spear in his hand; and then he cried with a loud voice, "Where art thou now, thou false traitor Sir Launcelot? why dost thou hide thyself within holes and walls like a coward? look out now, thou false traitor knight, and here I shall revenge upon thy body the death of my three brethren."

All this language heard Sir Launcelot, and his kin every deal; and then his knights drew about him, and they said all at once unto Sir Launcelot, "Sir Launcelot, now ye must defend you like a knight, or else ye be shamed for ever; for now ye be called upon treason, it is time for you to stir, for ye have slept over long, and suffered over much."

"So God me help," said Sir Launcelot, "I am right heavy of Sir Gawaine's words, for now he chargeth me with a great charge; and therefore I wot it as well as ye that I must defend me, or else to be a recreant knight."

Then Sir Launcelot commanded to saddle his strongest horse, and bade fetch his armor, and bring all unto the gate of the tower. And then Sir Launcelot spake on high unto King Arthur, and said, "My lord and noble king which made me knight, wit you well that I am right heavy for your sake, that ye thus sue upon me, and always I forbare you; for, and I would have been revengeable, I might have met you in the midst of the field, and there to have made your boldest knights full tame; and now I have forborne you half a year, and have suffered you and Sir Gawaine to do what ye would, and now I may endure it no longer; now must I needs defend myself, in so much as Sir Gawaine hath appealed me of treason, the which is greatly against my will, that ever I should fight against any of your blood; but now I may not forsake it, I am driven thereto as a beast to a bay."

And so the covenant was made, there should no man nigh them, nor deal with them, till the one were dead or yielden.

Then Sir Gawaine and Sir Launcelot departed a great way in sunder, and then they came together with all their horses' might as they might run, and either smote other in midst of their shields, but the knights were so strong, and their spears so big, that their horses might not endure their buffets, and so the horses fell to the earth. And then they avoided their horses, and dressed their shields afore them. Then they stood together, and gave many sad strokes on divers places of their bodies, that the blood brast out on many sides and places. Then had Sir Gawaine such a grace and gift that an holy man had given to him, that every day in the year, from underne till high noon, his might increased those three hours as much as thrice his strength, and that caused Sir Gawaine to win great honor. [And] there were but few knights that time living that knew this advantage that Sir Gawaine had, but King Arthur all only. Thus Sir Launcelot fought with Sir Gawaine, and when Sir Launcelot felt his might evermore increase, Sir Launcelot wondered, and dread him sore to be shamed. For Sir Launcelot wend, when he felt Sir Gawaine double his strength, that he had been a fiend and no earthly man, wherefore Sir Launcelot traced and traversed, and covered himself with his shield, and kept his might during three hours: and that while Sir Gawaine gave him many sad brunts and many sad strokes, that all the knights that beheld Sir Launcelot marvelled how he might endure him, but full little understood they that travail that Sir Launcelot had for to endure him. And then when it was past noon, Sir Gawaine had no more but his own might. Then Sir Launcelot felt him so come down; then he stretched him up, and stood near Sir Gawaine, and said thus, "My lord Sir Gawaine, now I feel ye have done, now my lord Sir Gawaine, I must do my part, for many great and grievous strokes I have endured you this day with great pain."

Then Sir Launcelot doubled his strokes, and gave Sir Gawaine such a buffet on the helmet, that he fell down on his side, and Sir Launcelot withdrew him from him.

"Why withdrawest thou thee?" said Sir Gawaine; "now turn again, false traitor knight, and slay me; for and thou leave me thus, when I am whole I shall do battle with thee again."

"Sir, I shall endure you by the grace of God," said Sir Launcelot; "but wit you well, Sir Gawaine, I will never smite a felled knight."

And so Sir Launcelot went into the city, and Sir Gawaine was borne into one of King Arthur's pavilions; and anon there was leeches brought to him, which searched his wound, and salved it with soft ointments. And then Sir Launcelot said, "Now have good day, my lord the king, for wit ye well ye shall win no worship at these walls; and if I would bring out my knights, there should many a man die. Therefore, my lord King Arthur, remember you of old kindness, and howsoever I fare, Jesu be your guide in all places."

"Alas," said the king, "that ever this unhappy war was begun, for ever Sir Launcelot forbeareth me in all places, and in likewise my kin, and that is seen well this day by my nephew Sir Gawaine."

Then King Arthur fell sick for sorrow of Sir Gawaine, that he was sore hurt, and because of the war betwixt him and Sir Launcelot. So then they on King Arthur's party kept the siege with little war and small force, and they within kept their walls, and defended them when need was. Thus Sir Gawaine lay sick about three weeks in his tents, with all manner of leech-craft that might be had; and as soon as Sir Gawaine might go and ride, he armed him at all points, and started upon a courser, and gat a spear in his hand, and so he came riding afore the chief gate of Benwick, and there he cried on high, "Where art thou, Sir Launcelot? come forth, thou false traitor knight, and recreant, for I am here, Sir Gawaine, will prove this that I say on thee."

All this language Sir Launcelot heard, and then he said thus, "Sir Gawaine, me repenteth of your foul saying, that ye will not cease of your language, for wit ye well, Sir Gawaine, I know your might, and all that ye may do, and well ye wot, Sir Gawaine, ye may not greatly hurt me."

"Come down, traitor knight," said he, "and make it good the contrary with thy hands; for it mishapped me the last battle to be hurt of thy hands, therefore wit thou well, that I am come this day to make amends, for I ween this day to lay thee as low as thou laidest me."

"Defend me," said Sir Launcelot, "that ever I be so far in your danger as ye have been in mine, for then my days were done. But Sir Gawaine," said Sir Launcelot, "ye shall not think that I tarry long; but sithence that ye so unknightly call me of treason, ye shall have both your hands full of me."

And then Sir Launcelot armed him at all points, and mounted upon his horse, and gat him a great spear in his hand, and rode out at the gate. And both the hosts were assembled of them without and of them within, and stood in array full manly; and both parties were charged for to hold them still to see and behold the battle of these two noble knights. And then they laid their spears in their rests, and they ran together as thunder. And Sir Gawaine brake his spear upon Sir Launcelot in an hundred pieces unto his hand. And Sir Launcelot smote him with a greater might, that Sir Gawaine's horse's feet raised, and so the horse and he fell to the earth. Then Sir Gawaine full quickly avoided his horse, and put his shield before him, and eagerly drew his sword, and bade Sir Launcelot "alight, traitor knight! for though this mare's son hath failed me, wit thou well that a king's son and a queen's son shall not fail thee."

Then Sir Launcelot avoided his horse, and dressed his shield before him, and drew his sword. And so they stood together and gave many sad strokes, that all men on both parties had thereof passing great wonder. But when Sir Launcelot felt Sir Gawaine's might so marvellously increased, he then withheld his courage and his wind, and kept himself wondrous covert of his might, and under his shield he traced and traversed here and there for to break Sir Gawaine's strokes and his courage. And Sir Gawaine enforced him with all his might and power to destroy Sir Launcelot, for ever as Sir Gawaine's might increased, right so increased his wind and his evil will. Thus Sir Gawaine did great pain unto Sir Launcelot three hours continually, that Sir Launcelot had great pain to defend himself. And after that the three hours were passed, then Sir Launcelot felt verily that Sir Gawaine was come to his own proper might and strength, and that his great power was done. Then Sir Launcelot said unto Sir Gawaine, "Now have I well proved you twice, that ye are a full dangerous knight, and a wonderful man of your might, and many wonderful deeds have you done in your days: for by your might increasing you have deceived many a full noble and valiant knight; and now I feel that ye have done your mighty deeds. Now wit you well I must do my deeds."

And then Sir Launcelot stood near Sir Gawaine, and then Sir Launcelot doubled his strokes, and Sir Gawaine defended him mightily. But nevertheless Sir Launcelot smote such a stroke upon Sir Gawaine's helm, and upon the old wound, that Sir Gawaine sank down upon his one side in a swoon. And anon as he was awake, he waved and foined at Sir Launcelot as he lay, and said, "Traitor knight, wit thou well I am not yet slain: come thou near me, and perform this battle unto the uttermost."

"I will no more do than I have done," said Sir Launcelot; "for when I see you on foot I will do battle upon you all the while I see you stand on your feet; but for to smite a wounded man that may not stand, God defend me from such a shame."

And then he turned him and went his way towards the city, and Sir Gawaine evermore calling him traitor knight, and said, "Wit thou well, Sir Launcelot, when I am whole, I shall do battle with thee again; for I shall never leave thee till that one of us be slain."

Thus as this siege endured, and as Sir Gawaine lay sick near a month, and when he was well recovered and ready within three days to do battle again with Sir Launcelot, right so came tidings unto King Arthur from England, that made King Arthur and all his host to remove.

As Sir Mordred was ruler of all England, he caused letters to be made as though they came from beyond the sea, and the letters specified that King Arthur was slain in battle with Sir Launcelot; wherefore Sir Mordred made a parliament, and called the lords together, and there he made them to choose him king. And so he was crowned at Canterbury, and held a feast there fifteen days. And afterwards he drew him to Winchester, and there he took Queen Guenever, and said plainly that he would wed her which was his uncle's wife; and so he made ready for the feast, and a day prefixed that they should be wedded. Wherefore Queen Guenever was passing heavy; but she durst not discover her heart, but spake fair and agreed to Sir Mordred's will. Then she desired of Sir Mordred for to go to London for to buy all manner thing that belonged unto the wedding; and because of her fair speech, Sir Mordred trusted her well enough, and gave her leave to go. And when she came to London, she took the Tower of London, and suddenly in all haste possible she stuffed it with all manner of victual and well filled it with men, and so kept it. Then when Sir Mordred wist how he was beguiled, he was passing wroth out of measure. And, a short tale for to make, he went and laid a mighty siege about the Tower of London, and made many great assaults thereat, and threw many great engines unto them, and shot great guns. But all might not prevail Sir Mordred, for Queen Guenever would never for fair speech nor for foul trust to come in his hands again. And then came the bishop of Canterbury, the which was a noble clerk and an holy man, and thus he said to Sir Mordred: "Sir, what will ye do, will ye first displease God, and sithen shame yourself and all knighthood? Is not King Arthur your uncle, no further but your mother's brother? Leave this opinion, or else I shall curse you with book, and bell, and candle."

"Do thou thy worst," said Sir Mordred, "wit thou well I shall defy thee."

"Sir," said the bishop, "and wit you well I shall not fear me to do that me ought to do. Also where ye noise where my lord Arthur is slain, and that is not so, and therefore ye will make a foul work in this land."

"Peace, thou false priest," said Sir Mordred, "for, and thou chafe me any more, I shall make strike off thy head."

So the bishop departed, and did the curse in the most orgulous wise that might be done. And then Sir Mordred sought the bishop of Canterbury for to have slain him. Then the bishop fled, and took part of his goods with him, and went nigh unto Glastonbury, and there he was as priest hermit in a chapel, and lived in poverty and in holy prayers: for well he understood that mischievous war was at hand. Then Sir Mordred sought on Queen Guenever by letters and by fair means and foul means, for to have her to come out of the Tower of London, but all this availed not, for she answered him shortly, openly and privily, that she had liever slay herself than to be married with him. Then came word to Sir Mordred that King Arthur had raised the siege from Sir Launcelot, and that he was coming homeward with a great host, for to be avenged upon Sir Mordred. Wherefore Sir Mordred made to write letters unto all the barony of this land, and much people drew unto him; for then was the common voice among them, that with King Arthur was none other life but war and strife, and with Sir Mordred was great joy and bliss. Thus was King Arthur depraved and evil said of, and many there were that King Arthur had made up of nought, and had given them lands, might not say of him then a good word.

Lo, we all Englishmen see what a mischief here was; for he that was the noblest king and knight of the world, and most loved the fellowship of noble knights and men of worship, and by him they were all upholden, now might not we

Englishmen hold us content with him. Lo, this was the old custom and usage of this land. And also men say that we of this land have not yet lost nor forgotten the custom and usage. Alas! alas! this is a great default of us Englishmen, for there may nothing please us no term. And so fared the people at that time. For they were better pleased with Sir Mordred than they were with King Arthur, and much people drew unto Sir Mordred, and said they would abide with him for better and for worse. And so Sir Mordred drew with a great host towards Dover, for there he heard say that King Arthur would arrive. And the most part of all England held with Sir Mordred, the people were so new-fangled.

And so, as Sir Mordred was at Dover with his host, there came King Arthur with a great navy of ships, galleys, and carracks. And there was Sir Mordred ready awaiting upon his landing, to let [*hinder*] his own [uncle] to land upon the land that he was king over. Then there was launching of great boats and small, and full of noble men of arms, and there was much slaughter of gentle knights, and many a full bold baron was laid full low on both parties. But King Arthur was so courageous, that there might no manner of knights let him to land, and his knights fiercely followed him. And so they landed, maugre Sir Mordred and all his power, and put Sir Mordred aback, that he fled and all his people. So when this battle was done, King Arthur let bury his people that were dead, and then was the noble knight Sir Gawaine found in a great boat lying more than half dead. When Sir Arthur wist that Sir Gawaine was laid so low, he went unto him, and there the king made sorrow out of measure, and took Sir Gawaine in his arms, and thrice he there swooned. And when he awaked he said, "Alas, Sir Gawaine, my sister's son, here now thou liest, the man in the world that I loved most, and now is my joy gone: for now, my nephew Sir Gawaine, I will discover me unto your person; in Sir Launcelot and you I most had my joy, and mine affiance, and now have I lost my joy of you both, wherefore all mine earthly joy is gone from me."

"Mine uncle King Arthur," said Sir Gawaine, "wit you well, my death day is come, and all is through mine own hastiness and wilfulness, for I am smitten upon the old wound the which Sir Launcelot gave me, on the which I feel well I must die, and had Sir Launcelot been with you as he was, this unhappy war had never begun, and of all this am I causer, for Sir Launcelot and his blood through their prowess held all your cankered enemies in subjection and danger: and now," said Sir Gawaine, "ye shall miss Sir Launcelot. But, alas, I would not accord with him, and therefore," said Sir Gawaine, "I pray you, fair uncle, that I may have paper, pen, and ink, that I may write unto Sir Launcelot a letter with mine own hands."

And when paper and ink was brought, Sir Gawaine was set up weakly by King Arthur, for he had been shriven a little before; and he wrote thus unto Sir Launcelot: "Flower of all noble knights that ever I heard of or saw in my days; I, Sir Gawaine, King Lot's son of Orkney, sister's son unto the noble King Arthur, send unto thee greeting, and let thee have knowledge, that the tenth day of May I was smitten upon the old wound which thou gavest me before the city of Benwick, and through the same wound that thou gavest me I am come unto my death day, and I will that all the world wit that I Sir Gawaine, knight of the Round Table, sought my death, and not through thy deserving, but it was mine own seeking; wherefore I beseech thee, Sir Launcelot, for to return again unto this realm and see my tomb, and pray some prayer more or less for my soul. Also, Sir Launcelot, for all the love that ever was between us, make no tarrying, but come over the sea in all the haste that thou mayest with thy noble knights, and rescue that noble king that made thee knight, that is my lord and uncle King Arthur, for he is full straitly bestood [*sore beset*] with a false traitor, which is my half brother Sir Mordred, and he hath let crown himself king, and he would have wedded my lady Queen Guenever, and so had he done, if she had not put herself in the Tower of London. And so the tenth day of May last past, my lord and uncle King Arthur and we all landed upon them at Dover, and there we put that false traitor Sir Mordred to flight. And there it misfortuned me for to be stricken upon thy stroke. And at the date of this letter was written but two hours and half before my death, written with mine own hand, and so subscribed with part of my heart's blood. And I require thee, most famous knight of all the world, that thou wilt see my tomb."

And then Sir Gawaine wept, and King Arthur wept. And the king made Sir Gawaine to receive his Saviour. And then Sir Gawaine prayed the king to send for Sir Launcelot, and to cherish him above all other knights. And so at the hour of noon, Sir Gawaine yielded up the spirit. And then the king let inter him in a chapel within Dover Castle; and there yet all men may see the skull of him, and the same wound is seen that Sir Launcelot gave him in battle. Then was it told King Arthur that Sir Mordred had pitched a new field upon Barendoune [*Barham Down*]. And upon the morn the king rode thither to him, and there was a great battle betwixt them, and much people were slain on both parties. But at the last King Arthur's party stood best, and Sir Mordred and his party fled into Canterbury.

And then the king let search all the towns for his knights that were slain, and interred them; and salved them with soft salves that so sore were wounded. Then much people drew unto King Arthur. And then they said that Sir Mordred warred upon King Arthur wrongfully. And then King Arthur drew him with his host down by the sea side, westward unto Salisbury, and there was a day assigned between King Arthur and Sir Mordred, that they should meet upon a down beside Salisbury, and not far from the sea side, and this day was assigned on a Monday after Trinity Sunday, whereof King Arthur was passing glad, that he might be avenged upon Sir Mordred. Then Sir Mordred raised much people about London, for they of Kent, Southsex [*Sussex*], and Southery [*Surrey*], Estsex [*Essex*], and Southfolk [*Suffolk*], and of Northfolk [*Norfolk*], held the most party with Sir Mordred, and many a full noble knight drew unto Sir Mordred and to the king; but they that loved Sir Launcelot drew unto Sir Mordred.

So upon Trinity Sunday at night King Arthur dreamed a wonderful dream, and that was this, that him seemed he sat in a chair, and the chair was fast unto a wheel, and thereupon sat King Arthur in the richest cloth of gold that might be made. And the king thought there was under him, far from him, a hideous and a deep black water, and therein was all manner of serpents and worms, and wild beasts foul and horrible; and suddenly the king thought that the wheel turned upside down, and that he fell among the serpents and wild beasts, and every beast took him by a limb; and then the king cried, as he lay in his bed and slept, "Help!"

And then knights, squires, and yeomen awaked the king; and then he was so amazed that he wist not where he was; and then he fell in a slumbering again, not sleeping nor thoroughly waking. So King Arthur thought that there came Sir Gawaine unto him verily, with a number of fair ladies with him; and so when King Arthur saw him, he said, "Welcome, my sister's son, I wend thou hadst been dead, and now I see thee alive, much am I beholden unto almighty Jesu; oh, fair nephew and my sister's son, what be these ladies that be come hither with you?"

"Sir," said Sir Gawaine, "all these be the ladies for whom I have fought when I was man living: and all these are those that I did battle for in righteous quarrel. And God hath given them that grace at their great prayer, because I did battle for them, that they should bring me hither unto you for to warn you of your death; for and ye fight as to-morrow with Sir Mordred, as ye both have assigned, doubt ye not ye must be slain, and the most part of your people on both parties. For within a month shall come Sir Launcelot, with all his noble knights, and rescue you worshipfully, and slay Sir Mordred and all that ever will hold with him." Then Sir Gawaine and all the ladies vanished.

So then were they condescended that King Arthur and Sir Mordred should meet between both their hosts, and every each of them should bring fourteen persons. And they came with this word unto King Arthur, and then said he, "I am glad that this is done." And so he went into the fields; and when King Arthur should depart, he warned all his host that, and they saw any sword drawn, "look that ye come on fiercely, and slay that traitor Sir Mordred, for I in no wise trust him."

In like wise Sir Mordred did warn his host that "if ye see any manner of sword drawn, look that ye come on fiercely, and so slay all that ever standeth before you, for in no wise I will not trust for this treatise, for I know well that my [uncle] will be avenged upon me."

And so they met as their appointment was, and were agreed and accorded thoroughly, and wine was fet [*fetched*] and they drank. Right so came an adder out of a little heath bush, and it stung a knight on the foot; and when the knight felt him stung, he looked down and saw the adder, and then he drew his sword to slay the adder, and thought of none other harm. And when the hosts on both parties saw that sword drawn, they blew trumpets and horns, and shouted grimly. And so both hosts dressed them together, and King Arthur took his horse, and said, "Alas, this unhappy day!" and so rode he to his party. And so Sir Mordred did in like wise; and never was there seen a more dolefuller battle in no Christian land, for there was but rashing and riding, foining and striking, and many a grim word was there spoken either to other, and many a deadly stroke. And ever they fought still till it was nigh night, and by that time was there an hundred thousand laid dead upon the down. Then was King Arthur wroth out of measure, when he saw his people so slain from him. Then the king looked about him, and then was he ware that of all his host, and of all his good knights, were left no more alive but two knights, that was Sir Lucan the Butler and Sir Bedivere his brother, and they were right sore wounded.

"Jesu mercy!" said King Arthur, "where are all my noble knights become? Alas! that ever I should see this doleful day; for now," said King Arthur, "I am come unto mine end; but would to God that I wist where that traitor Sir Mordred is, which hath caused all this mischief."

Then was King Arthur ware where Sir Mordred leaned upon his sword among a great heap of dead men.

"Now give me my spear," said King Arthur to Sir Lucan, "for yonder I have espied the traitor which hath wrought all this woe."

"Sir, let him be," said Sir Lucan, "for he is unhappy; and if ye pass this unhappy day ye shall be right well revenged upon him. My good lord, remember well your dream that ye had this night, and what the spirit of Sir Gawaine told you this night; yet God of his great goodness hath preserved you hitherto, therefore, for God's sake, my lord, leave off by this, for blessed be God ye have won the field; for here we be three on live, and with Sir Mordred is none alive. And if ye leave off now, this wicked day of destiny is done."

"Betide me death, betide me life," said the king, "now I see him yonder alone he shall never escape my hands, for at a better vantage shall I never have him."

"God speed you well," said Sir Bedivere.

Then the king gat his spear in both his hands, and ran towards Sir Mordred, crying, "Traitor, now is thy death day come."

And when Sir Mordred heard King Arthur, he ran unto him with his sword drawn in his hand. And then King Arthur smote Sir Mordred under the shield with a foin of his spear throughout the body more than a fathom. And when Sir Mordred felt that he had his death's wound, he thrust himself, with the might that he had, up to the bur of King Arthur's spear. And right so he smote [the king] with his sword holden in both his hands, on the side of the head, that the sword pierced the helmet and the brain-pan. And therewithal Sir Mordred fell stark dead to the earth. And the noble Arthur fell in a swoon to the earth, and there he swooned ofttimes. And Sir Lucan the Butler and Sir Bedivere ofttimes heaved him up, and so weakly they led him betwixt them both to a little chapel not far from the sea side. And when the king was there, he thought him well eased. Then heard they people cry in the field.

"Now go thou, Sir Lucan," said the king, "and do me to wit what betokens that noise in the field."

So Sir Lucan departed, and he was grievously wounded in many places. And so as he went, he saw and hearkened by the moonlight, how the pillers [*pillagers*] and robbers were come into the field to pill and to rob many a full noble knight of broaches and beads, of many a good ring, and of many a rich jewel; and who that were not dead all out [*entirely*], there they slew them for their harness and their riches. When Sir Lucan understood this work, he came to the king as soon as he might, and told him all what he had heard and seen.

"Therefore by mine advice," said Sir Lucan, "it is best that we bring you to some town."

"I would it were so," said the king.

"But I may not stand. Ah, Sir Launcelot," said King Arthur, "this day have I sore missed thee. Alas, that ever I was against thee, for now have I my death, whereof Sir Gawaine me warned in my dream."

Then Sir Lucan took up the king the one part, and Sir Bedivere the other part, and in the lifting, the king swooned, and Sir Lucan fell in a swoon with the lift, and therewith the noble knight's heart brast. And when King Arthur came to himself again, he beheld Sir Lucan how he lay foaming at the mouth.

"Alas," said the king, "this is unto me a full heavy sight to see this noble duke so die for my sake, for he would have holpen me, that had more need of help than I. Alas, he would not complain him, his heart was so set to help me. Now Jesu have mercy upon his soul."

Then Sir Bedivere wept for the death of his brother.

"Leave this mourning and weeping," said the king, "for all this will not avail me: for, wit thou well, and I might live myself the death of Sir Lucan would grieve me evermore; but my time hieth fast," said the king. "Therefore," said King Arthur, "take thou Excalibur, my good sword, and go with it to yonder water side, and when thou comest there, I charge thee throw my sword in that water, and come again, and tell me what thou shalt see there."

"My lord," said Sir Bedivere, "your command shall be done, and lightly bring you word again."

And so Sir Bedivere departed; and by the way he beheld that noble sword where the pommel and the haft were all of precious stones, and then he said to himself, "If I throw this rich sword into the water, thereof shall never come good, but harm and loss."

And then Sir Bedivere hid Excalibur under a tree, and as soon as he might he came again unto King Arthur, and said he had been at the water, and had thrown the sword into the water.

"What sawest thou there?" said the king.

"Sir," said he, "I saw nothing but waves and wind."

"That is untruly said of thee," said King Arthur, "therefore go thou lightly and do my command, as thou art to me lief [*beloved*] and dear; spare not, but throw it in."

Then Sir Bedivere returned again, and took the sword in his hand; and then him thought it sin and shame to throw away that noble sword. And so he hid the sword, and returned again and told to the king that he had been at the water and done his command.

"What saw ye there?" said the king.

"Sir," said he, "I saw nothing but the water wap and waves wane." [1]

"Ah, traitor untrue!" said King Arthur, "now hast thou betrayed me two times. Who would have wend that thou that hast been unto me so self [*loved like myself*] and dear, and thou art named a noble knight, and wouldest betray me for the rich sword? But now go again lightly, for thy long tarrying putteth me in great jeopardy of my life, for I have taken cold; and but if thou do as I command thee, and if ever I may see thee, I shall slay thee with my own hands, for thou wouldst for my rich sword see me dead."

Then Sir Bedivere departed, and went to the sword, and lightly took it up, and went to the water's side; and there he bound the girdle about the hilts, and then he threw the sword into the water as far as he might; and there came an arm and an hand above the water, and met it and caught it, and so shook it thrice and brandished.

And then the hand vanished away with the sword in the water. So Sir Bedivere came again to the king, and told him what he had seen.

"Alas!" said the king, "help me from hence, for I dread me I have tarried over long."

Then Sir Bedivere took King Arthur upon his back, and so went with him to the water's side. And when they were

[1] "Water wap and waves wane," *water lap and waves ebb.*

at the water's side, even fast by the bank hoved a little barge, with many fair ladies in it, and among them all was a queen, and all they had black hoods, and they wept and shrieked when they saw King Arthur.

"Now put me into the barge," said the king; and so he did softly; and there received him three queens with great mourning, and so these three queens [whereof one was King Arthur's sister Morgan le Fay, the other was the queen of Northgalis, and the third was the queen of the waste lands] set them down, and in one of their laps King Arthur laid his head. And then that queen said, "Ah! dear brother, why have ye tarried so long from me? Alas! this wound on your head hath taken overmuch cold."

And so then they rowed from the land, and Sir Bedivere beheld all those ladies go from him; then Sir Bedivere cried, "Ah! my lord Arthur, what shall become of me now ye go from me, and leave me here alone among mine enemies?"

"Comfort thyself," said King Arthur, "and do as well as thou mayest, for in me is no trust for to trust in; for I will into the vale of Avalon for to heal me of my grievous wound; and if thou never hear more of me, pray for my soul."

But evermore the queens and the ladies wept and shrieked that it was pity for to hear them. And as soon as Sir Bedivere had lost the sight of the barge, he wept and wailed, and so took the forest; and so he went all the night, and in the morning he was ware between two hills of a chapel and an hermitage.

Then was Sir Bedivere glad, and thither he went; and when he came into the chapel, he saw where lay an hermit grovelling upon all four there fast by a tomb newly graven. When the hermit saw Sir Bedivere, he knew him well, for he was, but a little before, [the] bishop of Canterbury that Sir Mordred banished away.

"Sir," said Sir Bedivere, "what man is there that ye pray so fast for?"

"Fair son," said the hermit, "I wot not verily, but by deeming, but this night, at midnight, here came a great number of ladies, and brought hither a dead corpse, and prayed me to bury him; and here they offered an hundred tapers and gave me an hundred besants."

"Alas," said Sir Bedivere, "that was my lord King Arthur, that here lieth buried in this chapel!"

Then Sir Bedivere swooned, and when he awoke he prayed the hermit he might abide with him still there, to live with fasting and prayers. "For from hence will I never go," said Sir Bedivere, "by my will, but all the days of my life here to pray for my lord Arthur."

"Ye are welcome to me," said the hermit, "for I know you better than ye ween that I do. Ye are the bold Bedivere, and the full noble duke Sir Lucan the Butler was your brother."

Then Sir Bedivere told the hermit all as ye have heard before. So there bode Sir Bedivere with the hermit, and there Sir Bedivere put upon him poor clothes, and served the hermit full lowly in fasting and in prayers. And when the Queen Guenever understood that King Arthur was slain, and all the noble knights, Sir Mordred and all the remnant, then the queen stole away, and five ladies with her, and so she went to Almesbury, and there she let make herself a nun and wore white clothes and black. And great penance she took as ever did sinful lady in this land; and never creature could make her merry, but lived in fastings, prayers, and alms deeds, that all manner of people marvelled how virtuously she was changed. Now leave we Queen Guenever in Almsbury, that was a nun in white clothes and black; and there she was abbess and ruler, as reason would. And turn we from her, and speak we of Sir Launcelot du Lake.

And when he heard in his country that Sir Mordred was crowned king in England, and made war against King Arthur, and would not let him to land in his own land; also it was told Sir Launcelot how that Sir Mordred had laid siege about the Tower of London, because the queen would not wed him; then was Sir Launcelot wondrous wroth.

Then they made them ready in all the haste that might be, with ships and galleys, with Sir Launcelot and his host for to pass into England. And so he passed over the sea, and arrived at Dover, and there he landed with seven kings, and their number was hideous to behold. Then Sir Launcelot inquired of the men of Dover where King Arthur was become.

Then the people told him how that he was slain, with Sir Mordred, and an hundred thousand died upon a day, and how Sir Mordred gave King Arthur there the first battle at his landing, and there was the good knight Sir Gawaine slain; and on the morrow Sir Mordred fought with King

Arthur upon Barendoune, and there King Arthur put Sir Mordred to the worst.

"Alas!" said Sir Launcelot, "this is the heaviest tidings that ever came to me. Now fair sirs," said Sir Launcelot, "I beseech you show me the tomb of Sir Gawaine."

And then certain people of the town brought him to the castle of Dover, and showed him the tomb of Sir Gawaine. Then Sir Launcelot kneeled down, and wept, and prayed full heartily for his soul. And that night he made a dole, and all they that would come had as much flesh and fish, wine and ale, as they might eat and drink, and every man and woman had twelve pence, come who would.

Then on the third day Sir Launcelot called to the kings, dukes, earls, and barons, and said thus: "My fair lords, I thank you all of your coming into this country with me. But we come too late, and that shall repent me while I live. But sithen it is so, I will myself ride and seek my lady Queen Guenever, for as I hear say she hath great pain and much disease, and I heard say that she is fled into the west country, therefore ye all abide me here, and but if I come within fifteen days, then take your ships and your fellowship, and depart into your country."

Then came Sir Bors de Ganis, and said, "My lord Sir Launcelot, what think ye for to do, now to ride in this realm? wit thou well, ye shall find few friends."

"Be as be may," said Sir Launcelot, "keep you still here, for I will forth on my journey, and no man nor child shall go with me."

So it was no boot to strive, but he departed and rode westerly, and there he sought a seven or eight days, and at the last he came unto a nunnery. And then was Queen Guenever ware of Sir Launcelot as she walked in the cloister; and when she saw him there, she swooned three times, that all the ladies and gentlewomen had work enough for to hold the queen up. So when she might speak, she called ladies and gentlewomen unto her, and said, "Ye marvel, fair ladies, why I make this cheer. Truly," said she, "it is for the sight of yonder knight which yonder standeth; wherefore I pray you all to call him unto me." And when Sir Launcelot was brought unto her, then she said: "Sir Launcelot, I require thee and beseech thee heartily, for all the love that ever was between us two, that thou never look me more in the visage. And furthermore I command thee on God's behalf right straitly, that thou forsake my company, and that unto thy kingdom shortly thou return again, and keep well thy realm from war and wreck. For as well as I have loved thee, Sir Launcelot, now mine heart will not once serve me to see thee. Therefore, Sir Launcelot, go thou unto thy realm, and there take thee a wife, and live with her in joy and bliss. And I beseech you heartily, pray for me unto our Lord God, that I may amend my misliving."

"Now, sweet madam," said Sir Launcelot, "would ye that I should now return again into my country, and there to wed a lady? Nay, madam, wit you well that shall I never do: but the same destiny that ye have taken you to, I will take me unto, for to please Jesu, and ever for you I cast me specially to pray. And if I had found you now so disposed, I had cast me to have had you into mine own realm."

[Then] there was lamentation as they had been stung by spears, and the ladies bare the queen to her chamber.

And Sir Launcelot took his horse and rode all that day and all that night in a forest, weeping. And at last he was ware of a hermitage and a chapel between two cliffs, and then he heard a little bell ring to mass.

[And it was here that the bishop and Sir Bedivere had served God together; and they knew Sir Launcelot, and told him all, and his heart was nearly brast for sorrow. And Sir Launcelot threw abroad his armor, and was shriven, and took the habit upon him, and abode at that chapel.

And there came Sir Bors, who had gone forth for to seek Sir Launcelot. And Sir Bors took the habit upon him. And within half a year there was also come] Sir Galihud, Sir Galihodin, Sir Bleoberis, Sir Villiers, Sir Clarrus, and Sir Gahalantine. So these seven knights abode there still. And when they saw that Sir Launcelot had taken him unto such perfection they had not list [*desire*] to depart, but took such an habit as he had, and their horses went where they would.

Thus they endured in great penance six years, and then Sir Launcelot took the habit of priesthood, and twelve months he sung the mass. [And he used] such abstinence that he waxed full lean. And thus upon a night there came a vision to Sir Launcelot, and charged him, in remission of his sins, to haste him unto Almesbury, "And by then thou come there, thou shalt find Queen Guenever dead: and therefore take thy fellows with thee, and purvey them of an horse-bier, and fetch thou the corpse of her, and bury her by her husband the noble King Arthur." So this vision came to Launcelot thrice in one night.

Then Sir Launcelot rose up or day, and told the hermit.

"It were well done," said the hermit, "that ye made you ready, and that you disobey not the vision."

Then Sir Launcelot took his seven fellows with him, and on foot they went from Glastonbury to Almesbury, the which is little more than thirty miles. And thither they came within two days, for they were weak and feeble to go. And when Sir Launcelot was come to Almesbury, within the nunnery, Queen Guenever died but half an hour before.

Then Sir Launcelot saw her visage, but he wept not greatly, but sighed; and so he did all the observance of the mass himself, both the dirige [*dirge*] at night and the mass on the morrow.

[And so with many holy rites, Queen Guenever was wrapped thirty-fold in cloth of Rheims, and put in a web of lead, and after in a coffin of marble. And when she was put in the earth Sir Launcelot swooned.]

Then Sir Launcelot never after eat but little meat, nor drank, till he was dead; for then he sickened more and more, and dried and dwined [*dwindled*] away; for the bishop nor none of his fellows might not make him to eat, and little he drank; for evermore day and night he prayed, but sometime he slumbered a broken sleep, and ever he was lying grovelling on the tomb of King Arthur and Queen Guenever. And there was no comfort that the bishop, nor Sir Bors, nor none of his fellows could make him, it availed nothing.

Oh, ye mighty and pompous lords, shining in the glory transitory of this unstable life, as in reigning over great realms and mighty great countries, fortified with strong castles and towers, edified with many a rich city; ye also, ye fierce and mighty knights, so valiant in adventurous deeds of arms; behold, behold, see how this mighty conqueror King Arthur, whom in his human life all the world doubted [*praised*], see also the noble Queen Guenever, which sometime sat in her chair adorned with gold, pearls, and precious stones, now lie full low in obscure fosse or pit, covered with clods of earth and clay; behold also this mighty champion Sir Launcelot, peerless of all knighthood, see now how he lieth grovelling upon the cold mould, now being so feeble and faint that sometime was so terrible. How and in what manner ought ye to be so desirous of worldly honor so dangerous! Therefore me thinketh this present book is right necessary often to be read, for in it shall ye find the most gracious, knightly, and virtuous war of the most noble knights of the world, whereby they gat praising continually. Also me seemeth, by the oft reading thereof, ye shall greatly desire to accustom yourself in following of those gracious knightly deeds, that is to say, to dread God, and to love righteousness, faithfully and courageously to serve your sovereign prince; and the more that God hath given you the triumphal honor, the meeker ye ought to be, ever fearing the unstableness of this deceitful world. And so I pass over and turn again unto my matter.

So within six weeks after Sir Launcelot fell sick, and lay in his bed; and then he sent for the bishop that there was hermit, and all his true fellows. Then Sir Launcelot said with dreary steeven [*voice*], "Sir bishop, I pray you give to me all my rights that longeth to a Christian man."

"It shall not need you," said the hermit and all his fellows, "it is but heaviness of your blood: ye shall be well amended by the grace of God to-morn."

"My fair lords," said Sir Launcelot, "wit you well, my careful body will into the earth. I have warning more than now I will say, therefore give me my rights."

So when he had all that a Christian man ought to have, he prayed the bishop that his fellows might bear his body unto Joyous Gard.

"Howbeit," said Sir Launcelot, "me repenteth sore, but I made mine avow sometime that in Joyous Gard I would be buried, and because of breaking of mine avow, I pray you all lead me thither."

Then there was weeping and wringing of hands among all his fellows. So at the season of night they went all to their beds, for they lay all in one chamber. So after midnight against day, the bishop that was hermit, as he lay in his bed asleep, he fell on a great laughter; and therewith the fellowship awoke, and came unto the bishop, and asked him what he ailed.

"Ah, Jesu, mercy," said the bishop, "why did you awake

me? I was never in all my life so merry and well at ease."

"Why, wherefore?" said Sir Bors.

"Truly," said the bishop, "here was Sir Launcelot with me, with more angels than ever I saw men upon one day; and I saw the angels heave up Sir Launcelot towards heaven; and the gates of heaven opened against him."

"It is but dretching [*fantasy*] of swevens [*dreams*]," said Sir Bors; "for I doubt not Sir Launcelot aileth nothing but good."

"It may well be," said the bishop. "Go to his bed, and then shall ye prove the sooth."

So when Sir Bors and his fellows came to his bed, they found him stark dead, and he lay as he had smiled, and the sweetest savor about him that ever they smelled. Then was there weeping and wringing of hands, and the greatest dole they made that ever made men. And on the morrow the bishop sung his mass of requiem; and after the bishop and all those nine knights put Sir Launcelot in the same horse-bier that Queen Guenever was laid in before that she was buried.

And so the bishop and they all together went with the corpse of Sir Launcelot daily till they came unto Joyous Gard, and ever they had an hundred torches burning about him.

And so within fifteen days they came to Joyous Gard; and there they laid his corpse in the body of the choir, and sung and read many psalters and prayers over him and about him; and ever his visage was laid open and naked, that all folk might behold him, for such was the custom in those days that all men of worship should so lie with open visage till that they were buried. And right thus as they were at their service, there came Sir Ector de Maris, that had sought seven year all England, Scotland, and Wales, seeking his brother Sir Launcelot.

And when Sir Ector de Maris heard such noise and light in the choir of Joyous Gard, he alighted, and put his horse away from him, and came into the choir; and there he saw men sing and weep. And all they knew Sir Ector, but he knew not them. Then went Sir Bors unto Sir Ector, and told him how there lay his brother Sir Launcelot dead. And then Sir Ector threw his shield, sword, and helm from him; and when he beheld Sir Launcelot's visage he fell down in a swoon. And when he awaked it were hard any tongue to tell the doleful complaints that he made for his brother.

"Ah, Sir Launcelot," he said, "thou were head of all Christian knights; and now I dare say," said Sir Ector, "that Sir Launcelot, there thou liest, thou were never matched of none earthly knight's hands; and thou were the courtliest knight that ever bare shield; and thou were the truest friend to thy lover that ever bestrode horse; and thou were the truest lover, of a sinful man, that ever loved woman; and thou were the kindest man that ever struck with sword; and thou were the goodliest person that ever came among press [*crowd*] of knights; and thou were the meekest man and the gentlest that ever ate in hall among ladies; and thou were the sternest knight to thy mortal foe that ever put spear in the rest."

Then there was weeping and dolor out of measure.

Thus they kept Sir Launcelot's corpse above the ground fifteen days, and then they buried it with great devotion. And then at leisure they went all with the bishop of Canterbury to his hermitage, and there they were together more than a month. Then Sir Constantine, that was Sir Cador's son, of Cornwall, was chosen king of England; and he was a full noble knight, and worshipfully he ruled this realm. And then this King Constantine sent for the bishop of Canterbury, for he heard say where he was; and so he was restored unto his bishopric, and left that hermitage; and Sir Bedivere was there ever still hermit to his life's end. Then Sir Bors de Ganis, Sir Ector de Maris, Sir Gahalantine, Sir Galihud, Sir Galihodin, Sir Blamor, Sir Bleoberis, Sir Villiers le Valiant, Sir Clarrus of Claremount, all these knights drew them to their countries, howbeit King Constantine would have had them with him, but they would not abide in this realm; and there they lived in their countries as holy men.

Here is the end of the whole book of King Arthur and of his noble knights of the Round Table, that when they were whole together there was ever an hundred and forty. Also, here is the end of the death of King Arthur. I pray you all, gentlemen and gentlewomen, that read this book of King Arthur and his knights from the beginning to the ending, pray for me while I am alive, that God send me good deliverance.

OF THE DEATH OF ARTHUR

And when I am dead, I pray you all pray for my soul. For this book was finished the ninth year of the reign of King Edward the Fourth, by Sir Thomas Maleor [*Malory*] knight, as Jesu help me for his great might, as he is the servant of Jesu both day and night.